MORE DIRT:
The New American Fiction

19

Editor: Bill Buford
Assistant Editor: Graham Coster
Associate Editor: Piers Spence
Advertising and Promotion: Monica McStay, Tracy Shaw
Executive Editor: Pete de Bolla
Design and Cover: Chris Hyde
Office Manager: Carolyn Harlock
Subscriptions: Claire Craig
Research: Margaret Costa
Editorial Assistant: Lauren Comiteau
Contributing Editor: Todd McEwen
Photo Editor: Harry Mattison
US Editor: Jonathan Levi

Editorial and Subscription Correspondence in the United States and Canada: Jonathan Levi, GRANTA, 13 White Street, New York, NY 10013.
All manuscripts are welcome but must be accompanied by a stamped, self-addressed envelope or they cannot be returned.

Granta/0017–3231 is published quarterly for $22 by Granta Publications Ltd, 44a Hobson Street, Cambridge CB1 1NL, England. Second class postage pending at New York, NY. POSTMASTER: send address changes to GRANTA, 13 White Street, New York, NY 10013.

Back Issues: $7.50 each. *Granta* 1–4, 9 and 12–13 are no longer available.

Granta is photoset by Lindonprint Typesetters, Hobson Street Studio Ltd and Goodfellow and Egan, Cambridge, and is printed by Hazell Watson and Viney Ltd, Aylesbury, Bucks.

Granta is published by Granta Publications Ltd and distributed by Penguin Books Ltd, Harmondsworth, Middlesex, England; Viking Penguin Inc., 40 West 23rd St, New York, New York, USA; Penguin Books Australia Ltd, Ringwood, Victoria, Australia; Penguin Books Canada Ltd, 2801 John Street, Markham, Ontario, Canada L3R 1B4; Penguin Books (NZ) Ltd, 182–90 Wairau Road, Auckland 10, New Zealand. This selection copyright © 1986 by Granta Publications Ltd.

Cover photograph by Eric Meola

SUPPORTED BY THE
EASTERN
Arts
ASSOCIATION

Granta 19, Fall 1986

ISBN 014–00–8595.5   ISSN 0017–3231

CONTENTS

The Ecco Press

FALL 1986/WINTER 1987

Antaeus 57 (Essays on Nature)
Paper $10.00

PAUL BOWLES
Points in Time
new in paper $7.50

ANTON CHEKHOV
The Schoolmaster & Other Stories
paper only $9.50

The Cook's Wedding & Other Stories
paper only $9.50

STUART DYBEK
Childhood and Other Neighborhoods
paper only $8.50

SONDRA STANG, EDITOR
The Ford Madox Ford Reader
paper only $13.50

BETTY FUSSELL
Eating In
paper only $8.95

DAVID LONG
The Flood of '64 and Other Stories
cloth $16.95

CECILY MACKWORTH
The Destiny of Isabelle Eberhardt
new in paper $9.50

CZESLAW MILOSZ
The Separate Notebooks
new in paper $12.50

HOWARD MOSS
Minor Monuments: Selected Essays
cloth $20.00
paper $10.50

CESARE PAVESE
Stories
paper only $12.95

FERNANDO PESSOA
Poems
cloth $19.95
paper $10.50

V.S. PRITCHETT
The Gentle Barbarian:
The Work and Life of Turgenev
paper only $9.50

LEON ROOKE
The Fat Woman
paper only $8.50

SUSAN SWAN
The Biggest Modern Woman of the World
paper only $9.50

IVAN TURGENEV
A Sportsman's Notebook
paper only $10.50

18 West 30th Street   New York/10001

Now they're finding out what life in America is *really* like

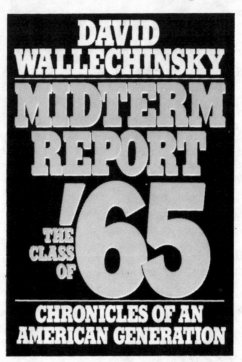

DAVID WALLECHINSKY

MIDTERM REPORT

THE CLASS OF '65

CHRONICLES OF AN AMERICAN GENERATION

Ten years ago David Wallechinsky, co-author of *What Really Happened to the Class of '65*, reported the effects of a turbulent decade on the members of his own high-school class. Now, a very different decade later, Wallechinsky renders a Midterm Report as the national class of '65 finds itself on the verge of middle age. To discover his generation anew, the author travelled across the country to interview men and women of all backgrounds. *Midterm Report* presents their stories—diverse, dramatic, happy and harrowing—vividly told in their own voices.

Viking

LSU Fiction

The Lost Get-Back Boogie
A Novel by JAMES LEE BURKE
A pitch-perfect, seamless performance, *The Lost Get-Back Boogie* is the story of one man's attempt to redirect his life, to exorcise the demons of his past. ''James Lee Burke writes with such thrusting force that the reader, carried along, forgets he has a book in his hands.''—A.B. Guthrie, Jr.
$16.95, November

Those Who Blink
A Novel by WILLIAM MILLS
''In *Those Who Blink,* William Mills plunges backward, from a Louisiana chemical plant to a family farm in the southern low-hill country, and his story is enough to raise the dead. Seldom have I been so caught up in a literary action as I was in this.''—James Dickey. ''This slender book keeps working long after the last page is turned.''—*Booklist*
$14.95

The All-Girl Football Team
Stories by LEWIS NORDAN
Lewis Nordan continues to explore a fictional territory he laid claim to in his first collection of stories, *Welcome to the Arrow-Catcher Fair,* a territory in which the bizarre and the grotesque assume a terrifying importance within the ordinary.
$15.95 cloth, **$9.95** paper, October

A World Quite Round
Two Stories and a Novella by GORDON WEAVER
In these fictions, about a young boy and an aging art professor, a Chinese interpreter in a prisoner-of-war camp in Korea, and the imagined fate of a timid high-school acquaintance, Gordon Weaver works themes of loss, failure, and the limitations of language into beautifully told truths. ''Weaver has a convincing and captivating style.''—*Publishers Weekly*
$15.95 cloth, **$9.95** paper

Louisiana State University Press   Baton Rouge 70893

RICHARD FORD
EMPIRE

Sims and his wife Marge were on the train to Minot from their home in Spokane. They had left Spokane at five, when Marge got off her shift, and it was after nine now and black outside. Sims had paid for a roomette which Marge said she intended to be asleep in by nine, but she wasn't in it yet. She had talked Sims into having a drink.

'How would you hate to die most?' Marge said, waggling a ballpoint in her fingers. She was working a crossword puzzle book that had been left on the seat. She had finished the hardest puzzle and gone on to the quiz in the back. The quiz predicted how long people would live by how they answered certain questions, and Marge was comparing her chances to Sims's. 'This will be revealing,' Marge said. 'I'm sure you've thought about it, knowing you.' She smiled at Sims.

'I'd hate to be bored to death,' Sims said. He stared out at the glassy darkness of Montana where you could see nothing. No lights. No motion. He'd never been here before.

'OK. That's *E*,' Marge said. 'That's good. It's ten. I'm ten because I said none of the above.' She wrote a number down. 'You can see the psychology in this thing. If *E* is your answer for all of these, you live forever.'

'I wouldn't like that,' Sims answered.

At the front of the parlor car a group of uniformed Army people were making a lot of noise, shuffling cards, opening beer cans and leaning over seats to talk loud and laugh. Every now and then a big laugh would go up and one of the Army people would look back down the car with a grin on his face. Two of the soldiers were women, Sims noticed, and most of the goings on seemed intended to make them laugh and to present the men with a chance to give one of them a squeeze.

'OK, hon.' Marge took a drink of her drink and repositioned the booklet under the shiny light. 'Would you rather live in a country of high suicide or a high crime rate? This thing's nutty, isn't it?' Marge smiled. 'Sweden's high suicide, I know that. Everywhere else is high crime, I suppose. I'll answer *E* for you on this one. *E* for me, too.' She marked the boxes and scored the points.

'Neither one sounds all that great,' Sims said. Outside, the train flashed through a small, Montana town without stopping—two crossing gates with bells and red lanterns, a row of darkened stores, an empty rodeo corral with two cows standing alone under a bright floodlight. A single car was waiting to cross, its parking lights shining. It all disappeared. He could hear a train whistle far off.

'Here's the last one,' Marge said. She took another sip and cleared her throat as if she was taking it seriously. 'The rest are…I don't know what. Weird. But just answer this one. Do you feel protective often, or do you often feel in need of protection?'

At the front of the car the Army people all roared with laughter at something one of them had said in a loud whisper. A couple more beer cans popped and somebody shuffled cards, cracking them together hard. 'Put your money where *your* mouth is, sucker. Not where *mine* is,' one of the women said, and everybody roared again. Marge smiled at one of the Army men who turned to see who else was enjoying all the fun they were having. He winked at Marge and made circles around his ear with his finger. He was a big sergeant with an enormous head. He had his tie loosened. 'Answer,' Marge said to Sims.

'Both,' Sims said.

'*Both*,' Marge said and shook her head. 'Boy, you've got this test figured out. That's an extra five points. *Neither* would've taken points off, incidentally. Ten for me. Fifteen for you.' She entered the numbers. 'If there weren't twenty taken off yours right from the start, you'd live longer by a long shot.' She folded the book and stuck it down between the seat cushions, and squeezed Sims's arm to her. 'Unfortunately, I still live five years longer. Sorry.'

'That's all right with me,' Sims said, and sniffed.

One of the Army women got up and walked back down the aisle. She was a sergeant, too. They were all sergeants. She was wearing a green Army blouse and a regulation skirt and a little black tie. She was a big, shapely woman in her thirties, an ash blonde with reddish cheeks and dark eyes that sparkled. She was not wearing a wedding ring, Sims also noticed. When she passed their seat she gave Marge a nice smile and gave Sims a smaller one. Sims wondered if she was the jokester. BENTON was the name on her brass name-tag. SGT. BENTON. Her epaulettes had little black and white sergeant's stripes snapped on them. The woman went back and entered the rest room.

'I wonder if they're on duty,' Marge said.

'I can't even remember the Army, now,' Sims said. 'Isn't that funny? I can't remember anybody I was even in it with.' The toilet door clicked locked.

'You weren't overseas. You'd remember things, then,' Marge said. 'Carl had a horror movie in his head. I'll never forget it.' Carl, Marge's first husband, lived in Florida. Sims had met him, and they'd been friendly. Carl was a stumpy, hairy man with a huge chest, whereas Sims was taller. 'Carl was in the Navy,' Marge said.

'That's right,' Sims said. Sims himself had been stationed in Oklahoma, a hot, snakey, hellish place in the middle of a bigger hellish place he'd been glad to stay in instead of shipping out to where everybody else was going. How long ago was that? Sims thought. 1969. Long before he'd met Marge. A different life altogether.

'I'm taking a snooze pill now,' Marge said. 'I worked today, unlike some people. I need a snooze.' She began fishing around inside her purse for some pills. Marge waitressed in a bar out by the airport, from nine in the morning until five. Airline people and manufacturers' reps were her customers, and she liked that crowd. When Sims had worked, they had had the same hours, and Sims had sometimes come in the bar for lunch. But he had quit his job selling insurance, and hadn't thought about working since then. Sims thought he'd work again, but he wasn't a glutton for it.

'I'll come join you in a little while,' Sims said. 'I'm not sleepy yet. I'll have another one of these, though.' He drank the last of his gin from his plastic cup and jiggled his ice cubes.

'Who's counting?' Marge smiled. She had a pill in her hand, but she took a leather-bound, glass flask out of her purse and poured Sims some gin while he jiggled his ice.

'Perfect. It'll make me sleepy,' Sims said.

Marge put her pill in her mouth. 'Snoozeroosky,' she said, and washed it down with the rest of her drink. 'Don't be Mr Night Owl.' She reached and kissed Sims on the cheek. 'There's a pretty girl in the sleeping car who loves you. She's waiting for you.'

'I'll keep that in mind,' Sims said and smiled. He reached across and kissed Marge and patted her shoulder.

'Tomorrow'll be fine. Don't brood,' Marge said.

'I wasn't even thinking about it,' Sims said.

'Nothing's normal, right? That's just a concept.'

'Nothing I've seen yet,' Sims said.

'Just a figure of the mind, right?' Marge smiled then went off down the aisle toward the sleeping car.

The Army people at the front of the car all laughed again, this time not so loud, and two of them—there were eight or so—turned and watched Marge go back down the aisle toward the sleeping car. One of these two was the big guy. The big guy looked at Marge, then at Sims, then turned back around. Sims thought they were talking about the woman in the rest-room, telling something on her she wouldn't like to hear. 'Oh, you guys. Jesus,' the remaining woman said. 'You guys are just awful. I mean, really. You're *awful*.'

All the worry was about Marge's sister, Pauline, who was currently in a mental health unit somewhere in Minot—probably, Sims thought, in a strait-jacket, tied to a wall, tranquilized out of her brain. Pauline was younger than Marge, two years younger, and she was a hippy. Once, years ago, she had taught school in Seattle. That had been three husbands ago. Now she lived with a Sioux Indian who made metal sculptures from car parts on a reservation outside of Minot. Dan was his name. Pauline had changed her own name to an Indian word that sounded like Monica. Pauline was also a Scientologist and talked all the time about getting 'clear'. She talked all the time, anyway.

At four o'clock yesterday morning the police had come and gotten Dan, she said, and arrested him for embezzling money using stolen cars. The FBI, too, she said. Dan was in jail down in Bismark now. She said she knew nothing about any of it. She was there in the house with Dan's dog, Eduardo, and the doors broken in from when the FBI had showed up with axes.

'Do you want this dog, Victor?' Pauline had said to Sims on the phone.

'No. Not now,' Sims had said from his bed. 'Try to calm down, Pauline.'

'Will you want it later, then?' Pauline said. He could tell she was spinning.

'I don't think so. I doubt it.'

'It'll sit with its paw up. Dan taught it that. Otherwise it's useless. It has nightmares.'

'Are you all right, honey?' Marge said from the kitchen phone.

'Sure, I'm fine. Yeah.' Sims could hear an ice cube tinkle. A breath of cigarette smoke blown into the receiver. 'I'll miss him, but he's a loser. A self-made man. I'm just sorry I gave up my teaching job. I'm going back to Seattle in two hours.'

'What's there,' Marge asked.

'Plenty,' Pauline said. 'I'm dropping Eduardo off at the pound first, though, if you don't want him.'

'No thanks,' Sims said. Pauline had not taught school in ten years.

'He's sitting here with his idiot paw raised. I won't miss that part.'

'Maybe now's not the best time to leave Dan,' Sims said. 'He's had some bad luck.' Sims could see the yellow light down the hall in the kitchen.

'He broke my dreams,' Pauline said. 'The Indian chief.'

'Don't be a martyr, hon,' Marge said. 'Tell her that, Vic.'

'You're not going to make it acting this way,' Sims said. He wished he could go back to sleep.

'I remember you,' Pauline said.

'It's Victor,' Marge said.

'I know who it is,' Pauline said. 'I want out of this. I'm getting the fuck out of this. Do you know how it feels to have FBI agents wearing fucking flak jackets, chopping in your bedroom with fire axes?'

'How?' Sims said.

'Weird, that's how. Lights. Machine guns. Loudspeakers. It was like a movie set. I'm just sorry.' Pauline dropped the receiver and picked it up again. 'Oh shit,' Sims heard her say. 'There it goes.' She was starting to cry. Pauline gave out a long, wailing moan that sounded like a dog howling.

'Monica?' Marge said. Marge was calling Pauline by her Indian name now. 'Get hold of yourself, sweetheart. Talk to her again, Vic.'

'There's no reason to think Dan's a criminal,' Sims said. 'No reason at all. The government harasses Indians all the time.' Pauline was wailing.

'I'm going to kill myself,' Pauline said. 'Right now, too.'

'Talk to her, Victor,' Marge said from the kitchen. 'I'm calling 911.'

'Try to calm down, Monica,' Sims had said from his bed. He heard Marge running out the back door, headed for the Krukows

19

next door. Death was not an idle notion to Pauline, he knew that. Pauline had taken an overdose once, back in the old wild days, just to make good on a threat. 'Monica,' Sims had said. 'This'll be all right. Pet the dog. Try to calm down.' Pauline was still wailing. Then suddenly the connection was broken, and Sims was left alone in bed with the phone on his chest, staring down the empty hall where the light was still on but no one was there.

When the police got to Pauline and Dan's house it was an hour later. Pauline was sitting by the phone. She had cut her wrists with a knife and bled all over the dog. The policeman who called said she had not hit a vein and couldn't have bled to death in a week. But she needed to calm down. Pauline was under arrest, he said, but she'd be turned loose in two days. He suggested Marge come out and visit her.

Sims had always been attracted to Pauline. She and Marge had been wild girls together. Drugs. Overland drives at all hours. New men. They had had imagination for wildness. They were both divorced; both small, delicate women with dark, quick eyes. They were not twins, but they looked alike, though Marge was prettier.

The first time he had seen Pauline was at a party in Spokane. Everyone was drunk or drugged. He was sitting on a couch talking to some people. Through a door to the kitchen he could see a man pressed against a woman, feeling her breast. The man pulled down the front of the woman's sundress, exposed both breasts and kissed them; the woman was holding on to the man's crotch and massaging it. Sims understood they thought no one could see them. But when the woman suddenly opened her eyes, she looked straight at Sims and smiled. She was still holding the man's dick. Sims thought it was the most inflamed look he had ever seen. His heart had raced, and a feeling had come over him like being in a car going down a hill out of control in the dark. It was Pauline.

Later that winter he walked into a bedroom at another party to get his coat, and found Pauline naked on a bed fucking a man who was naked himself. It had not been the same man he'd seen the first time. Later still, at another party, he had asked Pauline to go out to dinner with him. They had gone, first, on a twilight row-boat ride on a lake in town, but Pauline had gotten cold and refused to talk to him anymore, and he had taken her home early. When he met Marge, sometime later, he had at first thought Marge was Pauline. And when Marge later introduced Pauline to Sims, Pauline didn't seem to remember him at all, something he was relieved about.

S ims heard the rest-room door click behind him, and suddenly he smelled marijuana. The Army crew was still yakking up front, but somebody not far away was smoking reefer. It was a smell he didn't smell often, and hadn't for a long time. A hot, sweet, thick smell. Who was having a joint right on the train? Train travel had changed since the last time he'd done it, he guessed. He turned around to see if he could find the doper, and saw the woman sergeant coming back up the aisle. She was straightening her blouse as if she'd taken it off in the rest-room, and was brushing down the front of her skirt.

The woman looked at Sims looking at her and smiled a big smile. She was the one smoking dope, Sims thought. She'd slipped off from her friends and gotten loaded. He had smoked plenty of it in the Army. In Oklahoma. Everybody, then, had stayed loaded all the time. It was no different now, and no reason it should be.

'Where's your pretty wife?' the sergeant said casually when she got to Sims. She arched her brows and put her knee up on the arm rest of Marge's seat. She was loaded, Sims thought. Her smile spoke volumes. She didn't know Sims from Adam.

'She's gone off to bed,' Sims said.

'Why aren't you with her?' the woman asked, still smiling down over Sims.

'I'm not sleepy. She wanted to go to sleep,' Sims said. The woman smelled like marijuana. It was a smell he liked, but it made him nervous. He wondered what the Army people would think. Being in the Army was a business now. Businessmen didn't smoke dope.

'You two have kids?' the woman said to Sims.

'No,' Sims said. 'I don't like kids.' She looked down at her friends who were playing cards in two groups. 'Do you?' Sims said.

'None that I know about,' the woman said. She wasn't looking at Sims.

'Are you a farmer?'

'No,' Sims said. 'Why?'

'What else is there to do out here?' The woman's look unexpectedly turned sour. 'Do you say nice things to your wife?'

'Every day,' Sims said.

'You must really be in love,' she said. 'That's the coward's way out.' The woman quickly smiled. 'Just kidding.' She ran her fingers back through her hair and gave her head a shake as if she was clearing her thoughts. She looked down the aisle again and seemed, Sims thought, not to want to go back down there. He looked at the name BENTON on her brass tag. It also had tiny sergeant's stripes stamped into it. Sims looked at the woman's breast underneath the tag. It was in a big brassiere and couldn't be defined well. Sims thought about his own age. Forty-two.

'Your friends are having a good time, it sounds like.'

'They're not my friends,' she said.

This time the other Army woman in the group got up and looked back where Sergeant Benton was standing beside Sims's seat. She put her hands on her hips and shook her head in a mock disapproving way, then waved an arm in a wide wagon-train wave at Sergeant Benton. 'Get back down here, Benton,' the woman shouted. 'There's money to be made off these drunks.'

The other sergeants said, 'Whoa!' then laughed. Another beer can popped. Cards were shuffled. The other woman was fat and short with black hair.

'They think they're your friends,' Sims said.

'Let 'em think it. I just met them tonight,' the woman said. 'It's the easy-going camaraderie of the armed forces. They're all nice people, I guess. Who knows? Where're you going if you're not a farmer?'

'Minot,' Sims said.

'Which rhymes with why-not. I remember that from school. Pierre rhymes with queer.' She shook her head again and touched her palm to her forehead. She had big hands, red and tough-looking. Hands that had worked. Bigger than his own hands, Sims suspected. 'I feel a little light-headed,' the woman said.

'Must be that dope you smoked,' Sims said.

She grinned at Sims. 'Well, do tell.' The woman looked scandalized but wasn't scandalized at all. 'You're just full of ideas, aren't you?'

'I'm a veteran myself,' Sims said.

'What of? Modern life?'

'I was in Vietnam,' Sims said. The words just popped out of his mouth. They shocked him. He didn't want them back, but they shocked him. How many people had been there, after all? He tried to guess how old Sergeant Benton was. If she might've been there herself. Thirty. Thirty-five. It was a long time ago.

'When was that?' the woman said.

'When was what?' Sims said.

'Vietnam? Was that a war or what?' She looked disgustedly at Sims. 'I don't believe you were in Vietnam. Do you know how many of you guys I've met?'

'How many?'

'Two million,' the woman said, 'possibly three.'

'I was in the Navy,' Sims said.

'And you were probably on a boat that patrolled the rivers shooting blindly in the jungle day and night, and you don't want to discuss it now because of your nightmares, right?'

'I worked on an air base,' Sims said. This seemed safe to say.

'That's a new one,' Sergeant Benton said. 'The non-violent tactic.'

'What's your job in the Army?' Sims felt a big smile involuntarily crossing his face. He wished he'd never mentioned Vietnam. He wished he had that part of his life-story to tell over again. He was relieved Marge wasn't here.

'I'm in intelligence,' Sergeant Benton said brazenly. 'Don't I look smart?'

The fat woman sergeant stood up and faced Sergeant Benton again. 'Stop harassing the civilians, Benton,' she shouted. A laugh went up.

'You look plenty smart,' Sims said. 'You look great, if you ask me.' Sims realized he was still grinning and wished he weren't. He wished he'd told her to go to hell in a rickshaw.

'Well, aren't you nice?' the woman said in a voice Sims thought was vulgar. The sergeant kissed her finger tips and blew him a kiss. 'Sweet dreams,' she said and walked off down the aisle to where the other soldiers were laughing and drinking.

Sims took a walk back to the sleeping car to check on Marge. Two of the sergeants turned and watched him leave. He heard someone chuckle and somebody say, 'Gimme a break.'

When he stepped out on to the vestibule he noticed it was colder, a lot colder than Spokane. It was September the eighteenth. It could freeze tonight, he thought. Canada wasn't far north of where they were. That was not an appealing world, Sims thought. Cold and boring.

The train was coming into a station when he looked in on Marge. There was one main street that came straight up to the train tracks. The sky was cloudy in front of a big harvest moon. Down the street were red bar signs and Christmas lights strung across one intersection. Here was a place, Sims thought, you'd want to stay drunk in if you could.

Marge was asleep on top of the covers, still in her clothes. The reading light was on. She had a mystery novel open on her chest. She was dead to the world.

Sims took down the extra blanket and covered Marge up to her neck. He put the book on the window ledge and turned off the light. It was cold in the roomette. There was hardly room for him in the bed.

Out the window on the station platform he saw the one big sergeant walk past, then the other Army people. He could see a green Army van waiting in a parking lot, its motor running in the chilled air. A few Indian men were standing along the wall of the station in their shirt-sleeves. Two dogs sat in front of them. One of the Indians saw Sims looking out and pointed to him. Sims, leaning over Marge, waved and gave him the thumbs up. All the Indians laughed.

The Army sergeants, seven in all, carrying their bags, walked down to the parking lot and climbed in the van. The one fat woman was with them, and the big man was giving the orders. They looked cold. Where could they be going, Sims wondered. What was out here?

A bell sounded. The train moved away before the Army van left. Sims kept watching. The Indians all gave him the thumbs up and laughed again. They had bottles in Sneaky-Pete sacks.

'What's happening?' Marge said. She was still asleep, but she was talking. 'Where are we now?'

'Nowhere. I don't know,' Sims said softly, still leaning over her, watching the town slide by. 'Everything's fine.'

'OK,' Marge said. 'That's good news.'

She went back to sleep. Sims slipped out and headed back to his seat.

It was quieter in the car, now. A couple of new people had gotten on, but it seemed less smoky, the lights not as bright. Sims bought a ham sandwich and a soft drink at the snack bar and sat back in his seat and ate, watching the night go by. He thought he should've taken

Marge's mystery novel. That would put him to sleep fast. He wasn't going to be able to sleep in the roomette anyway.

Out the window, a highway went along with the train tracks. There were trucks running in the night, there. A big white Winnebago seemed to be trying to keep up with the train. Lights were on in the living quarters, and children's faces at the windows. The kids were pointing toy guns at the train and bouncing up and down. Their parents were up front, invisible in the dark. Sims made a pistol with his fingers and pointed it at the Winnebago. All the children—three of them—ducked from sight. Suddenly, the train was out on to a long trestle, over a bottomless ravine, and the Winnebago was lost from view in the dark.

Sergeant Benton rose out of a seat at the far end of the car and looked back toward the rest-room. She looked like she'd been asleep. She grabbed her shoulder purse and walked back toward Sims, pushing the sides of her hair up.

'What happened to your friends?' Sims said, though he knew perfectly well what had happened to them.

Sergeant Benton looked down at Sims as if she'd never seen him before. Her blouse was wrinkled. She looked dazed. It was the dope, Sims thought. He'd felt the same himself before. Like a criminal.

'Nothing but bars in these towns,' the woman said vaguely. 'All social life's in the bars. Where do you eat?' The woman shook her head and put her fingers over one eye, leaving the other looking at Sims. 'What's your name?'

'Vic,' Sims said and smiled.

'Vic,' The woman stared at him. 'How's your wife?'

'She's fine,' Sims said. 'She's locked away in dreamland.'

'That's good. My friends left in a hurry. They were loud-mouths. Especially that Ethel. She was too loud.'

'What's your name,' Sims asked. He was staring at the woman's breasts again.

Sergeant Benton looked at her name-tag and back at Sims. 'Can I trust you?' she said. She covered her other eye and looked at Sims with the one that had been covered.

'Depends,' Sims said.

'Doris,' she said. 'Wait a minute. Stay right here.'

'I'm up all night,' Sims said.

The woman went on down to the toilet and locked herself in

again. Sims wondered if she'd smoke another joint. Maybe he'd smoke one himself this time. He hadn't been loaded in ten years. He could stand it. If Marge were here, she'd want to get loaded herself. He wondered what Pauline had on her mind tonight. He wondered if she'd stopped howling yet. Maybe things would get better for Pauline. Maybe she'd go back and teach school some place, some small town in Maine, possibly, where no one knew her. Maybe Pauline was a manic depressive and needed to be on drugs.

He thought about Sergeant Benton, in the head now, washing up. His attitude toward 'lifers', which is what he assumed she was, had always been that something was wrong with them. The women, especially. Something made them unsuited for the rest of life, made them need to be in a special category. The women were always almost pretty, but not quite pretty. They had a loud laugh, or a moustache or enlarged pores, or some mannishness that went back to a farm experience with roughneck brothers and a cruel, strict father—something to run away from. Bad luck, really. Something somebody with a clearer outlook might just get over and turn into a strong point. Maybe he could find out what it was in Doris and treat her like a normal person, and that would make a difference.

Out the window, running along with the train, was the big white Winnebago again. The kids were in the windows, but they weren't shooting guns at him this time. They were just staring. Sims thought maybe they weren't staring at him, but at something else entirely.

Sergeant Benton came out of the toilet, and this time no dope smell came out with her. She had puffed up her hair, straightened her green blouse and her tie, and put on some lipstick. She looked better, Sims thought, and he was happy for her to come back. But then Sergeant Benton looked straight down the aisle past him, patted her hair again, raised her chin slightly but made no gesture to suggest she had ever known Sims was alive and on the earth at that moment. She turned and walked straight out through the door and into the next car.

Sims watched through the window glass as her blonde head crossed the vestibule and disappeared through the second door into the lounge car. He felt surprised and vaguely disappointed, but it was actually better, he thought, if she didn't come back. He'd wanted her to sit down and talk—all a matter of being friendly and passing the time—but it wasn't going any place. Killing time led to trouble, he'd found. It was even possible Sergeant Benton was travelling with someone else, somebody asleep somewhere. Another sergeant.

A year ago, Marge had gotten sick and had had to go in the hospital for an operation. Marge had seemed fine. Then suddenly she'd lost twenty pounds and gotten pale and weak, so weak she couldn't go to work. All in the space of what seemed like two weeks. The doctor who examined Marge told her and Sims together that Marge had a tumor the size of an Easter egg deep under her arm, and in all likelihood it was cancerous. After a dangerous operation, she would have to undergo prolonged treatments at the end of which she would probably die anyway, though nothing was certain. Sims took a leave from his insurance job and spent every day and every night until nine in the hospital with Marge, who needed to be there two weeks just to get strong enough for the surgery.

Every night Sims kissed Marge goodbye in her bed, then drove off into the night streets alone. Sometimes he'd stop in a waffle house, eat a sandwich, read the paper and talk to the waitresses. But most of the time he would go home, fix his own sandwich, eat it standing at the sink and watch TV until he went off to sleep, usually by eleven. Sometimes he'd wake up in his chair at three a.m.

When he'd been alone at home for three weeks, he began to notice, as he stood at the sink eating his sandwich and staring into the dark, that the woman in the house next door was always at her kitchen table at that time. A radio and an ash tray were on the table top, and as he stood and watched, she would start crying, put her head down on her bare arms and wag it back and forth as if there was something in her life, an important fact of some kind, she couldn't understand.

Sims knew the woman was the younger sister of Mrs Krukow, who owned the house with her husband, Stan. The Krukows were away on a driving trip to Florida, and the sister was watching the house for them. The sister's name was Cleo. She had dyed red hair and green eyes, and Mrs Krukow had told Sims that she was 'betwixt and between', and had no place to go at the moment. Sims had seen her in the backyard hanging out clothes, and often late in the day walking the Krukows' dachshund on the sidewalk. He had waved several times, and once or twice they exchanged a pleasant word.

When Sims had stood in the kitchen, drinking milk and eating a sandwich three days running and had seen Cleo alone and crying, he decided he should call over to the Krukows' and ask if there was something he could do. Maybe she was worried about the house. Or maybe something had happened to the Krukows and she was in shock about it and hadn't come out of the house for days. He didn't know what she did all day. It would be an act of kindness. Marge would go herself if she weren't in the hospital.

At ten-thirty on the fourth night, just as he saw Cleo's head go down on her folded arms on the kitchen table, he called the Krukows' number from the kitchen phone. He saw Cleo wagging her head in unhappiness, then saw her look at the phone ringing on the wall, then look at the kitchen window and out into the night, as if whoever was calling was watching her, which of course was the case, though Sims had turned off his own light and stood far back in the room so he couldn't be seen. Somehow he knew Cleo was going to look that way the moment the phone rang.

'Hi, it's Vic Sims from next door,' Sims said from the darkness. 'Are you OK over there?'

'It's what?' Cleo said harshly. Again she turned and furrowed her brow at the picture window above the sink. She frowned into the night, then her eyes seemed to widen as if she could see something specific.

'It's Vic Sims,' Sims said cheerfully. 'Marge and I were just concerned that you were all right over there. Stan and Betty asked us to check on you and see if you needed anything. I was up late over here anyway.' This was a lie, but Sims knew it could have been the truth. Stan and Betty were not good friends of theirs and had never asked them to do anything for Cleo at all.

'Where are you?' Cleo said.

'I'm at home. In my living-room,' Sims lied, staring at Cleo, who, he could see, had on shorts and a long T-shirt. She sniffed into the receiver.

'Are you watching me?' Cleo said, looking at the window, then up at the ceiling. She sniffed again, and then Sims thought he heard her sob softly and swallow. He couldn't tell from looking through the two windows and the dark. She was turned toward the wall phone now.

'Am I watching you?' Sims laughed. 'No, I'm not watching you. I'm watching the news. If you're fine, then that's all I'm calling to find out. Just checking. What are you crying about, anyway?'

'Nothing. Oh, Jesus,' Cleo said. Then she was overcome by tears and sobbing. 'I'm sorry,' she said after what seemed to Sims like a long time. 'I'm just at my wits' end over here. I have to hang up now. Goodbye.'

Sims watched her hang up the phone, then turn and lean against the wall and cry again. She wagged her head just as she had when she was seated at the table. Finally Sims saw her slide down and out of sight to the floor. It was a dramatic thing to see.

Sims stood in the dark against the kitchen wall of his own house. She could hurt herself, he thought. She could be in some real trouble and have no one to help her, whereas if someone would just talk to her she might work out whatever it was and be fine. Sims thought about calling back, but suspected she wouldn't answer now. And so he decided to go over, knock on the door and offer help. He took a bottle of brandy out of the cabinet, walked across the dark, grassy yard and up the back steps and knocked.

Cleo came to the back door with tears still fresh on her cheeks. Her red hair was frizzy and damp, and she was bare-footed. She looked grief-stricken, Sims thought. She also looked vulnerable and beautiful. Coming over and having a drink with red-headed Cleo seemed like a good idea for both of them.

'Who are you?' Cleo said suspiciously, through the screen. She glanced down at Sims's brandy bottle and hardened her mouth.

'Vic,' Sims said. 'From next door. Remember me? I thought you might like a drink. It sounded like you were crying. I can leave the bottle here.' He hoped leaving the bottle wouldn't be necessary, but he didn't want to seem to hope that. He hoped she'd ask him to come in.

'Come on in, I guess,' Cleo said and turned around and walked away, leaving Sims on the door-step, watching her through the screen as she disappeared back into the kitchen.

Cleo, whose last name was Middleton, told Sims her entire story. How she and Betty, who was five years older, had grown up on a farm in Iowa; that Betty had gone off to college and married Stan and Stan had enjoyed a nice, unexamined life of advancement and few financial worries working as an executive for a chain of hardware stores. She herself, Cleo, had gone to a cosmetology school and had somehow ended up in California hanging out with a motorcycle gang who robbed and beat people up for fun and sold drugs and generally rained terror on anybody they wanted to. She didn't say how this involvement had started. She showed Sims a tattoo of a Satan's head she had on her ass. She pulled up her shorts and turned her back to him from across the table, and smiled when she did it. This tattoo was involuntary, she told him, and later she showed him some cigarette burns on the soles of her feet. Cleo said she'd had two children in her life—she was twenty-nine, she said—but Sims didn't believe her. She looked much older in the dim, kitchen light. Forty, Sims guessed, though possibly younger. One child had died soon after birth. But the other, a little boy named Archie, was still living with his father down in Rio Vista, but Cleo couldn't see him because his father, who was a biker, had threatened to cut her head off if he ever so much as saw her again. 'The courts are helpless against that kind of attitude,' Cleo said and looked stern. She told Sims about waking up one night and finding herself being dragged out of her bed by a bunch of her husband's biker friends—Satan's Diplomats. They put her in the back of a car and drove off to the mountains. She could hear them talking about Satan, she said, and his evil empire, and she heard one man, a biker named Loser, say they were going to sacrifice her to Satan and then laugh about it. She said she'd screamed and yelled but no one paid attention. Eventually, she said, the car ran out of gas, and all the bikers had gotten out and abandoned it with her left in it. The next morning a policeman came along and that was how she got out. She said she hadn't gone back home after that, but that her husband, whose name was Savage, sent her a letter care of Betty telling her all he would do to her if he ever saw her.

Cleo shivered when she told this story, then she took out a cigarette and smoked it, holding it between her teeth. There was a sense about Cleo, Sims thought, that all she said might not be true. Yet she had obviously had a kind of life that made inventing such a story an attractive possibility, and that was enough.

Cleo told Sims she knew his wife was in the hospital, and she encouraged him to talk about that. Sims had no idea how she'd found out about Marge, but he didn't really want to talk about it. Marge's illness was his terrible worry, he thought, and he didn't know what to say. Marge was sick and might die. And he hated the whole thought of it. He loved Marge, and if she died his life would be over. No ifs or ands. It would just be over. He'd already decided he'd go out in the woods and hang himself so no one but animals would ever find him. That didn't make good conversation in the middle of the night, though. Nothing he or Cleo could say would help any of that. He was happy to sit across from Cleo, who was very pretty, and get peacefully drunk and forget about illness and hospitals and people's puny insurance claims he wasn't processing.

Cleo drank brandy and said that since she'd left California, five years before, she'd had several jobs but couldn't seem to find herself, 'couldn't get focused.' She'd lived in Boise, she said, doing hair. She'd lived in Salt Lake. She'd gone back to California and gotten married again, but that hadn't lasted. She'd gone to Seattle, then, and come as close as she ever would to a steady job in her field, in a shopping center up in Bellingham. After that she'd gone on unemployment for a year. And then she'd accidentally run into Stan one day on the Bellingham ferry. And that had panned out in her staying in Stan and Betty's house for a month. 'A real cross-patch life pattern.' Cleo shook her head, smiling. 'A long way from Iowa, though not in actual miles.'

'Things seem better now, though. Here, at least,' Sims said.

'Not really,' Cleo said. 'What's next? It's anybody's guess.'

'Maybe there'll be work here.'

'I don't ever want to touch another head professionally,' Cleo said. She looked down then, and Sims thought she might be ready to cry again. He didn't want that, though he didn't think he could blame her. She'd told him her whole life in ten minutes, and once the telling was finished the life itself seemed over, too. His was not that way. Not yet, anyway. Marge could get well. He could go back to work. Different and good things could happen to them. They were young. But that wasn't Cleo's lot in life. She had plenty to regret and cry about, and it wasn't over yet, not by any means.

Cleo started wagging her head again slowly, as if something had occurred to her that bewildered her, and he knew she was about to start sobbing, maybe even cracking up completely, and he would be there alone with her for that. He thought of himself waiting outside a dingy emergency room inside which Cleo, someone he didn't even know, lay strapped to a gurney, heavily sedated, while Marge, his own wife whom he loved, was asleep and dying and alone three floors up.

He could see Cleo's red head begin to lower toward the table top. Suddenly Sims stood up, leaned across the table over the brandy bottle, took Cleo's damp soft face in his hands. 'Don't cry now, Cleo,' he said. 'Things'll be all right. Things're going to be a lot better. You'll see. I'll see to it myself.'

'You will?' Cleo said, and blinked at him. 'How exactly will you do that?'

That night he slept with Cleo in Stan and Betty Krukow's big king-sized bed upstairs. Cleo insisted on leaving the television tuned to a rock music channel, but without the sound. This made the room flash with light all night long and made Sims regret he was there. Once or twice he saw Cleo peeping over his shoulder at something going on in the fantasy world where the silent music came from, a world of smoky, dark streets and halloween masks and doors opening and violent surprises. This was an act of kindness, Sims thought, and there was no use letting anything bother him. This was not his life and wouldn't ever be. None of it made any sense, but it didn't make any difference, either. Months from then, if Marge lived, he'd tell her about it and they'd have a big laugh together. Cleo would be long gone. Maybe he and Marge would've moved, too, to another house or to another state.

Sometime before dawn, when the light was gray and the room was still except for Cleo's breathing, Sims woke up startled out of a terrible dream. On the TV screen children were dancing and smiling around a man wearing a goat's head and playing an electric guitar. But in his dream he had hanged himself from a tall pine-tree limb in a forest somewhere. He'd written letters explaining everything—he'd already seen them being opened by his friends. 'When you read this,' the letter said, 'I, Vic Sims, will already be dead.' Yet, even though he was dead and hanging from a new rope with birds perched on top of his head, Marge was somehow still alive and in her hospital room, smiling out of a sunny window, looking better than she had in weeks. She would survive. But it was too late for him. All was lost and ruined forever.

When he woke up later in the morning, the TV was off and Cleo was gone. The dog was not downstairs, and Stan and Betty's other car was missing from the garage. Cleo had left the coffee pot on but no note.

Sims couldn't get out fast enough. He slipped out the back door and ran across the backyard—relieved not to see Cleo drive up in the Krukows' van. Inside, he took a long shower, shaved and put on a clean suit. Then he drove straight out to the hospital, arriving an hour late with a bunch of flowers. Marge said she'd assumed he'd slept in and just unplugged the phone. She said he looked exhausted and that her illness was having bad effects on him, too. Marge cried then, and afterward said she felt better.

Marge stayed in the hospital another three weeks. At home, Sims stayed inside and saw Cleo mostly out the window—the way he'd seen her before the night he'd slept with her in the Krukows' bed—walking the dog, hanging out laundry, driving into and out of the driveway with sacks of groceries. But Cleo had begun to seem different. She never called him, and on the times he couldn't avoid seeing her outside she never acted as if he was anything more than her sister's neighbor, which was a big relief. But she referred to Sims by his first name whenever she saw him. 'Hello, *Vic*,' she said, across the fence, where she was walking the dog. She would smile a kind of mean, derisive smile Sims didn't like, as if there was a joke attached to his name that he didn't know about. 'How's Marge, *Vic*?' she'd say other times, though he was certain Cleo had never seen Marge. Before, Cleo had seemed out-of-luck, vulnerable, vaguely alluring and desirable. A waif. Now she seemed experienced and cynical, a woman who had ridden with Satan's Diplomats and told about it. A hard woman, a woman who could cause you big trouble.

In two weeks, Sims noticed a big, black Harley-Davidson motorcycle in the Krukows' driveway. It was a low, sleek thing with chrome parts and high handlebars, and after a few minutes Cleo and a big, nasty-looking biker came out, got on and rode away with a terrible roar. The biker had on black leathers, ear-rings and a bandana over his head like a pirate. Cleo had on exactly the same clothes.

For a week, the biker hung out in the Krukows' house. The bike had California plates that said LOSER, and once or twice Sims saw

Cleo and the biker hanging clothes on the line in the back, smoking cigarettes and talking softly. The biker wore no shirt most of the time and drank beer, and kept on his pirate's bandana. His chest and arms were stringy and pale and hard-looking, with tattoos. Sims understood this was the friend of Cleo's former husband, the one who'd tried to sacrifice her to Satan. He wondered what the two of them could have in common.

The Krukows came back two days before Marge was released from the hospital. The biker disappeared the same day, and the next morning Sims saw Stan carry Cleo's bags and some boxes out to the car, drive away with Cleo, then in a little while come back alone. Sims never saw Cleo again, though he did see the biker in a gas station while he was on his way to the hospital to bring Marge home.

Marge stayed home in bed another three weeks, but as it turned out, she did not have to take the horrible and prolonged treatments the doctor had predicted. She started getting better almost immediately and in a month was ready to go back to her job at the bar. The doctor said that sometimes people with strong dispositions just couldn't be held down, and that Marge was lucky and would probably be fine and live a long life.

On the morning Marge was getting ready for her first day back at the bar, the phone rang in the kitchen and Sims answered it. It was almost nine and he was reading the paper while Marge was getting dressed.

'Vic,' a voice said, a man's voice, a voice he didn't know. There was a long pause, then, during which it sounded like the receiver was being muffled and talking went on.

'Yes,' Sims said. 'Who is it?' It occurred to him that it was probably Marge's boss calling from the bar, needling Sims about being a housewife or something like that. Marge's boss, George, was a fat, good-natured Greek guy everybody liked. 'Is this Big George?' Sims said. 'I know what you're going to tell me, George. You better watch your step out there.'

'Vic,' the voice said again. Sims somehow sensed it wasn't George—though it could've been—and in the same instant he realized he had no earthly idea who it was or could be, but that it wasn't good. And in the silence that followed his own name, the feeling of a vast outside world opened up in him, and scared him so that he stood up beside the wall phone and stared at his own phone number. 723-2772. This was somebody calling from far away.

'This is Vic,' Sims said stiffly. 'What do you want? What's this about?' He heard Marge's footsteps in another room, heard her closet door close, smelled her perfume in the air.

'We're going to kill Marge, Vic,' the man said. 'If you let her out of your sight, anywhere, we'll be waiting for her. The devil needs Marge, Vic. You've given up your right to her by being an asshole and a slime, by fucking somebody else. And now you have to pay for it.'

'Who is this?' Sims said.

'This is the devil calling,' the voice said. 'Everybody's a loser today.'

Someone, a woman in the background, laughed a long, witchy, raspy laugh until she started to cough, then laughed through the cough and laughed until she couldn't stop coughing. Then a door slammed in a room at the end of the line, very far away. Sims knew who it was now. He turned and looked out the window and across the yard between his house and the Krukows'. Betty Krukow was standing at the sink, her hands down and out of sight. She looked up after an instant and saw Sims looking at her. She smiled at him through the two panes of glass and across the sunny yard with the fence in between. When Sims stared at her a moment longer, she held up a plate up out of the sink, dripping with suds and dishwater and waved it in front of her face as if it were a fan. Then her face broke into a wide laugh and she walked away from the window.

'Cleo,' Sims said. 'Let me speak to Cleo. Let me speak to her right now. Right this instant.' Things didn't have to be this way, he thought.

'He wants to speak to Cleo,' the man said to someone there where he was.

'Tell him she died,' Sims heard a woman's voice say casually. 'Like Marge.'

'She died,' the man said. 'Like Marge. Who's Marge?' he heard the man say.

'His wife, you numb-nuts,' the woman said, then laughed raucously. 'Ha, ha, ha, ha.'

'Let me speak to her,' Sims said. 'If that's Cleo, I want to talk to her. Please.'

'Don't forget us,' the man's voice said suddenly very close to the receiver. Then almost immediately the connection was broken.

Sims stood holding the buzzing phone to his ear. And after a moment of looking out the window into the bright daylight, brightening the blue shingles of the Krukows' house and reflecting his own brown house in their kitchen window, reflecting, in fact, the very window he could see out of but not himself, Sims thought: this is not a thing that happened, not a thing I'll hear about again. Things you do pass away and are gone, and you need only to outlive them for your life to be better, steadily better. That is what you can count on.

In the chill night, the train passed slowly through another small Montana town. The business section ran along both sides of the track. Yellow crime lights were shining. Sims saw a bar with a sign that said LIVE ENTERTAINMENT, and two car lots with strings of white bulbs along the rows of older cars. A convenience store with cars parked into the curb was open at the end of the street. Several boys wearing football uniforms stood in front drinking beers, holding up the bottles in salute. In the rear windows of their cars, girls' faces were looking out at the train.

Down the highway, out of town, was a motel with a white neon sign that said SKYLARK. A soaring bird was outlined in delicate blue lights. He saw a woman and a man, the woman very fat and dressed in a white shift dress, walking down the row of motel rooms to where a door was ajar with light escaping. The woman was wearing high heels. Sims thought she was probably cold.

'Can you imagine a drink, Vic?' Sims looked up and Sergeant Benton was back and wearing a big grin. She was also wearing perfume and she looked fresher, Sims thought, as if she'd had a shower since he saw her.

'I thought you'd gone to sleep,' he said. She had her big hands on her hips, and she wasn't wearing shoes. Just stockings. Sims noticed her feet weren't particularly big.

'Are we going to argue about this all night, or what?' Sergeant Benton said.

'I'm fresh out here,' Sims said. He held up his plastic cup. 'I guess the bar's closed now.' He thought unhappily about the flask in Marge's purse.

36

'The Doris bar's still open,' Sergeant Benton said. 'No cover.'

'Where's the Doris bar?' Sims said.

'In Doris's suite.' Sergeant Benton raised her plucked eyebrows in an exaggerated way to let Sims know she was having some fun. 'Vic's wife wouldn't care if he had a drink, would she? A clear conscience is the same as no conscience, right?'

Marge would care, Sims thought. She'd care a lot, though Marge would certainly be happy to go herself with him and Doris if somebody were to ask her. She was asleep, though, and needed to get her rest for Pauline's next crisis. Meanwhile, he was here by himself, wide awake with no chance of sleep and nothing to do but stare at a dark, cheerless landscape. Anything he decided to do he would do, no questions asked. It had nothing to do with conscience.

'She wouldn't mind,' Sims said. 'She'd come herself if she wasn't asleep.'

'We'll drink a toast to her,' Doris held an imaginary glass up.

'Great,' Sims said, and held up a glass himself, and smiled. 'Here's to Marge.'

He followed Sergeant Benton into the lounge car, which was smoky. The snack bar was closed. Padlocks were on the steel cabinets. Two older men in cowboy hats and boots were arguing across a table full of beer cans. They were arguing about somebody named Helena, a name they pronounced with a Spanish accent. 'It'd be a mistake to underestimate Helena,' one of them said. 'I'll warn you of that.'

'Oh, fuck Helena,' the other cowboy said. 'That fat, ugly bitch. I'm not afraid of her or her family.'

Across from them a young Asian woman in a sari sat holding an Asian baby. They stared up at Sergeant Benton and at Sims. The woman's round belly was exposed and a tiny red jewel pierced her nose. She seemed frightened, Sims thought, frightened of whatever was going to happen next. He didn't feel that way at all, and was sorry she did.

Sergeant Benton led him out into the second, rumbling vestibule, tip-toeing across in her stocking feet and into the sleeping car where the lights were turned low. As the vestibule door closed, the sound of the moving train wheels was taken far away. Sergeant Benton turned smiling and put her finger to her lips. 'People are sleeping,' she said.

Marge was sleeping, Sims thought, right across the hall. It made his fingers tingle and feel cold. He walked right past the little silver door and didn't look at it. She'll go right on sleeping, he thought, and wake up happy tomorrow.

At the far end of the corridor a black man stuck his bald head out between the curtains of a private seat and looked at Sims and Doris. Doris was fitting a key into the lock of her compartment door. The black man was the porter who'd helped Marge and him with their suitcases and offered to bring them coffee in the morning. Sergeant Benton waved at him and went 'shhhh.' Sims waved at him, too, though only half-heartedly. The porter, whose name was Lewis, said nothing, and drew his head back inside the curtains.

'Give me your tired, right?' Doris said, and laughed softly as she opened the door. A bed-light was on inside, and the bed had been opened and made up—probably by Lewis. Out the window Sims could see the empty, murky night and the moon chased by clouds, and the ground shooting by below the glass. It was dizzying. He could see his own face reflected, and he was surprised to see that he was smiling. '*Entrez-vous*,' Doris whispered behind him, 'or we'll have tomorrow on our hands.'

Sims climbed in, then slid to the foot of the bed, while Doris crawled around on her hands and knees reaching for things and digging in her purse behind the pillow. She pulled out an alarm clock. 'It's twelve o'clock. Do you know where your kids are?' She flashed Sims a grin. 'Mine are still out there in space waiting to come in. Good luck to them, is what I say.' She went back to digging in her bag.

'Mine, too,' Sims said. He was cold in Doris's roomette, but he felt like he should take his shoes off. Keeping them on made him uncomfortable, but it made him uncomfortable to be in bed with Doris in the first place.

'I just couldn't stand it,' Doris said. 'They're just other little adults. Who needs that? One's enough.'

'That's right,' Sims said. Marge felt the same way he did. Children made life a misery, and once that was over, they did it again. That had been the first thing he and Marge had seen eye to eye on. Sims put his shoes down beside the mattress and hoped they wouldn't start to smell.

'Miracles,' Doris said, and held up a pint bottle of vodka. 'Never fear, Doris is here,' she said. 'Never a dull moment. Plus there's glasses, too.' She rumbled around in her bag. 'Right now in a jiffy there'll be glasses,' she said. 'Never fear. Are you just horribly bored already, Vic? Have I completely blown this? Are you antsy? Are you mad? Don't be mad.'

'I couldn't be happier,' Sims said. Doris, on her hands and knees in the half-light, turned and smiled at him. Sims smiled back at her.

'Good man. Excellent.' Doris held up a glass. 'One glass,' she said, 'the fruit of patience. Did you know I look as good as I did when I was in high school? I've been told that—recently, in fact.'

Sims looked at Doris's legs and her rear end. They were both good-looking, he thought. Both slim and firm. 'That's easy to believe,' he said. 'How old *are* you?'

Sergeant Benton narrowed one eye at him. 'How old do you think? Or, how old do I look? I'll ask that.'

She was taking all night to fix two drinks, Sims thought. 'Thirty. Or near thirty, anyway,' he said.

'Cute,' Sergeant Benton said. 'That's extremely cute.' She smirked at him. 'Thirty-eight is my correct age.'

'I'm forty-two,' Sims said.

Doris didn't seem to hear him.

'Glass,' she said, holding up another one for him to see. 'Two glasses. Let's just go on and have a drink, what do you say?'

'Great,' Sims said. He could smell Doris's perfume, a sweet flowery smell he liked and that came from her suitcase. He was glad he was here.

Doris turned and crossed her legs in a way that stretched her skirt across her knees. She set both glasses on her skirt and poured two drinks. Sims realized he could see up her skirt if the light in the compartment was any better.

She smiled and handed Sims a glass. 'Here's to your wife,' Doris said. 'May sweet dreams descend.'

'Here's to that,' Sims said and drank a gulp of warm vodka. He hadn't known how much he'd wanted a drink until this one was down his throat.

'How fast do you think we're going now?' Doris said, peering toward the dark window where nothing was visible.

'I don't know,' Sims said. 'Eighty, maybe. I'd guess eighty.'

'Hurtling through the dark night,' Doris said and smiled. She took another drink. 'What scares you ought to be interesting, right?'

'Where've you been on this trip?' Sims said.

Sergeant Benton pushed her fingers through her blonde hair and gave her head another shake, then sniffed. 'Visiting a relative.' She stared at Sims and her eyes seemed to blaze at him suddenly and for no reason Sims could see. Possibly this was a sensitive subject. He would be happy to avoid those.

'And where're you going? You told me but I forgot. It seems like a long time ago.'

'Would you like to hear a little story?' Sergeant Benton said. 'A recent and true-to-life story?'

'Sure.' Sims raised his vodka glass to toast a story. Doris extended the bottle and poured in some more, then more for herself.

'Well,' she said. She smelled the vodka in her glass, then pulled her skirt up slightly to be comfortable. 'I go to visit my father, you see, out on San Juan Island. I haven't seen him in maybe eight years, since before I went in the Army—since I was married, in fact. And he's married now himself to a very nice lady. Miss Vera. They run a boarding kennel out on the island. He's sixty something and takes care of all these noisy dogs. She's fifty something. I don't know how they do it.' Doris took a drink. 'Or why. She's a Mormon, believes in all the angels, so he's more or less become one, too, though he drinks and smokes. He's not at all spiritual. He was in the Air Force. Also a sergeant. Anyway, the first night I get there, we all eat dinner together. A big steak. And right away my father says he has to drive down to the store to get something, and he'll be back. So off he goes. And Miss Vera and I are washing dishes and watching television and chattering. And before I know it, two hours have gone by. And I said to Miss Vera, "Where's Eddie? Hasn't he been gone a long time?" And she just said, "Oh, he'll be back pretty soon." So we pottered around a little more. Each of us smoked a cigarette. Then she got ready to go to bed. By herself. It was ten o'clock, and I said, "Where's Dad?" And she said, "Sometimes he stops and has a drink down in town." So when she's in bed I get in the other car and drive down the hill to the bar. And there's his station-wagon in front. Only when I go in and ask, he isn't there, and nobody says they know where he is. I go back outside and this guy steps to the door behind me and says, "Try the trailer, hon. That's it. Try the trailer." Nothing else. And across the road is a little house trailer with its lights on and a car sitting out front. And I just walked across the road—I still had on my uniform—walked up the steps and knocked on the door. There're some voices inside and a TV. I hear people moving around and a door close. The front door opens then and here's a woman who apparently lives there. She's completely dressed. I'd guess her age to be fifty. She's younger than Vera anyway, with a younger face. She says, "Yes. What is it?" And I said I was sorry, but I was looking for my father, and I guessed I'd gotten the wrong place. But she said, "Just a second," and turned around, and said, "Eddie, your daughter's here."

'And my father came out of a door to the next room. Maybe it was a closet, I didn't know. I didn't care. He had his pants on and an undershirt. And he said, "Oh, hi, Doris. How're you? Come on in. This is Sherry." And the only thing I could think of was how thin his shoulders looked. He looked like he was going to die. I didn't even speak to Sherry. I just said, No, I couldn't stay. And I drove on back up to the house.'

'Did you leave then?' Sims said.

'No, I stayed around a couple more days. *Then* left. It didn't matter to me. It made me think, though.'

'What did you think,' Sims asked.

Doris put her head back against the metal wall and looked up. 'Oh, I just thought about being the other woman, which I've been that enough. Everybody's done everything twice, right? At my age. You cross a line. But you can do a thing and have it mean nothing but what you feel that minute. You don't have to give yourself away. Isn't that true?'

'That's exactly true,' Sims said and thought it was right. He'd done it himself plenty of times.

'Where's the real life, right? I don't think I've had mine yet, have you?' Doris held her glass up to her lips in both hands and smiled at him.

'Not yet, I haven't,' Sims said. 'Not entirely.'

'When I was a little girl in California and my father was teaching me to drive, I used to think, "I'm driving now. I have to pay strict attention to everything; I have to notice everything; I have to think about my hands being on the wheel; it's possible I'll think only about this very second forever, and it'll drive me crazy." But I'd already thought of something else.' Doris wrinkled her nose at Sims. 'That's my movie, right?'

'It sounds familiar,' Sims said. He took a long drink of his vodka and emptied the glass. The vodka tasted metallic, as if it had been kept stored in a can. It had a good effect, though. He felt like he could stay up all night. He was seeing things from the outside, and nothing bad could happen to anyone. Everyone was protected. 'Most people want to be good, though,' Sims said for no reason. Just words under their own command, headed who-knows-where. Everything seemed arbitrary.

'Would you like me to take my clothes off?' Sergeant Benton said and smiled at him.

'I'd like that,' Sims said. 'Sure.' He thought that he would also like a small amount more of the vodka. He reached over, took the bottle off the blanket and poured himself some more.

Sergeant Benton began unbuttoning her uniform blouse. She knelt forward on her knees, pulled her shirt tail out and began with the bottom button first. She watched Sims, half-smiling. 'Do you remember the first woman you ever saw naked?' she said, opening her blouse so Sims could see her white brassiere and a smooth line of belly over her skirt.

'Yes,' Sims said.

'And where was that?' Sergeant Benton said. 'What state was that in?' She took her blouse off, then pulled her strap down off her shoulder and uncovered one breast, then the other one. They were breasts that went to the side and pushed outward. They were nice breasts.

'That was California, too,' Sims said. 'Near Sacramento, I think.'

'What happened?' Sergeant Benton began unzipping her skirt.

'We were on a golf course. My friend and I and this girl. Patsy was her name. We were all twelve. We both asked her to take off her clothes, in an old caddy house by the Air Force base. And she did it. We did too. She said we'd have to.' Sims wondered if Patsy's name was still Patsy.

Sergeant Benton slid her skirt down, then sat back and handed it around her ankles. She had on only panty hose now. Nothing beyond that. You could see through them even in the dim light. She leaned against the metal wall and looked at Sims. He could touch her now, he thought. That was what she would like to happen. 'Did you like it?' Sergeant Benton said.

'Yes. I liked it,' Sims said.

'It wasn't disappointing to you?'

'It was,' Sims said. 'But I liked it. I knew I was going to.' Sims moved close to her, lightly touched her ankle, then her knee, then the soft skin of her belly and came down with the waist of her hosiery. Her hands touched his neck but didn't feel rough. He heard her breathe and smelled the perfume she was wearing. Nothing seemed arbitrary now.

'Sweet, that's sweet,' she said, and breathed deeply once. 'Sometimes I think about making love. Like now. And everything tightens up inside me, and I just squeeze and say *ahhhh* without even meaning to. It just escapes me. It's just that pleasure. Someday it'll stop, won't it?'

'No,' Sims said, 'that won't. That stays forever.' He was near her now, his ear to her chest. He heard a noise, a noise of releasing. Outside, in the corridor, someone began talking in a hushed voice. Someone said, 'No, no. Don't say that.' And then a door clicked.

'Life's on so thin a string anymore,' she whispered, and turned off the tiny light. 'Not that much makes it good.'

'That's right, isn't it?' Sims said, close to her. 'I know that.'

'This isn't passion,' she said. 'This is something different now. I can't lose sleep over this.'

'That's fine,' Sims said.

'You knew this would happen, didn't you?' she said. 'It wasn't a secret.' He didn't know it. He didn't try to answer it. 'Oh you,' she whispered, 'Oh you.'

Sometime in the night Sims felt the train slow and then stop, then sit still in the dark. He had no idea where he was. He still had his clothes on. Outside there was sound like wind, and for a moment he thought possibly he was dead, that it would feel like this.

Sergeant Benton lay beside him, asleep. Her clothes were around her. She was covered with a blanket. The vodka bottle was empty on the bed. What had he done here? Sims thought. How had things exactly happened? What time was it? Out the window he could see no one and nothing. The moon was gone, though the sky was red and wavering with a reflected light, as though the wind moved it.

Sims picked up his shoes and opened the door into the corridor. The porter didn't appear this time, and Sims closed the door softly and carried his shoes down to the wash room by the vestibule. Inside, he locked the door, ran water on his hands, wet his face, then rubbed soap on his face and his ears and his neck and into his hair-line, then rinsed them with water out of the silver bowl until his face was clean and dripping, and he could stand to see it in the dull, little mirror; a haggard face, his eyes red, his skin pale, his teeth gray and lifeless. A deceiver's face, he thought. An adulterer's face, a face to turn away from. He smiled at himself and then couldn't look. He was glad to be alone. He wouldn't see this woman again. He and Marge would get off in a few hours, and Doris would sleep around the clock.

Sims let himself back into the corridor. He thought he heard noise outside the train, and through the window on to the vestibule he saw the Asian woman, standing and staring out, holding her little boy in her arms. She was talking to the conductor. He hoped there was no trouble. He wanted to get to Minot on time, and get off the train.

When he let himself into Marge's roomette, Marge was awake. And out the window he saw the center of everyone's attention. A wide fire was burning on the open prairie. Out in the dark, men were moving at the edges of the fire. Trucks were in the fields and high tractors with their lights on, and dogs chasing and tumbling in the dark. Far away he could see the white stanchions of high voltage lines travelling off into the distance.

'It's thrilling,' Marge said and turned and smiled at Sims. 'The tracks are on fire ahead of us. I heard someone outside say that. People are running all over. I watched a house disappear. It'll drive you to your remotest thoughts.'

'What about us?' Sims said, looking out the window toward the fire.

'I didn't think of that. Isn't that strange?' Marge said. 'It didn't even seem to matter. It should, I guess.'

The fire had turned the sky red and the wind blew it upwards, and Sims imagined he felt heat, and his heart beat faster with the sight—a fire that could turn and sweep over them in a moment, and they would all be caught, asleep and awake. He thought of Sergeant Benton alone in her bed, dreaming dreams of safety and confidence. Nothing was wrong with her, he thought. She should be saved. A sense of powerlessness and despair rose in him, as if there was help but he couldn't offer it.

'The world's on fire, Vic,' Marge said. 'But it doesn't hurt anything. It just burns until it stops.' She raised the covers. 'Get in bed with me, sweetheart,' she said, 'you poor thing. You've been up all night, haven't you?' She was naked under the sheet. He could see her breasts and her stomach and the beginnings of her white legs.

He sat on the bed and put his shoes down. His heart beat faster. He could feel heat now from outside. But, he thought, there was no threat to them, to anyone on the train. 'I slept a little,' he said.

Marge took his hand and kissed it and held it between her hands. 'When I was in my remote thoughts, you know, just watching it burn, I thought about how I get in bed sometimes and I think how happy I am, and then it makes me sad. It's crazy, isn't it? I'd like life to stop, and it won't. It just keeps running by me. It makes me jealous of Pauline. She makes life stop when she wants it to. She doesn't care what happens. That's just a way of looking at things. I guess I wouldn't want to be like her.'

'You're not like her,' Sims said. 'You're sympathetic.'

'She probably thinks no one takes her seriously.'

'It's all right.' Sims said.

'What's going to happen to Pauline now,' Marge said, close to him. 'Will she be all right? Do you think she will?'

'I think she will,' Sims said.

'We're out on a frontier here, aren't we, sweetheart? It feels like that.' Sims didn't answer. 'Are you sleepy, hon?' Marge said. 'You can sleep. I'm awake now. I'll watch over you.' She reached and pulled down the shade and everything, all the movement and heat outside, was gone.

He touched Marge with his fingers—the bones in her face and her shoulders, her breasts, her ribs. He touched the scar, smooth and rigid and neat under her arm, like a welt from a mean blow. This can do it, he thought, this can finish you, this small thing. He held her to him, her face against his as his heart beat. And he felt dizzy then and insufficient, without any memory of life having changed in that peculiar way.

Outside on the cold air, flames moved and divided and swarmed the sky. And Sims felt alone in a wide empire, removed and afloat, calmed, as if life was far away now, as if blackness was all around, as if stars held the only light.

PICADOR

OUTSTANDING INTERNATIONAL WRITING

The Bone People
Keri Hulme
Winner of the 1985
Booker Prize

'A profoundly interesting novel which brings to life another continent, another people and a problem which most of us try to avoid thinking about'
Sunday Times

Paperback £3.95   Published 4 July

The Haunted House
Rebecca Brown

Robin's family was always on the move. They had no home. But it is a home above all else that Robin desires; a home that is safe and secure and one where the inhabitants display a constancy of purpose. As she and her lover set about building their dream house, Robin is haunted by the ghosts of her past. Her old fears take on a new meaning.

Hardback £8.95   Published 6 June

Theatre of Sleep
An Anthology of Literary Dreams
Guido Almansi & Claude Béguin

Bringing together a wide selection of dreams drawn from all ages and many cultures, some translated into English for the first time, this is a hugely entertaining work of some of the most bizarre, imaginative and perplexing passages ever written.

Hardback £10.95   Published 4 July

The Madwoman's Underclothes
Germaine Greer

From sources as diverse as *Spare Rib*, *Forum*, the *Sunday Times*, *Oz*, the *Spectator* and the *New York Times*, this mosaic of essays, long and short, some of which are appearing for the first time in print, is both a reflection of an era and the changing ideas and styles of Germaine Greer.

Hardback £9.95   Published 5 Sept.

Home Before Dark
Susan Cheever

The moving and brilliantly restrained account of John Cheever's life and work, from his early days as a penniless *New Yorker* writer to the 1960s when he was showered with prestigious awards and fellowships, by his daughter.

Paperback £3.95   Published 4 July

States of Desire
Edmund White

From Florida to LA, White sets out to investigate the way in which individual gays and gay communities feel about themselves and about the rest of society.

'White writes about his world and that of the men he meets with humour, open-mindedness and moral imagination'
Time Out

Paperback £3.95   Published 4 July

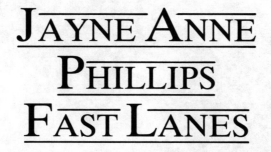

1975

W e walked down a grassy knoll to the lake.
'The truck should be OK there,' he said. 'Place is deserted.'
Behind us the pick-up sat squat and red in the sun, a black tarp roped across the boxes and trunks in the bed. Hot and slick, the tarp shimmered like a dark liquid. The rest stop was a small gravel lot marked by a low wooden fence and three large aluminium trash cans chained to posts. Beyond it the access road, unlined and perfectly smooth, glittered in a slant of heat.

'Where are we?' I asked.

'Somewhere in east Georgia.'

I could close my eyes and still feel myself across the seat of the moving truck, my head on his sour thigh and my knees tucked up. The steering-wheel was a curved black bar close to my face, its dark grooves turning. We hadn't spoken since pulling out of the motel lot in New Orleans. Now I stumbled and he drew me up beside him. The weeds were thick and silky. Pollen rose in clouds and settled in the haze. The incline grew steeper and we seemed to slide into the depths of the grass, then the ground leveled and several full elms banded the water. The bank was green to its edge. We entered the shade of the trees and felt the coolness through our shoes. He stepped out of his unlaced sneakers, pulled off his shirt and jeans. The belt buckle clanked on stones. Then he stood, touching the white skin of his stomach. His eyes were blue as blue glass, and bloodshot. He hadn't slept.

'You all right?' he said.

I didn't answer.

'You've got no obligation to me,' he said, 'I don't tell you who to pick up in a bar. But at eight o'clock this morning I began to wonder if I was going to have to leave you, and dump all that crap of yours in the middle of Bourbon Street.'

He turned, moving through high grass to the water. I saw him step in and push out, sinking to his shoulders. 'Thurman,' I said, but he was under, weaving long and pale below the surface.

I took off my dress and let it fall into the grass white and wrinkled, smelling of rum. The lake seemed to grow as I got closer, yawning like a cool mouth at the center of the heat. I was in it; I sank to my knees as water closed over me, then felt the settling mud as I lay flat and tried to stay down. I held my knees and swayed, hearing nothing. Their faces were fading, and the lines of white coke across the gleaming desk top. I rolled to my side and the water pushed, darkening, purple. It was Thurman, moving closer, changing the colors, and I felt his hands on my arms. He pulled me up and the air cracked as we surfaced, streaming water.

I wasn't crying but I felt the leaden air move out of my chest. I felt how hard he was holding me and I knew I was shaking. My heart beat in my throat and ears, pounding. He held my heavy hair pulled back and bunched in one hand, and with the other he poured water down my neck and shoulders, stroking with the warmth of his palm in the coolness. He said low disconnected words, mother sounds and lullabyes. I felt my teeth in my lips and my forehead moving slowly against his chest.Holding to his big shoulders, I could feel him with all my body.

'I drew a map to the motel on that napkin and you lost it, didn't you,' he said. 'I knew you would. We were both drunk when I gave it to you.'

Behind his voice there was a hum of insects and locusts and the faraway sound of the highway. The highway played three chords beyond his reddened arms: a low thrum, a continual median sigh, and a whine so shrill it was gone as it started. The sounds separated and converged, like the sounds of their voices in the room last night and the driftings of music from the club below. There was a discreet jarring of dishes or silver at a long distance, and the sound of the bed, close, under me, but fake, like a sound through a wall that might after all be a recording, someone's joke.

I was talking then, because Thurman said, 'No, no joke.' As he said it I could feel the water again, around us, between us.

'I lose track of where I am,' I said.

'Stand still. You're OK now. No one's trying anything. It's me. Remember me? The driver?'

'Yeah. I remember you. You're the one born in Dallas.'

'Right. That's good. Now listen. We're going to walk out of the water and dry off for five minutes. I'm not going to touch you. You'll feel fine in the sun and I'll smoke a joint.' He turned in the water, holding my wrist, pulling me gently towards the shore.

'I can't put that dress on again,' I said.

'Then leave it for the next refugee. Leave it where it is.'

'No one should wear it.'

'You can wear my shirt,' he said. 'You'll look great in blue denim and no pants, like Doris Day in a pajama movie.'

Thurman had seen a lot of Doris Day movies in Dallas, in neighbourhood theaters that weren't the Ritz. His two older brothers kissed girls in the balcony while he sat in the back row downstairs with the Mexicans. Blue-eyed Doris flickered in a bad print to the tune of bubbly music and wetback jeers. Thurman said he liked Doris in those days because she was so out-of-it she made no sense to anyone, and she kept right on raising her eyebrows, perky, not quite smart, as wads of paper and popcorn boxes bounced off the screen. Afterward he walked home with his brothers across the freeway, up long sidewalks to what was just a few houses then, not yet a suburb. His brothers told tales on the girls and teased him about sitting with the Mexicans. At home they sometimes shook him by his heels over the toilet, flushed it, and threatened to drop him in. That, said Thurman, was a precursor to all of Dallas in the 50s and early 60s: fringed shirts, steaming sidewalk grates globbed with saliva in the summer, first-time gang-bangs in a whore-house with steers' heads on the walls. Not just the horns, he said, the whole fucking head, stuffed, like it was a lion from Africa. And football, always football; Thurman's father was a successful high school coach who took pride in featuring his own sons on his teams. One after another, he'd coached, punished, driven them all to a grueling and temporary stardom.

When I met Thurman he was floating and I was floating home. He drove a Datsun pick-up and he lived in the foothills near Denver. He had a small wooden house with a slanted kitchen, a broken water heater, and a new skylight framed in white pine against old ceiling boards and dangling strips of flowered wallpaper. He played music with friends of mine and did carpentry and called me up once to eat with him at a good Indian restaurant. He'd been in the Peace Corps in Ceylon and he said you should eat this food right out of the bowls with your hand, but only one hand. The other stayed in your lap to prove you used separate hands for eating and for cleaning yourself.

He stayed with me that night, mostly because I liked the way he looked from the back as he bought oranges later, threading his way through the panhandlers at an open-air market. He had a cloth bag swinging at his hip but none of them asked for change. He was big and broad-shouldered in a blousey white shirt, red-headed and ruddy; he'd gotten slightly dressed-up and called me without really knowing me to pretend a good dinner was no big deal. He was probably lonely, but he moved nicely, mannish, not arrogant, tossing the oranges into a bag with the casual finesse of an ex-athlete still in shape at thirty. The sun was going down; it was early summer; the fruit was stacked in green trays like pretty ornaments. I didn't really want Thurman but I liked him and it was time to sleep with someone. I knew he'd be patient and slow and if I got a little high it would be OK, I'd feel better. But he went on too long, he woke me again in the night, and the next morning he wanted to stay around. He'd lived with someone quite a while in San Antonio; it had broken up three years ago, but he still dated history from that time: all the towns he'd lived in since, Berkeley, Austin, Jackson, Eugene, Denver, all the western floater's towns. We talked about money—how I'd spent mine having mono I'd caught waitressing and eating off plates, how he was making a lot building houses in the mountains with a crew of dealers from Aspen. Finally he drank his orange juice and left. I didn't think of him much until a month later when I read his notice advertising for riders on a bookstore bulletin board. He was taking off for a while, down through Texas and Louisiana, then up the coast. I went looking and found him installing wooden doors on a cold storage cabinet at a natural foods store.

'You leaving for good?' he asked. 'Going home?'

'Leaving here for good. I won't stay home long.'

'Then why go? For the hell of it?'

'It's a long story. I'd rather not go into it here by the plum nectar and the juice cartons advertising Enlightenment.'

'You're a cynic,' he said, measuring the blond frame of the door. 'That's why you're leaving. You can't take it here in paradise where everyone is beautiful and girls aren't allowed to wear make-up.'

'You've got it. I want to go back to my home town and buy mascara.'

'You wouldn't be caught dead in mascara.' He lifted the piece of glass against the frame, checking the fit, then set it down again.

Looking at me through the open door of the cabinet, he held the lock in one hand and rummaged in his apron for screws. 'I accept you as my rider.'

I looked at the floor, then back up at him. 'The thing is, I need to get there pretty quickly. My father is sick.'

'How sick?'

'Just sick. He has to have an operation in two or three weeks.'

'Well,' he said, and ran his hand along the wood, 'you'd almost get there in time. Three weeks would be the best I could do. Stopovers on the way. But you won't have to worry about money. Just pay for your food.' He looked away from me, leaning back to fit the lock. 'Is it a deal?'

'It's the best deal I've got.'

'Good. I'm leaving in four days.'

'Thurman,' I said, 'is this a kissey-poo number?'

He tested the hinges and shrugged. 'It's no particular number. Whatever works out. Besides, you can handle me. I'm a pushover.'

'Fine. I'm going home to pack.'

I turned and walked out, and as I hit the street I heard him yelling behind me, 'Listen, can you sing with the radio? Can you carry a tune?'

We pulled out of town at dawn. I had the feeling, the floater's only fix: I was free, it didn't matter if I never saw these streets again; even as we passed them they receded and entered a realm of placeless streets. Even the people were gone, the good ones and the bad ones; I owned whatever real had occurred, I took it all. I was vanished, invisible, another apartment left empty behind me, my possessions given away, thrown away, packed away in taped boxes fit into an available vehicle. The vehicle was the light, the early light and later the darkness.

'Hey dreamer,' Thurman said, 'What are you doing?'

'Praying,' I said.

He smiled. 'I did some speed, I'm going to just keep going. Sleep when you want to.'

'OK,' I said.

'New Mexico, tomorrow morning.'

'Good. That will be pretty.'

Thurman drove straight to an all-night stop in Albuquerque, the apartment of a stewardess he'd known in college. It was the first floor of a complex right off the freeway, motel terraces and a naugahyde couch. She was gone and it seemed she'd never been there, empty shelves and pebbly white walls with no marks. I sat up in bed while my legs still shook from holding him.

'You could be such a good lover,' he said, 'I can feel you have been, but you're so busy stepping out.'

'This mattress is too soft.' I moved away from him. 'The sheets feel heavy. I'm going to sleep in the other room on the floor.'

'The floor,' he said. He lit a cigarette. 'It's a shame you can't levitate, so that even the floor couldn't touch you.'

I went into the living-room and pushed the furniture against the walls. There were only three pieces; the black couch and chair and a formica table. They all seemed weightless, like cardboard. I lay down in the middle of the carpeted floor with my arms out and my feet together, counting each breath, counting with the hum of the air conditioner. I went away. I heard nothing until I felt him in the room. He was sitting beside me, cross-legged, in the dark.

'What are you scared of?' he said.

'I don't know. Going back.'

'Explain. Tell Thurman.'

'I can't. Sometimes it's hard to breathe, like living under blankets.'

'Hot?'

'Hot, but cold too. Shaking.'

'Then don't go back.'

'I have to,' I said. 'It doesn't help any more to stay away.'

He stood up and went to the bedroom. I heard him pull the sheet off the bed in one motion, the sheet coming clear with a soft snap. He brought a pillow too, stood at my feet, and furled the white sheet out so it settled over me like the rectangular flag of some pure and empty country.

'It's midnight,' he said. 'Get some sleep. We need to be out of here early.'

By nine a.m. we were two hours south of the city on Route 25. We didn't talk; the road was a straight two-lane, the light still clear but thickening with heat to come later. Both of us had

wanted out of that apartment by dawn; we'd drunk a half-carton of
orange juice we'd found in the spotless refrigerator, drunk it as we
pulled out of the parking lot, shrouded in a half-stupor of fatigue.
Thurman held the wheel steady with one knee, staring ahead. 'Can
you drive a standard shift?'

'Maybe,' I said, 'except I haven't for a while. I'm not sure I still
know how.'

'What?' His voice was flat. 'You're twenty-three and American
and you can't drive?'

'I have a license. Just never used it.'

'Why not?'

'Because when I was sixteen I pulled into the driveway in my
mother's car, sideswiped my father's car, and rear-ended my
brother's car.'

Thurman shook his head. 'Wonderful.'

'I was only going ten miles an hour—there wasn't much damage.
Scratches and dented chrome. But afterwards my driving was a
family joke and no one would let me behind the wheel.'

'I can imagine.'

'Besides, it was a small town. My boyfriends had cars.'

'Well,' he said, 'this is no small town and there's no boyfriend in
sight. You're going to learn how to drive.'

'Thurman, are you going to liberate me?'

'No, you're going to liberate me. I plan to spend exactly half this
trip pleasantly stoned, playing with the radio and reading girlie
magazines.'

'I didn't know you read girlie magazines.'

'Only the really sleazy ones, the ones with no pretensions. And I
don't want any shit about it.'

He pulled off the road near Cuchillo and took a left off the exit.
We could see the town in the distance, brown and white and hunched.
Thurman drove in the opposite direction. The land was absolutely
flat, wavering with heat, a moony unreal surface even as mirrors.
Light glanced off like knife glare. The far mountains were blue and
beige, treeless. 'Pinos Altos,' Thurman said, 'or the Mimbres range, I
don't know which. We aren't far from Elephant Butte and the
Reservation.' He steered onto the berm of the narrow road, slowed
and stopped as yellow dust rose around us. 'Good spot for a
ceremony.' He turned off the ignition and faced me. He seemed

55

amazingly defined in that early, hot light, a film of moisture on his forehead, his big hands opening towards me in even gestures, describing small spheres as he talked.

'Now,' he said, 'this is going to take twenty minutes. Remember a standard is always the best transmission—it allows you to feel the machine and the road more efficiently than an automatic. Nobody who knows much about cars drives an automatic.'

'Automatics are for cherries, right?'

He got out of the truck and stood looking in at me from the road. 'Slide over.'

'Do we have to be so serious? It was a joke.'

'I'm not laughing. In thirty minutes this pleasant eighty-degree interlude will be over and the temperature will be climbing right up to about a hundred and ten. It's early September in Texas. We will need to be moving. So pay attention.'

'OK.'

'It's easy.'

'Nothing mechanical is easy.'

He sighed. 'Are you ready?' He watched my face as I slid into the driver's seat, then slammed the door of the truck and walked around to the cab. He got in and sat motionless, waiting.

'I'll need a few instructions, if you don't fucking mind.'

'Look, it's hot in Texas. Let's both take it easy.'

'I'm trying to.'

He looked away to where the road disappeared in mirage past a nothingness, and recited, 'Right foot, gas and brake. Left foot, clutch. Now, push in the clutch, put the transmission in neutral, and turn the ignition.'

The engine turned over and caught. I wanted to get out of the truck and walk into the brown fields, keep walking. Far off, wheeling birds moved like a pattern of circular dashes in the sky. Something was dead out there, yellowed like the dust and lacey with vanishing. Thurman's voice continued, but closer. He had moved over next to me. 'Let the clutch out slowly. Give it gas as you let it out, enough gas at the precise moment, or you'll stall. Now try it, that's right, now the gas...' The truck jerked forward, coughed, jerked, stalled. 'Try it again,' he said, 'a little smoother, gauge the release a little more, there you go—now.'

He talked, we jerked and moved, rolled cautiously forward, stopped. The fields remained silent. A mongrel dog ambled out of the brush and sat in the middle of the opposite lane, watching and panting. The dog was maybe twenty pounds of rangy canine, immobile, a desert stone with slit eyes. 'Do it again,' Thurman murmured, 'there you go, give it gas, not too much. OK, OK, we're moving, don't watch the dog, watch the road. Good, good, now—if you go too slow in a gear, you force the engine to lug. Hear that? That's lugging. Give it some gas...'

He kept talking in the close room of the truck, both of us sweating, until the words were meaningless. I repeated the same movements: clutch, gas, shift, brake, downshift, up and down the same mile stretch of road. The mongrel sat watching from one side of the pavement or the other, and the last time we came by, got up and ambled back into the field toward nothing. I pulled jerkily onto the entrance ramp of the freeway as Thurman shifted for me, then onto the highway itself as he applauded.

'Do you forgive me?' I asked.

'For what?' He was watching the road, sitting near enough to grab the wheel. 'Check your mirrors. Always know what's coming up on you.'

I checked. 'For last night,' I said, 'I'm sorry.'

'Don't be sorry. What happened was as likely in this scheme as anything else.' He reached under the seat for a pack of cigarettes, still watching the road. 'I like you.'

'You know something? That one time we slept together in Denver was my first time in six weeks.'

'I figured.'

'What do you mean?'

'Pay attention—stay in your lane.' He turned and glanced behind us. 'I mean it seemed like you barely remembered how. There are several like you around. Where are all the girls who were smart and feisty and balled everyone all the time?'

'They got older,' I said. 'I used to ball anyone too, just based on his eyes or his arms. It's easy when you do it a lot. You get stoned and you don't even think about it. Easy. Like saying hello.'

'Guess I missed the boat,' he said. 'You must have been great to say hello to in the old days. I wish I'd known you then.'

'Yeah, I bet you do.'

He smiled and lit a cigarette. 'But don't you ever miss it? Weren't those days *fun* sometimes? Think about it for a minute. Everyone laughed a lot, didn't they? Group jokes and the old gang. All the dope, everyone with a nickname. Food and big meals and banjos and flutes. People weren't stupid; they just didn't *worry*. The war was over, no one was getting drafted. The girls had birth control pills and an old man, and once in a while they fucked their best friend's old man, or they all fucked together, and everything was chummy. Right?'

'Sure. That's right.'

'Ha,' he said.

If I remember right, what we did was this: Route 25 from Denver to Albuquerque, 10 to El Paso, 20 to Dallas, 35 to Austin, back on 10 to San Antonio, Houston, Beaumont, New Orleans, 65 to Montgomery, 85 to Atlanta and Charlotte, 21 to Wytheville, Virginia, 77 to Charleston and West Virginia; passing through, escaping gravity in a tinny Japanese truck, an imported living quarters. Love in a space capsule, Thurman called it, hate in Houdini's trunk. But there was the windshield and the continual movie past the glass. It was good driving into the movie, good the way the weather changed, the way night and day traded off. Good to camp out for a day or two in a park or a motel, buy a local paper, go to a rummage sale. It was good stopping at the diners and luncheonettes and the daytime bars, or even Hojo's along the interstates: an hour, a few hours, taking off as we'd walked in, like we had helium in our shoes. Everyone else lived where they stood. They had to live somewhere, and they'd ended up in Tucumari or Biloxi or Homer, Georgia. All of them, waitresses and bartenders, clerks standing behind motel desks in view of some road, and the signs, place names, streets, houses, were points on a giant connect-the-dots. The truck is what there really was: him and me and the radio, the shell of the space, thin carpet over a floor that reverberated with a hollow *ping* if you stamped down hard. There were the rear-view mirrors turning all that receded sideways, holding the light in glints and angles and the pastels in detached, flat pictures so that any reflected object—car, fence, billboard—seemed just a shape, miraculous in motion. There was a steering-wheel, the dash with its square illuminations at night, a few red needles registering numbers. The glove compartment: a flashlight, the truck registration, an aspirin bottle full of white crosses, dope and an aluminium foil envelope of crystal meth in the first aid box, two caramel bars, a deck of cards. Under the seat were some maps and a few paperbacks, magazines, crumpled wrappers of crackers and health food cookies and popsicles, Thurman's harmonica. The radio whined and popped and poured out whatever it caught in the air. In the desert there was nothing but rumbling crackles and shrills; we turned the volume way up till the truck was full of crashing static and rode fast with the roar for miles, all the windows open streaming hot air. But mostly the radio was low. He talked. I talked. We told stories. We argued. We argued a lot as we approached Dallas, where we were going to spend a couple of days with his parents.

'Where did you come from?'

'Thurman, I came from where I'm going.'

'I mean in the beginning, like Poland or Scandinavia.'

'Wales. But there, in West Virginia, since the 1700s. A land grant. So much land they parcelled it out for two hundred years of ten-child families, and only sold the last of it as my father was growing up.'

'Sold it to who?'

'The coal companies. Pennsylvania and New York coal companies.'

'Uh huh.' He adjusted the rear view mirror. 'Why aren't you back there mobilizing against strip mining?'

'Mobilizing? You make it sound like a war.' I turned on the radio, and turned it off. 'I guess it is a war—New York hippies against New York coal companies.' I looked away from him, out of the window. 'I don't have any excuse, I just wanted to get out.'

'You know West Virginia is the only state left where there are no nuclear reactors?' He took a drag on his cigarette and smiled at me across the seat.

'They couldn't put a reactor there,' I said. 'The land would open like a boil, like an infected Bible, and swallow it.' I caught his eye and smiled back. 'Impressive. You're up on your eco-lit.'

'I'm a good hippie carpenter.'

'There are no hippies anymore. There's a fairy-tale about working-class visionaries.'

'Just a fairy-tale? No vision in the working class?'

'Vision everywhere. But in the real working class, vision is half blind. It's romantic to think they really know—'

'You don't think they *know*? He flicked his cigarette out the window and raised his voice. 'They know—they just don't *talk* about it. My grandfather was an Irish Catholic plumber who died of cirrhosis. He used to sit in his chair while the news was on the radio and fold his newspaper into squares. Then he'd unfold it and roll it into a tube, a tight tube the width of a blacksnake. He'd whack it against the arm of the chair on a 4/4 time, while the announcer kept going and my skinny grandmother grated cabbage in the kitchen by the plates.' He checked the mirror and pulled out around a cattle truck. 'They knew plenty, sweetheart. You don't know what you're talking about.'

'Don't call me sweetheart, and I didn't say they weren't perceptive or frustrated. I said their isolation was real, not an illusion. They stayed in one place and sank with whatever they had. But us—look at us. Roads. Maps into more of the same. It's a blur, a pattern, a view from an airplane.'

'You're a real philosopher, aren't you? What do you want? You want to sink, righteous and returned, to your roots? Is that it?'

'I can't.'

'Can't what?'

'Sink. I don't know how.'

'Oh, Christ. Will you shut up and light that joint before we pull into Dallas?'

I took the joint out of his cigarette pack and looked for matches.

'Here,' he said, and threw them at me. 'No wonder you live alone and sleep on floors. You're ponderous and depressed. Nothing is any worse than it's ever been.'

'No,' I said, 'only more detached.'

'Detachment is an ageless virtue. Try a little Zen.'

'I am,' I said, and lit the joint. 'I'm living in Zen, highway Zen, the wave of the future.'

He didn't laugh. We pulled into Dallas and Thurman finished

the joint at a roadside park in sight of three Taco Bells, a McDonald's, and a Sleepytime Motel. He squinted behind the smoke, drawing in. 'What does your dad do?' he asked.

'Retired.'

'OK. What *did* he do?'

'Roads. He built roads.'

'Highways?'

'No. Two-lane roads, in West Virginia. Hairpin turns.'

The joint glowed in his fingers. Dusk had fallen, a grey shade. The air was heavy and hot, full of random horns and exhaust. I could see the grit on Thurman's skin and feel the same sweaty pallor on my face.

'What is your father like?' I asked him.

He exhaled, his eyes distanced. 'My father is seventy-five. Lately he's gone a little flaky.'

We sat in silence until the dope was gone. Thurman turned on the ignition. 'You'll have your own bedroom at my parent's house,' he said, 'and I sure hope your sheets aren't too heavy.'

The house was a big old-fashioned salt box on an acre of lawn, incongruous among the split-levels, badly in need of paint. Drain-pipes hung at angles from the roof and the grass was cut in strange swaths, grown tall as field weeds in patches. An old Chevy station-wagon sat on blocks in front of the garage. Thurman and I sat in the driveway, in the cab of the Datsun, looking.

'They've gotten worse, or he has. I've hired kids to cut the grass for him and he won't let them on the property.'

'Did they know we were coming?'

'Yes.'

The front door opened and Thurman's mother appeared. She was small and thin, her arms folded across her chest, and it was obvious from the way she peered into middle distance that she couldn't really see us.

'You go first,' I said, 'she'll want to see you alone.'

He got out of the truck and approached her almost carefully, then lifted her off the ground in an embrace. She didn't seem big enough to ever have been his mother, but a few minutes later, as she looked into my face, her handshake was surprisingly firm.

The inside rooms smelled of faded pot-pourri and trapped air despite the air-conditioner. Only the smallest downstairs rooms seemed lived-in; the kitchen, a breakfast nook, a small den with a television and fold-out couch made up as a bed. The large living-room was empty except for a rocking-chair in the middle of the naked floor. The room had been dismantled and holes in the plaster repaired; three large portraits in frames of uniform size were covered with painter's cloths and propped against the wall. Above them were the faded squares of space where they'd hung.

'Oh,' I said, 'you're painting.'

'Well.' She surveyed the room. 'We were going to paint three years ago, but we never did.' She smiled.

Upstairs the hall was dusty. Plaster had fallen off the walls in chunks and exposed the wooden wallboards. Bits of newspaper and chips of paint littered the floor; the master bedroom was clean but unused, and the other bedrooms seemed deserted: furniture pushed to the center of the floor, beds filmed with a fine dust.

'You take this room,' Thurman said, 'I'll be across the hall.' He picked up a broom and began sweeping off the mattress. 'I'll get you some sheets.'

I said nothing.

He put the broom down. 'Look, it was me who got the living-room ready for painting—two years ago, not three. I'd hired painters to do that room and the outside; my father called them and told them not to come.' Thurman stepped over to the window, looked down at the lawn through streaked glass. 'But that grass... Still, he's known I was coming for six weeks, maybe he planned this whole scenario. He won't let me buy him a power mower or do any chores for him. We fight about it every time I come home. This time I'm not fighting.'

'Why is he mad at you?'

Because I bailed out fifteen years ago. Fifteen years is a lot of mad.' Thurman looked up at me. 'And don't be surprised if he doesn't talk to you. His hearing isn't really so bad but he pretends to be deaf. He'll act busy the whole time we're here.'

We sat at the edge of the concrete patio in deck-chairs. 'My father was famous. He was known as the best high school football coach in the history of the state of Texas.

Universities offered him jobs, but he wouldn't move his family, he wouldn't leave this house.' Thurman shook the ice in his empty glass and looked levelly towards the old wooden garage. His father stood in the open doorway with the push mower, frowned down at the turning blades as he pushed the contraption into the grass of the side lawn. 'I knew he was famous from the time I was a kid. And my brothers were famous, six and eight years older than me, both of them drafted to play ball at SMU after starring on his teams. And later I was famous, but not as famous as them. I played on my father's last team and we went to the play-offs; he was sixty years old.'

The mower made its high scissoring whirr as the old man shoved it back and forth. The slender wooden handle was as gray and weathered as barn board.

'His kids aren't going to cart him off anywhere, and no one in this posh neighborhood had better try it either,' Thurman said. 'He was here first. And there are still people around who remember my father. If he wants to let his house fall down, or set it on fire or blow it up, I guess he's entitled.'

I watched Thurman's father. He'd barely acknowledged my presence, though he'd discussed the mower with Thurman as they both knelt to wipe the blades clean with a rag. The old man was lean and stooped but he didn't seem fragile.

Thurman picked up the pint bottle between our chairs and colored the ice in his glass with bourbon.

'Did you win?' I asked him.

'What?'

'Win the championships, the last ones.'

'By the skin of our teeth. We were behind and tried a long last-resort run as the clock ran out. I played end and blocked for our quarterback, a fast little Mexican named Martinez. I was the last one with him, thought it was over and took two of their backs as Martinez jumped the pile of us. I wanted to knock myself out, too much of a coward to stay conscious if we lost. I came to ten minutes later with a concussion, and we'd won.'

'Was your father standing over you?'

'No, he was up there accepting the trophy. Then he came and balanced it on my chest as they lifted me onto the stretcher—big gold monstrosity with three pedestals that multiplied and looked like infinity. I wasn't seeing too clearly. That was 1964; things were just beginning to focus.' He looked over at me. 'You were about eleven years old then.'

I looked back at him. 'You didn't go to SMU.'

'Not a chance. Football nearly killed me. I couldn't read print for two weeks.' He sank lower in the deck-chair, stroking the lush grass with his foot. His legs were long and muscular and fair. 'If I'd hit an inch more to the right, I'd have bought myself a box. But even without the concussion, I was sick of it. I went to Colorado and ski-bummed and ran dope up from Mexico and went to school, did the Peace Corps trip. Didn't see my father for years.'

'Why didn't the war get you? The concussion?'

'No. Knees. Got my brother though, the middle one. Killed him. He didn't even have to go. He was almost thirty years old and enlisted, like a fool. My father thought it was the right thing to do. They shipped him over there and killed him in nine weeks. 1968. Saw my father at the funeral. Kept saying to me, "Barnes was on drugs, wasn't he. They're all on drugs over there. He wouldn't have died otherwise, he was an athlete. Still worked out every day. Drugs killed him." I said, "Dad, the war killed him. War doesn't give a shit about athletes." I did two years in the Peace Corps after that. I just wanted to stay the fuck out of the country.'

'Thurman... Thurman?' His mother's voice wavered out across the lawn. I turned and saw her at the kitchen window.

'Supper,' she called, 'come on in now—' Her every phrase was punctuated with a silence.

Thurman didn't move.

'Do you come back here often?' I asked. 'How much do you see them?'

'Once a year, maybe twice. He's old. There's not much more time to figure it out, any of it.'

I couldn't sleep. I crept down the stairs to get a glass of water. Disoriented, I turned the wrong corner into the dim living-room and found myself facing the shrouded portraits. I knelt beside the last. If I looked now, no one would know; carefully, silently, I pulled the cloth away. First, a shine of glass, then, in moonlight, the features of a face. I thought it was Barnes, the dead brother, serious and young in his black suit, already marked—but no, the eyes—it was Thurman. I stared, puzzled.

'High school graduation,' he said behind me. 'We were all seventeen.' The rocking-chair creaked. 'What are you doing up?'

'I couldn't sleep.'

'No one sleeps much in this house.'

'Who else is awake?'

'My mother. I heard her in the kitchen. When I came downstairs, she went back to bed. That's the way we do it around here.' He nodded at the closed door of the little den. 'She seems to have had a few drinks.'

'Is that usual?'

'Who's to say? Her drinking progresses, like everything.' He took a drag off his cigarette, and the glow of the ash lit his face for an instant. 'She forgets things when she drinks. Conveniently.'

'I doubt it's just convenience.'

'What else would it be?'

I shrugged. 'Pain?'

Thurman sighed. 'You never know when to keep your mouth shut. Do you think I want to sit here in this house at three in the morning and talk about pain?'

'No.' I could see him very clearly in the darkness. I moved closer and touched his forehead. 'You talk, Thurman, and let me know when I should speak. I'll say whatever you want.'

He stood, and put his arms around my shoulders and held me. We turned to go upstairs, then Thurman paused. We heard broken words, a murmuring. He stepped closer to the den and stood listening, then pushed the door softly open. His mother stood near us in her bathrobe, an empty glass in her hand. She seemed unaware of us and looked up slowly. The dim little room was crowded with furniture and smelled faintly of bourbon. Thurman's sleeping father was in shadow.

'Mom, you should be in bed. You might fall.' He walked over to her and took the glass. 'I'll put this in the kitchen for you.'

She stopped Thurman and grabbed his wrist. 'Listen,' she said slowly, in a secretive tone. 'Barnes never answers a letter, never calls. Where is he?'

Thurman led her to the bed. 'Don't pull that on me.'

'She isn't,' I whispered, 'she really—'

Now she was sitting on the edge of the mattress. Thurman put his hands on her shoulders and shook her once, gently. She looked him in the eye. 'Who is that girl?' she said.

'A friend of mine, Mom, you met her earlier today. Here, lie down before you wake Dad.'

She said nothing and clutched Thurman's hands; he leaned closer involuntarily. Her eyes widened, her face caught in the light of the one lamp. For a moment I could see how he favoured her, how she must have looked at twenty-five: the clear ruddy complexion, the cast and blue directness of the eyes, the thick auburn hair, maybe worn in a braid to her waist. This close, their faces nearly touched. Her profile was a broken, feminine version of his. I turned away.

'Mom, lie down.'

'Don't you be leaving again now.'

'Go to sleep, get some rest.'

'I don't sleep. Don't you be leaving.'

'Thurman,' I said. I heard him staighten. Her body shifted in the bed, then he was beside me in the hallway, pulling their door shut. He stood breathing quietly, listening. No sound. The mottled living-room walls lightened as our eyes took in the dark again. Colors of dun and gray, cracked. In one corner, patches of missing plaster were ragged star shapes where the boards showed through. I reached for him.

'I shouldn't come here,' he said.

'It's all right.'

He stood there, looking at their closed door. 'Who saves who?' he said.

I pulled his head down, close to me, touching him, his face. 'Let's sleep outside.'

I got some blankets and we spread them in the yard. The acacia bushes were a thick bank, bulbous and shadowy, smelling of sweet dust.

Then we hit New Orleans. Checked into a motel. Went to that bar where everyone was dancing.

What happened was scary and stupid, and whirling and sick and drunkenly predictable, and in the cards from the first. Afterward things were different, and Thurman had no illusions about saving me. He must have worked things out himself after he left the bar alone, while he was waiting for me all night in that motel, the aqua drapes moving over the air vents behind the blue glow of the television. I remember almost all the motel rooms, and I remember that one especially, the big Zenith console TV and those cheap drapes blue as fired gas. In seven hours, Thurman could have watched three movies and twelve sets of commercials. He left me at the bar at two a.m. and I pulled into the motel parking-lot in a taxi at nine. He was just drawing tight the ropes of the tarp and the door to the room was standing open. I got in the truck after exchanging one look with him, and nothing else passed between us until Georgia when we got in the lake.

Then, we kept going.

'D on't drive in the fast lane unless you're passing.' Thurman, his voice gravelly with wakefulness.

'Why not? I pass everything anyway, so I might as well stay in the fast lane. I like fast lanes.'

'Oh, you do. Well. Someone even faster is going to come roaring up and eat your ass. How will you like that?' He switched off the radio. 'Godammit, will you listen to me for a minute?'

I pulled off on the berm and shifted into neutral. A cattle truck passed us doing eighty, rocking the cab. There was a bawl and a smell and it was gone. Thurman sat with his back to the passenger door. 'Take your hands off the wheel,' he said.

'Thurman, what is this?'

'I'll tell you what it is. You're in trouble, and no fast lane is going to help.'

'I don't want help. I'll just keep going until I find a way to get off.'

'Good for you, sweetheart.'

'Screw you.'

'Hey, don't worry. You'll get no help from me. Last time I quit fast lanes I made myself a promise—no more Samaritan crap.'

'You're all heart.'

'You'd better worry about your own heart. You're the one with the racing pulse and the shakes, sleeping on floors and getting picked up by three jokers in a disco. What the hell happened that night, anyway?'

'Not what you think. I talked my way out of most of it.'

'Lucky you're so good at talking.'

'OK, Thurman.'

'Not OK. I've been there, I know what you're doing. You spend half your time in a full-throttle heat and the other half holding on when you realize how fast you're going. You don't even come up for air. Your insides are blue because you're suffocating. Your guts shake because you scare yourself. You get close enough to see death doesn't give a shit about you.'

I turned off the ignition and the truck was silent. Noises of the highway went by, loud vibrations that took on the quality of musical tones. I don't know how long we sat there, maybe only a few minutes.

'Death isn't supposed to give a shit,' I said, 'is it? Death is a zero. Blue like ice is blue. Perfect. Barnes is perfect. Your father will be perfect, my father. All of us, cold and perfect.' Thurman moved close to me across the seat. We were both sweating. He pulled his damp T-shirt away from his body and touched my face with the cloth. I whispered, like someone was listening to us, 'I don't mind the heat. I guess I want the heat.'

'I know, I know. And we got heat. We got plenty of heat for you here in the USA.'

The cotton of his shirt was soft and worn. 'Let's drive,' I said, 'who's driving?'

'What the hell. You drive.'

'Do you want me to stay in the slow lane?'

'I don't care. Drive on the berm, drive up the median, drive upside down.'

I pulled onto the highway with a few jerks but no grinding of gears. Thurman turned the radio back on to a gospel broadcast. There was a choir singing strong and heavy about a land on high in the sunshine; their group vibrato wavered in the dashboard.

'You're something else,' came Thurman's voice. 'You never did take your fucking hands off the wheel.'

'I guess I didn't.'

'Jesus. I don't know why I should worry about you. You'll probably come out of this with a new refrigerator and a trip to Mexico.'

'Sure I will. A trip to the Gringo Hotel in Juarez, where they eat dog and hand out diseases.'

He lit a cigarette and gazed out of the window.

Close home, we drove through Virginia mountains in the rain. I had moments of total panic in which I seemed to be falling, spread-eagled, far away from myself, my whole body growing rapidly smaller and smaller. I could feel the spinning, the sensation of dropping. I held tightly to the door handle and concentrated on the moving windshield wiper in front of me, carefully watching its metal rib and rubber blade. I willed myself into the sound, the swish of movement and water, dull thwack as the blade landed on either side of its half-rotation. Runnels of rain and the tracks of their descent took me in; I could smell rain through the glass, smell clean water and washed leaves. I sat very still and the spinning of my own body slowed; the aperture of my senses widened, opened in a clear focus. Then I could feel the seat under my hips again and my feet on the floor of the truck, the purr, the vibration of the engine. The capsule of the truck's cab existed around me; damp leather, a faint musk of bodies. Close to me, Thurman would be humming tunelessly to himself, staring ahead into the rainy mountains and the twisting road.

The last night, we camped out in a National Forest. Nearly dusk already, and the ground was damp; I raked leaves into a broad pile to make us a softer bed, provide some insulation. Up here in the mountains there was a smell of autumn, soil, rich mulch.

'Sit down here and get warm.' Thurman piled more wood on the fire. 'Enjoy the wide open spaces. Tomorrow you're safe, if not sound. Remember safe? You'll get used to it again real fast.' He blew into the fire, then leaned back and gazed at me through a wavering column of heat. 'You scared?'

I touched the border of stones we'd built to surround the campfire. The stones were rough, and warming. 'The shakes are coming, right now,' I told him. 'I can feel them.'

'No,' he said, 'you're OK. I'm sitting right here looking at you.'

'You can't always see them. Sometimes they're just in my gut.'

He took one of my hands and squeezed it, then kneaded my palm and worked down each finger. He pulled hard on each joint and talked as though neither of us was paying any attention to how hard he was pulling. 'You're fine,' he said. 'We're going to lay down in the leaves and take some deep breaths, then all those jangles will go somewhere else.'

I closed my eyes and I could feel the shade creeping across the leaves. They dropped slowly at intervals; they kept dropping with a papery sound. 'I think it's better if I sit here and cry,' I said.

'You can't. You're not a crier.'

'Let me try. Tell me a bad story.'

'I got no bad stories.' He picked me up in his arms and knelt to put me on the ground. The leaves were thick under us, old leaves smelling of dry mud. 'Only one story,' Thurman said, 'we've been in that truck three weeks. A few more hours, and you're home.' I remembered a song that used to play on AM radio when I was gawky and twelve, the tallest girl in the class. *Be my little baby, Won't you be my darling, be my baby now* ... I laughed. That's what I was, a baby, a frozen twelve-year-old baby going back to the start of the cold.

'Funny story, huh?' He kissed my eyes. 'Don't get hysterical. I won't force you. Male pride, the Code—'

'You couldn't rape anyone. You might get mad enough to start, but at the crucial moment your equipment would fail you.'

'You're right. I was born with a kindly cock.' I felt his legs against me, his hard stomach, the buckle of his belt. He unfastened it to keep the metal from hurting me and touched me low on my hips.

'You get turned on when you're paternal,' I said. 'You're going to be hell on your daughter.'

'You're hell on me,' he said. 'You'll be someone's good lover someday when I'm drinking beer alone in a tavern and hearing the pinball machines.'

I opened his shirt and pants and slid down against him. Lake smell, like Georgia, taste of a bruise. He was in my mouth, his hands in my hair, then he moved to stop me and turned my face up. He bent over me, holding my arms, his eyes angry and surprised and wet. 'No,' he said.

'Thurman.' I was crying. 'I just want you to drop me off tomorrow. Me and the suitcases and the box of books. I don't want to see you meet my mother, none of that. All right? Please.'

Later, the cold was moving up through the ground. He felt me shiver in the dark and pulled me on top of him. I lay there and he held me with one arm. His chest was wider than my shoulders, smelling of the cold tinge of the leaves. He was awake, smoking a cigarette and staring into the trees. He exhaled with a long breath.

'It's all timing,' he said. 'This whole joke. Timing and the shakes.'

'You're better off without me. No more fast lanes.'

He moved his warm heavy hand to the back of my head. 'I'll tell you this about fast lanes. Don't close your eyes. Keep watching every minute. Watch in your sleep. If you're careful you can make it: the fast shift, the one right move. Sooner or later you'll see your chance.'

ff

faber and faber

NEW AMERICAN WRITING

WALTER ABISH
How German Is It
£3.95 FPB

GARRISON KEILLOR
Lake Wobegon Days
£9.95

MAX APPLE
Free Agents
£9.95

ANDREA LEE
Sarah Phillips
£2.95 FPB

AMY CLAMPITT
What the Light Was Like
£4.00 FPB

LORRIE MOORE
Self-Help
£8.95   (£3.95 FPB   November)

DEBORAH EISENBERG
Transactions in a
Foreign Currency
£9.95

FLANNERY O'CONNOR
Everything that Rises
Must Converge
£2.95 FPB

ELLEN GILCHRIST
Victory Over Japan
£3.50 FPB

JAYNE ANNE PHILLIPS
Machine Dreams
£2.95 FPB

RACHEL INGALLS
The Pearlkillers
£9.95

MARILYNNE ROBINSON
Housekeeping
£7.95

DENIS JOHNSON
Stars at Noon
£9.95   Spring 1987

SAM SHEPARD
Motel Chronicles and
Hawk Moon
£3.95 FPB

KATHRYN KRAMER
A Handbook for Visitors
from Outer Space
£9.95   (£4.95 FPB   October)

EUDORA WELTY
One Writer's Beginnings
£2.95 FPB

RICHARD RUSSO
FISHING WITH WUSSY
WUSSY

My father, unlike so many of the men he served with, knew just what he wanted to do when the war was over. He wanted to drink and whore and play the horses. 'He'll get tired of it,' my mother said confidently. She tried to keep up with him during those frantic months after the men came home, but she couldn't, because nobody had been shooting at her for the last three years and when she woke up in the morning it wasn't with a sense of surprise. For a while it was fun—the late nights, the drinking, the photo finishes at the track—but then she was suddenly pregnant with me and she decided it was time the war was over for real. Most everybody she knew was settling down, because you could only celebrate, even victory, so long. I don't think it occurred to her that my father wasn't celebrating victory and never had been. He was celebrating life. His. She could tag along if she felt like it, or not if she didn't, whichever suited her.

'He'll get tired of it,' she told my grandfather, himself recently returned, worn and riddled with malaria, to the modest house in Mohawk he had purchased with a 200 dollar down payment the year after the conclusion of the earlier war he'd been too young to enlist for legally. He liked to think there couldn't be more than a handful of men who had lied about their age in both wars. The others had lied to get out, not in. This second time around he felt no urge to celebrate victory or anything else. From his hospital bed in New London, Connecticut, he read books and wrote his memoirs while the younger men, all malaria convalescents, played poker and waited for weekend passes from the ward. In their condition it took little enough to get good and drunk, and by early Saturday night most of them had the shakes so bad they had to huddle in the dark corners of cheap hotel rooms to await Monday morning and re-admission to the hospital. But they'd lived through worse, or thought they had. My grandfather watched them systematically destroy any chance they had for recovery and so he understood my father. He may even have tried to explain things to his daughter when she told him of the trial separation that would last only until my father could get his priorities straight again, little suspecting he already had.

'Trouble with you is,' my father told her, 'you think you got the pussy market cornered.' Unfortunately, she took this observation to be merely a reflection of the fact that in her present swollen condition she was not herself. Perhaps she couldn't corner the market just then, but she'd cornered it once, and would again. And she must have figured too that when my father got a look at his son it would change him, change them both. Then the war would be over.

The night I was born my grandfather tracked him to a poker game in a dingy room above the Mohawk Grill. He was holding a well-concealed two pair and waiting for the seventh card in the game of stud. The news that he was a father did not impress him particularly. The service revolver did. My grandfather was wheezing from the steep, narrow flight of stairs and he stopped to catch his breath, hands on his knees. Then he took out the revolver and stuck the cold barrel in my father's ear and said, 'Stand up, you son of a bitch.' This from a man who'd gone two wars end to end without uttering a profanity. The men at the table could smell his malaria and they began to sweat.

'I'll just have a peek at this last card,' my father said. 'Then we'll go.'

The dealer rifled cards around the horn and everybody folded lickety-split, including a man who had three deuces showing.

'Deal me out a couple a hands,' my father said, and got up slowly because he still had a gun in his ear.

At the hospital, my mother had me on her breast and she must have looked pretty, like the girl who'd cornered the pussy market before the war. 'Turn it over,' my father said, and when she did he grinned at my little stem and said, 'What do you know?' It must have been a tender moment.

Not that it changed anything. Six months later my grandfather was dead, and the day after the funeral, for which my father arrived late, my mother filed for divorce, thereby losing in a matter of days the two men in her life.

Until I was six I thought of my father the way I thought of 'my heavenly father', whose existence was a matter of record, but who was, practically speaking, absent and therefore irrelevant. My mother never did end up getting her divorce. When my father heard what she was up to, he went to see her lawyer. He didn't exactly have an appointment, but then he didn't need one out in the parking lot where he strolled back and forth, his fists thrust deep into his pockets, waiting until F. William Peterson, Attorney-At-Law, closed up. It was one of the bleak, dead days between Christmas and New Year. I don't think my mother specifically warned F. William there would be serious opposition to her design and that the opposition might conceivably be extra-legal in nature. F. William Peterson had been selected by my mother precisely because he was not a Mohawk native. He had moved there just a few months before to join as a junior partner a firm which employed his law school room-mate. F. William Peterson was a soft man of some bulk, well-dressed in a knee-length overcoat with a fur collar, when he finally appeared in the deserted parking lot at quarter to six. Never an athletic man, he was engaged in pulling on a fine new pair of gloves, a Christmas gift from Mrs Peterson, while trying at the same time not to lose his footing on the ice. My father never wore gloves. For warmth, he blew into his cupped hands, steam escaping from between his fingers, as he came toward F. William Peterson, who, intent on his footing and his new gloves, hadn't what a fair-minded man would call much of a chance.

Finding himself suddenly seated on the ice, warm blood salty on his lower lip, the attorney's first conclusion must have been that somehow, despite his care, he had managed to lose his balance. Just as surprisingly, there was somebody standing over him who seemed to be making a point of not offering him a hand up. It wasn't even a hand that dangled in F. William's peripheral vision, but a fist. A clenched fist. And it struck the lawyer in the face a second time before he could account for its being there.

F. William Peterson was not a fighting man. Indeed, he had not been in the war, and had never offered physical violence to any human. He loathed physical violence in general, and this physical violence in particular. Every time he looked up to see where the fist was, it struck him again in the face, and after this happened several times, he considered it might be better to stop looking up. The snow and ice were pink beneath him, and so were his new gloves. He thought about what his wife would say when she saw them and concluded right then and there, as if it were his most pressing problem, that he would purchase an identical pair on the way home.

Had he been able to see his own face, he'd have known that the gloves were not his most pressing problem.

'You do *not* represent Jenny Hall,' said the man standing in the big work-boots with the metal eyelets and leather laces.

He *did* represent my mother though, and if my father thought that by beating F. William Peterson up and leaving him in a snowbank, that would be the end of the matter he had an imperfect understanding of F. William Peterson and, perhaps, the greater part of the legal profession. My father was arrested half-an-hour later in the Mohawk Grill in the middle of a hamburger steak. F. William Peterson identified the workboots with the metal eyelets and leather laces, and my father's right hand was showing the swollen effects of battering F. William Peterson's skull. None of which was the sort of identification that was sure to hold up in court, and the lawyer knew it, but getting my father tossed in jail, however briefly, seemed like a good idea. When he was released, pending trial, my father was informed that a peace bond had been sworn against him and that if he, Sam Hall, were discovered in the immediate proximity of F. William Peterson, he would be fined a thousand dollars and incarcerated. The cop who told him all this was one of my father's buddies and was very apologetic when my father wanted to know what the hell kind of free country he'd spent thirty-five months fighting for would allow such a law. It stank, the cop admitted, but if my father wanted F. William Peterson thrashed again, he'd have to get somebody else to do it. That was no major impediment, of course, but my father couldn't be talked out of the premise that in a truly free country he'd be allowed to do it himself.

So, instead of going to see F. William Peterson, he went to see my mother. She hadn't sworn out any peace bond against him that he knew of. Probably she couldn't, being his wife. It might not be perfect, but it was at least some kind of free country they were living in. Here again, however, F. William Peterson was a step ahead of him, having called my mother from his hospital room so she'd be on the look-out. When my father pulled up in front of the house, she called the cops without waiting for pleasantries, of which there turned out to be none anyway. They shouted at each other through the front door she wouldn't unlock.

My mother started right out with the main point. 'I don't love you!' she screamed.

'So what?' my father countered. 'I don't love you either.'

Surprised or not, she did not miss a beat. 'I want a divorce.'

'Then you can't have one,' my father said.

'I don't need your permission.'

'Like hell you don't,' he said. 'And you'll need more than lawyers and a cheap lock to keep me out of my own house.' By way of punctuation, he put his shoulder into the door, which buckled but did not give.

'This is my father's house, Sam Hall. *You* never had anything and you never will.'

'That's how come I married you,' he said. 'If you aren't going to open that door, you'd better stand back out of the way.'

My mother did as she was told, but just then a police cruiser pulled up and my father vaulted the porch railing and headed off through the deep snow in back of the house. One of the cops gave chase while the other circled the block in the car, cutting off my father's escape routes. It must have been quite a spectacle, the one cop chasing, until he was tuckered out, yelling, 'We know who you are!' and my father shouting over his shoulder, 'So what?' He knew nobody was going to shoot him for what he'd done (what *had* he done, now that he thought about it?) A man certainly had the right to enter his own house and shout at his own wife, which was exactly what she'd keep being until *he* decided to divorce *her*. It must have looked like a game of tag. All the neighbors came out on their back porches and watched, cheering my father, who dodged and veered expertly beyond the outstretched arms of the pursuing cops, for within minutes the backyards of our block were lousy with uniformed men who finally succeeded in forming a wide ring and then shrinking it, the neighbors' boos at this unfair tactic ringing in their ears. My mother watched from the back porch as the tough, wet, angry cops closed in on my father. She pretty much decided right there against the divorce idea.

It dawned on her much later that the best way of ensuring my father's absence was to demand he shoulder his share of the burden of raising his son. Until then, life was rich in our neighborhood. When he got out of jail, my father would make a bee-line for my mother's house (she'd had his things put in storage and changed the locks, which to her mind pretty much settled the matter of

79

ownership), where he'd be arrested again for disturbing the peace. His visits to the Mohawk County jail got progressively longer, and so each time he got out he was madder than before. Finally, one of his buddies in the force took him aside and told him to stay the hell away from Third Avenue, because the judge was all through fooling around. Next time he was run in, he'd be in the slam a good long while. Since that was the way things stood, my father promised he'd be a good boy and go home, wherever that might be. Since one place was as good as another, he rented a room across from the police station so they'd know right where to find him. He borrowed some money and got a couple things out of storage and set them in the middle of the rented room. Then he went out again.

Eight years later he kidnapped me.

I had left Aunt Rose's and was on my way home when I saw a white convertible. It was coming toward me up the other side of the street, travelling fast. I didn't think it would stop, but it did. At the last moment it swerved across the street to my side and came to a rocking halt, one wheel over the kerb.

'What's the matter?' my father wanted to know. I must have looked like something was the matter. He had a grey chin and his hair looked crazy until he ran his black fingers through it, which helped only a little.

I said nothing was the matter.

'You want to go for a ride?'

I figured he must mean for ice-cream or something.

'Come here,' he said.

I started around the car to the passenger side.

'Here,' he repeated. 'You know what "here" means?'

Actually, I don't think I did. At least I couldn't figure out what good it would do me to walk over and stand next to him outside the car. I found out though, because suddenly he had me under the arms, and then I was high in the air, above the convertible's windshield, where I rotated 180 degrees and plopped into the seat beside him. My teeth clicked audibly, but other than that it was a smooth landing.

He put the convertible in gear and we thumped down off the curb and up the street past Aunt Rose's in the opposite direction from the dairy. I figured he'd turn around when we got to the intersection, but he didn't. We just kept on going, straight out of Mohawk. My father's hair was wild again, and mine was too, I could feel it.

The car smelled funny. My father didn't seem aware of it until finally he sniffed and said, 'Oh, shit,' and pulled over so that he was half on the road and half on the shoulder. First he flung up the hood, then the trunk. With the hood up, the funny burning smell was even worse. My father got two yellow cans out of the trunk and punched holes in them. Then he unscrewed a cap on the engine and poured in the contents of the two cans. I could see his black fingers working in the gap between the dash and hood. I thought about my mother, who would be just about putting her key in the front door lock and wondering how come I wasn't on the front porch to greet her. I started to send her a telepathic thought, 'I'm with my father,' until I remembered that wouldn't exactly be a comfort if she received it.

He slammed the hood and trunk and got back in the car.

'Ever see one of these?' He dropped something small and heavy in my lap. A jack-knife, it looked like. I knew my mother wouldn't want me to touch it. 'Open it,' my father said.

I did. Every time I opened something, there was something else to open. There were two knives, a large one and a small one, the can opener I'd seen him use, a pair of tiny scissors you could actually work, assuming you had something that tiny that needed scissoring, a thing you could use to clean your nails with and a file. There were other features too, but I didn't know what they were for. With all its arms opened up, the gadget looked like a lopsided spider.

'Don't lose it,' he said.

We were pretty well out in the country now and, when he pulled into a long dirt driveway, I was sure he just meant to turn around. Instead, he followed the road on through a clump of trees to a small, rusty trailer. A big, dark-skinned man in a shapeless hat was seated on a broken concrete block. I was immediately interested in the hat, which seemed full of shiny metallic objects that reflected the sun. He stood when my father jerked the car to a stop, crushed stone rattling off the trailer.

'Well?' my father said.

The man consulted his watch. 'Hour late,' he said. 'Not bad for

81

Sam Hall. Practically on time. Who's this?'

'My son. We'll teach him how to fish.'

'Who'll teach you?' the man said. 'Howdy, Sam's kid.'

He offered a big, dark-skinned hand.

'Go ahead and shake his ugly paw,' my father said.

I did, and then the man gathered up the gear that was resting up against the trailer. 'You want to open this trunk, or should I just rip it off the hinges?' he said when my father made no move to get out and help.

'Kind of ornery, ain't he?' my father said confidentially, tossing the keys over his shoulder.

'Hey, kid,' the man said. 'How'd you like to ride in the back?'

'Tell him to kiss your ass,' my father advised. 'You got enough gear for three?'

The man reluctantly got in the back. 'Enough for me and the kid anyways. Don't know about you. Can he talk or what?'

My father swatted me. 'Say hello to Wussy. He's half colored, half white, and all mixed up.'

Wussy leaned forward so he could see into the front seat. 'He ain't exactly dressed for this.' I was wearing a thin T-shirt, shorts, sneakers. 'Course, you ain't either. You planning to attend a dance in those shoes?'

'I didn't have time to change,' my father shrugged.

'Where the hell were you?'

My father started to answer, then looked at me. 'Some place.'

'Oh,' the man called Wussy said. 'I been there. Hey, Sam's kid, you know what a straight flush is?'

I shook my head.

'His name is Ned.'

'Ned?'

My father nodded. 'I wasn't consulted.'

'Where were you?'

'Some place,' my father said. 'Which reminds me.'

We were on the highway and there was a small store, a shack really, up ahead. We pulled in next to the telephone booth. I heard part of the conversation. My father said she could kiss his ass.

When he got back in the car, my father looked at me and shook his head as if he thought maybe *I'd* done something. 'Don't lose that,' he said. I was still fingering the spider gadget.

'As long as we're stopped,' Wussy said, 'what do you say we put the top up?'

'What for?' my father said.

Wussy tapped me on the shoulder and pointed up. The sun had disappeared behind dark clouds, and the air had gone cool.

'Your ass,' my father said, jerking the car back onto the highway.

It was half-an-hour before the skies opened.

'Your old man is a rock-head,' Wussy observed after they finally got the top up. It had stuck at first and we were all soaked. 'No wonder your mother don't want nothing to do with him.'

It was nearly dark when we got to the cabin. We had to leave the convertible at the end of the dirt road and hike in the last mile, the sun winking at us low in the trees. We followed the river, more or less, though there were times when it veered off to the left and disappeared. Then after a while we'd hear it again and there it would be. Wussy—it turned out that his name was Norm—led the way, carrying the rods and most of the tackle, then me, then my father, complaining every step. His black shoes got ruined right off, which pleased Wussy, and the mosquitos ate us. My father wanted to know who would build a cabin way the hell and gone off in the woods. It seemed to him that anybody crazy enough to go to all that trouble might better have gone to a little more and poured a sidewalk, at least, so you could get to it. Wussy didn't say anything, but every now and then he'd hold onto a branch and then let go so that it whistled over the top of my head and caught my father in the chin with a thwap, after which Wussy would say, 'Careful.'

I was all right for a while, but then the woods began to get dark and I felt tired and scared. When something we disturbed scurried off underfoot and into the bushes, I got to thinking about home and my mother, who had no idea where I was. It occurred to me that if I let myself get lost, nobody would ever find me, and the more I thought about it, the closer I stuck to Wussy, ready to duck whenever he sent a branch whistling over my head.

'I hope you didn't bring me all the way out here to roll me, Wuss,' my father said. 'I should have mentioned I don't have any money.'

'I want those shiny black shoes.'

'You would, you black bastard.'

'Nice talk, in front of the kid.' A branch caught my father in the chops.

'What color is he, bud?' My father poked me in the back.

I was embarrassed. My mother had told me about Negroes and that it wasn't nice to accuse them of it. Wussy's skin was the color of coffee, at least the way my mother drank it, with cream and sugar. 'I don't know,' I said.

'That's all right,' my father said. 'He's none too sure either.'

And then suddenly we were out of the trees and there was the cabin, the river gurgling about forty yards down the slope.

Wussy tossed all the gear inside and started a fire in a circle of rocks a few feet from the porch. When it got going, he brought out a big iron grate to put over it. With the sun down, it had gotten cool and the fire felt good. My father fidgeted nearby until Wussy told him he could collect some dry sticks if he felt like it. 'You could have brought a pair of long pants and a jacket for him at least,' he said.

'Didn't have a chance,' my father said.

'Look at him,' Wussy said critically. 'Knees all scraped up . . .'

'How the hell did I know we were going to blaze a trail?' my father said. 'You cold?'

'No,' I lied.

Wussy snorted. 'I think I saw blankets inside.'

My father dropped his armload of sticks and went to fetch some. 'Your old man's a rock-head,' Wussy told me confidentially. 'Otherwise, he's all right.'

He didn't seem to need me to agree, so I didn't say anything. He opened three cans of chilli into a black skillet and set it on top of the grate. Then he chopped up two yellow onions and added them. You couldn't see much except the dark woods and the outline of the cabin. We heard my father banging into things and cursing inside. After a few minutes the chilli began to form craters which swelled, then exploded. 'Man-color,' Wussy said. 'That's what I am.'

My father finally came back with a couple rough blankets. He draped one over me and threw the other around his own shoulders.

'No thanks,' Wussy said. 'I don't need one.'

'Good,' my father said.

'And you don't need any of this chilli,' Wussy said, winking at me. 'Me and you will have to eat it all, Sam's kid.'

My father squatted down and inspected the sputtering chilli. 'I hate like hell to tell you what it looks like.'

It looked all right to me and it smelled better than I knew food could smell. It was way past my normal dinner time and I was hungry. Wussy ladled a good big portion on to a plate and handed it to me. Then he loaded about twice as much on to a plate for himself.

'What the hell,' my father said.

'What the hell is right,' Wussy said. 'What the hell, eh, Sam's kid?'

My father got up and went back into the cabin for another blanket. When he returned, Wussy said no thanks, he was doing fine, but didn't my father want any chilli? 'You better get going,' he advised. 'Me and the kid are ready for seconds.'

We weren't, exactly, but when he finished giving my father some, he ladled more on to my plate and the rest of the skillet on to his own.

'I bet there's a lot of shallow graves out here in the woods,' my father speculated, pretending not to notice there was no more chilli whether he hurried up or not. 'You suppose anybody would miss you if you didn't come home tomorrow?'

'Women, mostly,' Wussy said. 'I feel pretty safe though. Mostly I worry about you. Anything happened to me, you'd starve before you ever located that worthless oil guzzler of yours.'

'Your ass.'

When I couldn't eat any more, I gave the rest of my chilli to my father, who looked like he was thinking of licking the hot skillet. 'The kid's all right,' Wussy said. 'I don't care *who* his old man is.'

It was so black out now that we couldn't even see the cabin, just each other's faces in the dying fire.

Wussy blew the loudest fart I'd ever heard. 'What color's my skin?' he said, as if he hadn't done anything at all.

I had been almost asleep, until the fart. 'Man-color,' I said, wide awake again.

'There you go,' he said.

I woke with the sun in my eyes next morning. There were no curtains on the cabin's high windows. I was still dressed from the night before. My legs, all scratched from the long walk through the woods, felt heavy and a little unsteady when I stood up. I looked around for a bathroom, but there wasn't one.

My father and his friend Wussy were face down on the other two bunks. My father's face and arms were coffee-colored, like Wussy's, but his legs and back were fish-white. Wussy had taken the trouble to crawl under the covers, but my father lay on top. The cabin had been warm the night before, but it was chilly now, though my father wasn't aware of it. I was, and it made me wish there was a bathroom even more. In the center of the small table was an empty bottle and a deck of cards fanned face up. They'd kept score in long uneven columns labeled N and S on a brown paper bag. The S columns were the longer ones, and the number 85 was circled at the top of the bag with a dollar sign in front of it. I had awakened several times during the night when one of them yelled 'Gin!' or 'You son of a bitch!' but I was too exhausted to stay awake. I watched the two sleepers for a while, but neither man stirred, so I went outside.

The iron skillet, alive with bright green flies, still sat on the grate. There were so many flies, and they were so furious, that their bodies pinged against the surface like small pebbles. I watched with interest for a while and then went down to the river. We were so far upstream that it wasn't very deep in most spots, a river in name only. Rocks jutted up above the surface of the water and it looked like you'd be able to jump from one to the next all the way to the opposite bank. I tried it, but only got part way, because when you got out toward the middle, the rocks weren't as close together as they looked. One solid-looking flat rock tipped under my weight and I had to plunge one sneakered foot deep into the cool current to keep from falling in. The water ran so fast that the shoe was nearly sucked off, and I was scared enough to head back to shore on a squishy sneaker, aware that if my mother had been there she'd have thrown a fit about my getting it wet. I doubted my father and Wussy would even notice. I found a comfortable rock on the bank and had another look at my father's knife gadget, trying to pretend I didn't have to go to the bathroom. Having the river right there made the necessity to pee hard to ignore. I wasn't sure I could hold it all day.

After a while the door of the cabin opened and Wussy appeared in his under-shorts. 'Hello, Sam's kid,' he said. He tip-toed over to the spot where he'd built the fire, yanked himself out of his shorts and watered the bushes for a very long time. I could hear him above the sound of the river.

When he saw me watching, he said, 'Gotta go, Sam's kid?'

I shook my head. I could hold out a while longer, and I wanted it to seem like my own idea when I went. I was relieved to learn that peeing in the weeds was permissible, though it was one more thing I didn't think I 'd mention to my mother.

'First thing every morning for me,' Wussy explained. 'Can't wait.'

When he was finished, he went back inside for his pants and shoes. I went over to where he'd stood, as if it were an officially designated area, and released my agony.

Wussy came out with the rods and his tackle box. 'Better get our ass going and catch breakfast,' he said. 'Your old man ain't going to be no help. I see you got your shoe wet.'

'Fell in,' I admitted, surprised that I had been wrong about him not being the type to notice.

'River runs pretty quick out there in the middle,' he observed without looking at me, and I was suddenly sure he'd seen me out there, though he wasn't going to say anything.

At the water's edge, he attached the spinning reels to the rods and ran line through the eyelets all the way to the tips. I watched, full of interest. 'Ever fish before?'

I shook my head.

'It's about the best thing there is until you're older and can do some other stuff, and it's better than most of the other stuff too.'

I watched him tie on the hooks, and he did it slow so I could see. He pointed to the little wing on each hook. 'Called a barb,' he said. 'So the fish can't slip off once he's on. Works the same way on your finger if you aren't careful.'

We walked up river about a hundred yards so that when my father woke up there'd be nobody around. 'Serve him right,' Wussy said, without explaining what for.

When we got to a spot that looked lucky to Wussy, where there was a good safe rock for me to sit on, he handed me a rod. Then he opened up a can that looked like it was full of dirt, but when he fished around with his brown index finger I could see the bottom was alive and writhing. He pulled out an astonishingly long worm and hooked him three times until he oozed yellow and twisted angrily. I must have looked a little yellow myself, because Wussy baited my hook with two bright pink salmon eggs. Then he taught me how to release the bail and let the current carry the bait downstream, and how to reel in.

'How will I know when there's a fish?' I said when he started out toward the middle.

He said not to worry about it, I'd know, though that didn't strike me as a satisfactory explanation. Then I was by myself with only the sound of the running water for company. The sun was high and warm and when I saw Wussy had taken off his shirt I did the same. I watched Wussy for a while, then studied the reflected sun on the water near the drooping tip of my rod.

I couldn't have been asleep more than a few minutes when I felt the excited tugging. For some reason it was not what I had expected. The jerks came in short bursts, like a coded message: 'STAY-ALERT-THERE-ARE-FISH-IN-THE-RIVER.' Thirty yards downstream a fish jumped, but I didn't immediately associate this phenomenon with my now frantic rod tip. Wussy had waded further upstream and did not hear when I shouted 'Agh!' in his general direction.

I was not at all certain I wanted to reel in the fish. Every time I tried, he seemed to resent it and tugged even harder. When he did this, I stopped and waited apologetically for the tugging to stop. I only reeled in when I felt the line go slack. When the fish jumped, or rather flopped onto the surface, a second time, he was much closer, and my already considerable misgivings grew. I was thinking I might just let him stay where he was until Wussy came back, whenever that might be. But then I got my courage up and reeled in a little more, all the time watching the spot on the surface where my line disappeared into the stream, beads of rainbow water dancing off it with the tension.

Then I saw the fish himself off to the side in a spot far from where I had imagined him to be. He was no longer tugging so frantically, but he darted first left, then right in the large pool of relatively calm water beneath my rock. Then he must have got a gander at me sitting there, because he was full of flight again. I stopped pulling at him and just watched his colors in the clear water. After a while he stopped trying to get away and just stayed even with the current, his tail waving gently, like a flag in the breeze. Then I looked up and Wussy was there, and he had my fish out of the water and flopping in the green netting so that cold water sprayed on my knees. I examined the fish without pride as Wussy extracted him from the net and probed his gullet for the hook he'd practically digested.

'Well, Sam's kid,' Wussy said, 'you're about the most patient fisherman I ever saw. Nobody won't ever accuse you of not giving a trout a chance. If I was him, I'd have had about three separate heart attacks.'

Tired of the fish's unco-operative squirming, Wussy took out his knife and brained my trout with the handle. The fish shuddered and was still.

'There,' Wussy said. 'Now you won't have no more heart attacks.'

Wussy then handed me the jar of salmon eggs, reminding me to be careful of the barb when I baited up. He slipped my fish on to his stringer next to a larger trout already dangling from it. 'We got us *our* breakfast, anyhow. I guess we should catch one for the rock-head if we can.'

He watched me while I baited my hook and released the line into the current the way he'd taught me. 'You're a fisherman,' Wussy said. 'A good, patient fisherman.'

We fished until the sun was directly overhead. I didn't have any more luck, for which I was grateful, but Wussy's fat worms located two more trout, and then we headed back downstream to the cabin. My father was standing in the doorway, scratching his groin. 'Where's the bacon and eggs?' he wanted to know.

'Back in Mohawk,' Wussy said. 'Your kid caught a fish.'

'That's good,' my father said, studying the stringer, as if mine might be recognizable. 'I could eat about three.'

'So happens I got some for sale,' Wussy said. 'What's three into eight-five?'

'Your ass.' Then my father studied me. 'What're you scratching about?'

'Itch,' I said. I'd been scratching most of the morning, first one spot and then another. For some reason one scratch just wasn't enough, no matter how hard. After a minute or so, the itching would be even worse.

'You could go wash that pan in the river,' Wussy said to my father, 'and keep from being *completely* worthless.'

'I had *my* fish on the line last night,' my father said. 'Cleaned him too.' But he grabbed the pan and headed for the river. When it was clean, or clean enough so the flies weren't interested in it any more, we returned to the cabin. Wussy was cleaning the last of the fish, tossing its string of insides off into the bushes. My father found some oil in the cabin and before long the four fish were sputtering in the big skillet. Then we ate them right down to their tiny bones and drank from the icy river. Even my father had stopped complaining.

We fished some more that afternoon. Wussy was good at it. Between pulling them in, baiting up, stringing the catch, and tending to me, he was pretty busy. My father could have used some help too, but Wussy ignored him and my father, who claimed to know how to fish, refused to ask. Every time we looked at my father, he was either trying on a new hook, or re-baiting it, or trying to figure out why there was a big nest of monofilament line jamming his reel. After a while my father took his act up around the bend in the river where he could fight his gear in private.

'With most fishermen,' Wussy remarked, 'the contest is between the man and the fish. With your old man, it's between him and his reel.'

I caught two more trout during the afternoon and would have been among the world's truly happy boys if I could have just stopped itching. In addition to my legs, my stomach and shoulders were now covered with angry red blotches. 'Looks like you found some poison ivy all right,' Wussy remarked. 'You'd be better off not scratching if you could avoid it.'

I couldn't though, and after another hour of watching me dig myself, Wussy said he was going to fish his way up river and tell my father we'd better head back before I drew blood. I reeled in, leaned Wussy's rod up against the cabin porch and jumped from rock to rock along the river edge to where I found my father seated on the bank. Wussy was standing thigh deep in the river, about twenty yards away, calmly reeling in a trout and smiling, no doubt at the fact that my father was engaged in extracting a barbed hook from his thumb by swearing at it. Swearing was about the only thing he did that didn't work the hook deeper into his thumb. To make matters worse, there was only an inch or two of line at the end of the rod, which kept falling off his knee, setting the hook even further. By the time he washed the blood away so he could see what he was doing, and balanced the rod on his knee, the bright blood was pumping again and he'd have to stop and wipe the sweat off his forehead. He looked like he was mad enough to toss everything into the woods, and he probably would have if he himself hadn't been attached to it.

When Wussy had landed, cleaned and strung his last trout, he came over and surveyed the situation. 'Where you got all your fish hid?' he said. 'There's a little room left on this stringer.' He sat down on a rock out of striking distance, but close enough to observe what promised to be excellent entertainment.

My father didn't bother answering him about the fish.

'Your old man looks like he could use some cheering up,' Wussy said. 'Tell him how many fish you caught, Sam's kid.'

I wasn't sure it would cheer him up, but I told him three, and I was right; it didn't.

'Anything I can do?' Wussy said.

My father gave him a black look. 'How you planning to get home?' he said weakly.

'I figure I'll just sit right here till you pass out from loss of blood and then take your car keys. Somebody will find you along about Labor Day and that hook will still be right where it is now.'

'You better hope so, because if I get it out it's going up your ass.'

'Of course you know best,' Wussy said slowly, 'but if that hook was in my thumb, the first thing I'd do is release my bail.'

My father looked at him, not comprehending. I was close enough, so I leaned over and tripped the bail, releasing the line. My father flushed.

'Now you got room,' Wussy continued, 'I'd bite that line in two.'

Humbled, my father did as he was told. Wussy picked up the rod and reeled in the slack.

'And?' my father said.

'And now I got the majority of my gear back,' Wussy said, turning back toward the cabin. 'You can just go ahead and keep that hook.'

I think my father would have chased Wussy, hook and all, except that he'd noticed me for the first time and it scared him so he forgot all about his thumb. I had been scratching non-stop and the patches of poison ivy skin were everywhere, including my face. 'Look at you,' he said. 'Your mother's going to shoot us for sure.'

'Shoot *you*,' Wussy said over his shoulder. 'Come with me, Sam's kid. Stay a safe distance from that rock-head. He's a dangerous man.'

M y father got back at Wussy by refusing to carry anything out of the woods. I helped a little, but by the time we got back to the convertible Wussy was beat and trying hard not to show it. 'What's that streaming from your thumb?' he asked when we were back on the highway heading for Mohawk. The monofilament line took the breeze and fluttered like a cobweb from my father's black thumb.

About that time I noticed the car smelling funny again, and my father pulled over onto the shoulder. He took two cans of oil from the trunk and headed around to the front via the passenger side. I stopped scratching myself when he held out his hand. 'Let me see that thing a minute.'

I felt an awful chill. I could see the gadget in my mind's eye and it was sitting on the last rock I fished from. I pretended to look for it. 'I . . .' I began.

But he already knew. 'What'd I tell you when I gave it to you?'

I tried to speak, but could only stare at my patchy knees.

'Well?'

'Don't lose it,' I finally croaked.

'Don't lose it,' he repeated.

I was suddenly very close to tears, even though all the way home I'd been feeling as happy as I thought it possible to feel. I had caught fish and peed in the woods and not complained about my poison ivy. I had felt proud and important and good. Now, it came home to me that, having betrayed my father's simple trust, I was a disappointment to him—a little boy to be taken home to his mother where he belonged.

My father walked around to the driver's side and kicked the convertible hard. 'Let me see that knife,' he said to Wussy.

'You aren't using my good knife to punch holes in no oil cans,' Wussy said.

There was nothing to do but kick the car again, so my father did. Then he did it five more times all down the driver's side of the car. That was all right with Wussy, in as much as it wasn't his car, but I began to cry, even though it wasn't my car either. When my father was through kicking the convertible, he said, 'Come on, dumb-bell. Help me find a sharp rock.'

Then he felt the monofilament line flapping in the breeze, wrapped it between the thumb and forefinger of his good hand, and yanked. The hook came out all right, and along with it a hunk of flesh. Fresh blood began to pour out of the wound and on to the ground. My father swore and flung the line and hook with all his might. It landed about five feet away.

We started looking along the shoulder for a jagged rock, my father kicking the round ones for not being pointed. When my father was a ways up the road, Wussy went back to the car and plunged his knife into the two oil cans. By the time my father got back with a jagged rock, Wussy was tossing the empty cans into the neighboring field and wiping the knife blade on his pants. My father dropped his rock and we all got back in the car.

'Hey!' he said, looking over at me before putting the convertible back on the road. 'Smile. I'm the one with something to cry about.'

After his walk he wasn't mad any more and he let me see his thumb. It really was an ugly-looking thumb.

When we pulled up in front of the house, my mother was sitting on one of the front porch chairs with a blanket over her lap, looking like she'd been there for days. Her face was absolutely expressionless.

'Uh-oh,' Wussy said. 'Don't forget to take your fish,' he added when I got out, probably hoping that three nice trout might appease my mother.

Let me try to view through her eyes what she saw when we pulled up at the curb that afternoon.

First, she saw my father at the wheel, looking a tad nervous but far from repentant.

Next, she saw a large man of indeterminate breed wearing an absurd hat full of fish hooks, just the sort of companion she imagined my father would select for his son.

And finally, she saw me. My rumpled shirt and shorts were filthy, my hair wild from the ride in the convertible. My arms and legs were red and raw, my eyes swollen nearly shut from scratching and crying.

And she saw too that under the law she was completely helpless, since, as F. William Peterson had that day informed her, a father could not be guilty of kidnapping his own son.

She did not get up at first. My father got out of the car to walk me as far as the porch steps, though he looked a little pale, even before he saw my grandfather's service revolver, the same one that had already been stuck in his ear once. He stopped, his head cocked, as if listening for something, as my mother stood and raised the gun. I heard Wussy say 'Jesus!' and he slumped as far down into the back seat as his big body would allow. The first explosion surprised my mother so, she almost dropped the gun. After that, she did better. She shot my father's car five more times, taking out the windshield and the front tire, neither of which she was particularly aiming at.

'God damn you, Jenny!' my father exclaimed when the shooting stopped. He had scooted behind the car and was now peering tentatively over the hood. 'I think you shot Wussy.'

'Nope,' Wussy's voice came from the floor of the rear seat. 'Except for the heart attack, I'm OK. She isn't re-loading, is she?'

'Look at my car,' my father said. The glass from the windshield was all over the street, but for some reason he didn't look as mad as he'd been when he discovered I'd lost his gadget, though a lot more surprised.

'Look at my son,' my mother said.

'Our son,' my father said.

'You can't have him.' She was still aiming the gun in his direction, empty now, though she probably didn't know it. She had just stopped shooting when it seemed she'd made her point.

My father seemed pretty sure she was through, but he couldn't be certain. The neighbors had all come out on the porches, and he was looking increasingly self-conscious about being pinned down behind his own ruined car. He'd been shot at before and must have guessed that my mother wasn't really trying to hit him, but those were precisely the situations that got you shot. He'd have felt safer if she'd been aiming at his skull. Since there was nothing to do but test the water, he slowly stood, and when she didn't shoot he got back in the car. Naturally, it wouldn't start. 'Jesus,' Wussy said from the floor of the back seat.

Finally the engine turned over. My father leaned over the back seat. 'You want to ride up front with me?'

'I'm fine.'

'Which is how come I call you Wussy,' my father said.

ELLEN GILCHRIST
MEMPHIS

Her horror and fascination with his size. His power, his hands, feet, mouth, dick, all that stuff that carried her across the door of that little frame-house on T Street and kept her there until her neck snapped. That's part of it. I have to tell you that part so you'll believe she stayed. I can't believe it and I was there. Katherine Louise Wheeler, Baby Kate, my niece, the daughter of a famous author and a Delta beauty. 'Cat,' he called her, and 'Baby, Baby,' all the time when they were doing it. They were always doing it.

'Wait till you meet him,' she said. 'And you will understand.'

'All right. Bring him by.'

'Wait till you see his shoulders. Three people could hide behind his shoulders. His people cleared this land. We owe them their share.'

'When's he coming?' I folded my hands in my lap. I stretched my mind. I am the family intellectual. I am supposed to be able to see beyond my fears. Then he was there. Coal black, powerful, full of laughter. I pictured the children. Light brown with that soft dusty cloudlike hair the children have when black men and blondes breed together. You've seen it. As if a wash of Clorox had been poured across a piccaninny. Piccaninny, what kind of a word is that?

'How are you?' I said. 'Baby Kate told me all about you.'

'What did she say? What does she know to tell?' He took my hand. It slid into his like a trout returning to water. I decided he was a nice man. I was sure he was the nicest black man she could have found.

'You fix apartments? She said you do it all alone. Make the plans and all.'

'Could I have a drink of water? I've been in the sun all morning. I was playing tennis with some people from the mayor's office.'

I went to get the water. When I returned she was sitting in his lap. 'I have to get on to school,' I said. 'I have to give exams today. I wish I never had to give them. It hurts me more than it hurts you, that's what I always say.'

'It's nice of you to let us use your place, Miss Wheeler. It's really nice of you.'

'Thank you, Aunt Allie,' she said, her eyes as solemn as an owl's. She walked me to the door. 'He has to work tonight. You and

I'll cook dinner. I'll go shopping.' She kissed me. I could smell her perfume. What was I doing in this? I am fifty-four years old. I'm as crazy as a loon.

So first they were doing it in my apartment. The musk from those encounters rose up and invaded the walls. Hours after he was gone I could feel his breath on everything.

I am only a few blocks from the Memphis State campus where I teach. I walked home slowly all that summer. I would stop and inspect trees, read the memorial plaques on benches. Class of 1903. Veterans of World War II, In Memory of Carmen Carson Garth, Class of 1915. Site of the First Earth Science Class, 1923.

It was hot that summer. Hot and dry. The rain stayed above the Ozarks and left us dry. At night the jasmine and catalpa and honeysuckle turned the town into a bordello. The students walked the streets in twos and threes and licked ice-cream cones and hardly seemed to speak and by the twenty-ninth of June my desk was littered with pathetic little notes and scraps of paper. Miss Wheeler, can you forgive me? Miss Wheeler, can I see you after class to explain where I have been? Professor Wheeler, you won't believe the mess I'm in. I am so sorry I couldn't come yesterday. If you could wait till Friday for the paper . . . and so on. Fine, I told them. Sure. Of course, I understand.

I turned my office radio onto WKSS—'Nothing But Love Songs'—and thought about them doing it on my bed.

He came from West Memphis in a rented white Chevrolet and found her on the university track and told her he was a real-estate developer. She believed him. She had done it with him a dozen times before she noticed the scars on his neck or finally got stoned or drunk enough to ask for details. He told her the truth. I'll say that for him. He never told any of us a lie. And it was true he knew the mayor.

His name was Franke Brown and his father was a janitor and his mother collected welfare and Baby Kate thought she had finally found a way to get her father to notice her, to acknowledge she was here. Her father, my brother, Hailey Wheeler. He wrote all those books about man's inhumanity to man. He sat on Big Hodding's right hand when they integrated the Delta schools. He knew Walker Percy and Shelby Foote and all the big ones. He was the hit of a thousand New York cocktail parties telling anyone who would listen where he stood and what it had cost him in family and friends and inheritance, and now here he was confronted with Baby Kate doing it with the biggest black man who had ever stood as a guest in our entrance hall. Well, he lost it, as the children say. The whole pack of cards came down.

'Get out,' he told her. 'How dare you bring that trash into my house.' He let her take her clothes. Whatever she could fit into her car.

She came to me. What's an old maid for but to take in the strays. 'He can't live here too,' I told her. 'The place is too small. But you can do it while I'm gone to class.'

B aby Kate. Long bones, long undulations, arms swinging free, gold hair like Hailey's, the sweetest voice in the world, a voice like music. Why couldn't her father love her? He loves me, an ugly older sister whose only grace is that I can read his books. Hailey Wheeler, poet, novelist; Memphis, Tennessee's bright troubled darling son.

I read his books and I loved his wife, Baby Kate's and Cauley's mother. I loved her every drunken moment she was here, every drunken afternoon and night until she died. I found the body myself, or found it seconds after Celestine. I was the one to wipe the vomit off the pillow before the others came.

The coroner was 'worried' about that, as he told me several times in the mess that followed. 'Not deeply worried,' as he said. 'Troubled. Of course, we all knew Mrs Wheeler drank.'

Anyway, Hailey loved me and I wasn't beautiful in any way, so why couldn't he love his daughter, or pretend to love her, or say he loved her or even quit criticizing her long enough to let her love herself? She spent more time getting dressed than anyone I have ever known.

'If only I were prettier,' she was always saying. 'If only my face wasn't so thin. If only I had been a beauty like my mother.'

Hailey was sitting in the police chaplain's car when I drove up. He was in the back seat with his head bowed. This little shabby-looking chaplain was in the front, twisted around, talking to him. I didn't know what to do. I decided to wait.

'They took the guy away already.' A black girl perched on top of a Fuji bicycle was holding court on the sidewalk facing the murder door. A white frame-house with a porch and a door with long windows on each side. Through the gauze curtains you could see men standing in the yellow light. The sun was going down behind the roof. The black girl spoke again. 'She's lying in the door. They have to step over her every time they go in. You watch when they open the door. You can see her feet or something covered with a sheet. She's right there. It could have been an accident.'

'Aunt Allie, you must believe me, I am doing all I can to keep it at bay.' That's what she told me in the beginning. 'I keep talking all the time and I barely let him do it to me. I'm not good at doing it with him. I bet he wishes I was a black girl, a passionate woman. I'm trying not to love him. I know I'm trying not to. Something's holding me back.'

I turned from the stove where I was making breakfast. It must have been a Sunday, right after she moved in with me. Before they got the place on T Street. 'Then why are you doing it at all?'

'I have to,' she said. 'I just have to.'

So I let them use my apartment all those weeks and this is on my hands as surely as it is on his. Where was my mind? What took my mind away?

There were no beatings here. That started after she went to T Street to be his wife. Oh, yes, she married him. That's how the Wheelers do things. Went down the day before they moved in together and said, I do. She was paying for everything by then, even her own ring. She had an income from the Delta land. Not much, but it must have seemed like a lot to him.

Did I know what was coming? Did Hailey know? Answer, we all know everything. It's just a matter of how much of it we're going to let drift up into our conscious mind at any given moment. At least she didn't die in that mausoleum out on Roundtree. Where the rest of them finished their drunken lives. Three generations of drunks. That's the real history of this family. I escaped by being ugly. Hailey tried to write his way out. Well, it got us too at last.

Here's the tradition Baby Kate found herself in. Her mother choked to death on absinthe. She should have stuck to bourbon. She could put bourbon away. Memphis, it's a hard town. Are they better off in Boston? I don't know.

Baby Kate, when she was small I would dress her up and take her for walks or to the park or to shows the auxiliary put on to raise money. The first telephone number she learned was mine. She would call me when she needed me. 'Come and get me, Allie,' she would say in her little voice. 'I need you to come get me.' Meaning her mother was breaking the dining-room furniture into pieces or melting Hailey's phonograph records in the oven or throwing a television set out of a third-floor window or running naked through the streets, a few of the things she did that I was called in on.

Sally, she was so very beautiful. Even at the last, constantly drunk and full of vitriol and screaming insults even at me or anyone she could get to stay on the phone. In repose, the mouth would begin its trembling, that imperceptible tremor and those violet eyes would pin you down. 'Help me, Allie. Why can't you help me?' She choked to death in the bed that had been the general's.

Now it's Baby Kate's turn and Hailey isn't talking to anyone, not even to me, and Franke Brown's in jail who probably wasn't even a bad man and I wouldn't talk about it either except I have to. I can't get rid of it until it's told.

She had this little banjo. She would sit on the steps and sing 'Rabbit In A Gum Tree, Coon In A Holler'. He must have loved her, even if he killed her. She was a princess, a king's child, thrown down upon his bed like a ransom.

I should visit him in jail. What did you do to her? I'd say. How did you do it? How could it happen? No one could want to hurt her. Could they? Could they?

Ellen Gilchrist

Hailey came home from the University of Virginia in the summer of 1953 and asked Sally Peets to marry him and she did. They were both drunk at the wedding and Shine Phillips handcuffed himself to her at the reception and they had to take him along to the Peabody until someone found a sheriff with a key. Harvey Trump had wanted to marry her, as later Harvey Trump Junior wanted to marry Baby Kate. They own this town, the Trumps do. Baby Kate wouldn't let him touch her, even at a dance. 'He's a fairy,' she said. 'He smells like a girl.'

She could have had any of them at first, until she went off to Newcomb and got in all that mess. After that it narrowed down and she came home and enrolled at Memphis State and started drinking at night with English department people who idolized her father. She'd get drunk and tell them how cold he was to her and they would eat it up. Knowing Hailey was a bad father made up to them for his books. The books did all right. He was 'legit', as he was fond of saying. Of course that wasn't what he wanted. He wanted to be great.

The black girl was perched precariously on the seat of the Fuji with her feet on the back wheel. Only the kickstand was holding her up. The good-looking coroner in the beige suit with the built-up heels kept running in and out of the house conferring with the policemen. He was so angry, I loved him for being angry. I could not get mad. I could not register this death. This death was one too many. All I wanted to do all afternoon was laugh.

The coroner kept stepping over the obstruction in the door and coming out and going over to the policemen and raising his arms like wings and snapping them down, like he was breaking somebody's back. Let it be her neck, I'd think each time he did it. Not her back. Not her precious back.

The crowd around the Fuji. Mothers and their children. The sun going down behind the death house. A long time seemed to be going by. Mosquitoes began to bite. An old friend of Baby Kate's named Saint John Wells came walking up the sidewalk wearing a Police concert T-shirt. He was coming to borrow some dope. He didn't have the vaguest notion what he was walking into. There were police cars all over the place. He just kept walking up, smiling like an idiot. What was he smiling about? Hailey got out of the chaplain's car and ran out into the street and grabbed Saint John and started crying in his arms. A mother slapped a child for pointing. 'Don't point,' she said, in a cold tight voice.

'I'm scared,' the child said.

'You have a right to be,' I said. I patted the child on the shoulder and went over and took my brother's hand but he was burrowed into Saint John's faded T-shirt.

'She's dead,' he kept saying. 'A nigger killed her.'

All those weeks while they were doing it in my apartment. He was so nice, as nice as he could be. Helpful, bringing flowers and wine. He told me he'd been in some trouble. 'What happened?' I asked Baby Kate later. 'What was he talking about?'

'He fixes apartments. He buys one and fixes it up, then sells it and buys another one. The reason he got in trouble was because someone burned one down and tried to blame it on him. Black people have so much trouble when something like that happens. They can't just call a lawyer like we do. So he lost a lot of money. He's just starting over.'

'How does he have so much free time in the daytime?'

'He makes it up at night. Don't you notice he isn't around much at night?'

'Oh,' I said. 'Of course. I understand.'

The faces around the Fuji. They didn't give a damn. They weren't surprised. What had they heard? What did they know?

'It's going to be on Channel Six at ten,' the man from the panel truck was saying to the rest. 'You can see it then.'

Anybody in my family could tell a version of this. This is the real story. Of whiskey and slaves and bored women and death. Two hundred years of slavery and still going on and still paying for it.

Here's the way it was. Here's the first thing I see when I try to understand, try to find a series of events to follow. That house, Roundtree, at the end of the cold lawns. Sally, drunk in the den, the stereo blaring, Leontyne Price singing Aïda. Hailey writing in his den, standing at a stand-up desk, reminiscent of you-know-who. Big glass of bourbon by his side, you-know-who, long half-comprehensible sentences, you know who. The servants smoking on the back veranda. Baby Kate on her little wooden rocking-horse. Black faces all around her. She is eating a popsicle, or a bowl of potato chips, anything she wants.

'Come on, honey,' I would say and she would drag the wooden horse across the floor and take it with us.

I am watching my angel die. Through that door. Every time the good-looking club-footed coroner steps over the door. 'It's right there,' the girl on the Fuji says. 'It's right in the door. They said he beat her with a horse. They took it off when they took him. Some horse toy.'

I walk over to the girl. 'Don't say any more about this,' I say. 'Get out of here. All of you, get out of here. That's my niece over there. My baby, my little girl. Get out of here. Get the hell out of here.' I am yelling now. At all of them, at every one of them. 'Go back inside your houses. Stop watching this. You goddam stupid worthless pointless television-watching idiots, get back inside, get out of my sight. I cannot bear the sight of you.'

Three officers had me by the arms. 'Why are you so angry?' the chaplain said. 'Why are you so full of anger?'

'Oh, Allie.' Hailey was behind them. 'For God's sake, don't make a scene.'

The first time Franke beat her up was not in my apartment. It was in July after the cocktail party she dragged him to at the museum.

'It was my fault,' she told me. We were in my car. I was taking her to the dentist to get her teeth fixed. 'I took him there to show him off. To make them look at him. It wasn't fair. It wasn't his fault. I forgive him.'

'No,' I said, 'Forgiveness is for what you can't understand. You are part of this. If you understand you are part of it. Are you part of it, Baby Kate? Of beating yourself up? Of breaking your teeth? Didn't you have enough of that when your mother was alive?'

'I don't care. It doesn't matter. Those are only words. I love him, which is not words, which is real. Which I will stand by.'

'Y'ou must go to her,' I told Hailey. 'He beat her up. He broke two of her teeth.'

    'She has made her bed,' he said. 'I'm done with it.'

'No, you have to intervene. Someone has to.'

'Leave me alone,' he said. He went upstairs. I heard the door to his office close. I went out onto the back porch looking for her horse. 'Where's that wooden horse of Miss Baby Kate's?' I said to Celestine, who was sitting at the table pretending to shell peas. 'Where'd you put her horse?'

'It's upstairs on the third floor with her stuff. He said not to let her have none of it.'

'Well, I'm getting that horse.' I went upstairs and found it and picked it up. It was a wonderful handcarved creature, a golden palomino with a dark gold mane and a red saddle with a design like coins. Where the paint was chipped away above the eyes the grain of the wood showed through. Mahogany or cypress. I patted it on the head. It will bring her to her senses, I decided. It will remind her to ride away.

I picked it up and carried it down the stairs, my mother's stairs, my grandmother's stairs. What is that law? Primogeniture? I'm getting so bad about language. I can't remember the words I need. I carried the horse down the stairs and out to my car. When she was little she would set it up in my front hall and pretend to be out west. 'Dat west,' she called it. 'I'm at dat west, Allie, bring me dat sandwich den.' And I would pretend to be the old chuck-wagon cook and serve her wild steer and Nebraska grass and buffalo and she would ride 'dem hills'. 'I'm widing dem hills some more,' she would call out and I would say, 'slow down, slow down.'

'H'e has confessed,' Channel Six informs me. 'Wife murderer begs to be allowed to go to funeral. Family refuses his request.' Confess, what does that mean? What did he say? What did he say he did to her? Have the grave-diggers covered the grave?

I dreamed last night the coffin was sitting beside the grave and all the people left the cemetery and when they were gone the funeral parlor came and took the coffin back to their store and opened it and took her out and returned her to us.

'What a tacky dress,' she said. 'It's torn all the way up the back. Someone get me something else to wear.'

'I will make you a dress of cowslips,' I said. 'A dress of blue flowers.'

The second time he beat her up was on the Mississippi coast, at Hailey's spare house in Biloxi. They had gone down there without permission. The caretaker was rude to them. He told them they could stay only one night. Then they were treated badly in a seafood restaurant. The waitress wouldn't bring them a menu. Baby Kate was scared. She acted badly. Afterwards he took her to a black oyster bar. She danced with the owner. They walked out on the dunes. Franke hit her in the face. He threw her down in the sand and left her there and took her car and drove home alone.

She came to me and stayed two days. She got up at twelve o'clock the third night and went back to him. She called a cab and went back to T Street. 'I made him do it,' she said. 'I pretended I didn't know him. I flirted with his friend.'

'You can't go back over there. I won't let you go.' I had thrown myself in front of the door. 'You are not going back over there.'

She pushed past me wearing a raincoat over her nightgown and went out into the night and I did not see her after that until I saw her dead. Although she called me. 'I'm fine,' she said when she called. 'We're both working. We're doing fine.'

'I'm coming over there to see about you. Tell me the address.'

'Don't come here. Don't any of you come here. I don't want you here.' She paused. 'It would get me in trouble.'

'What do you mean, in trouble? In what kind of trouble? What's going on, Baby Kate? Tell me what's going on.'

'I have to go now, Allie. I have to start dinner. He'll be home in a while.' She was going away. And I could not hold her.

'What are you doing? Tell me what you do.'

'At night we lie on the floor and listen to the crickets and the sound of the people in the neighborhood and I tell him my stories and he tells me his. We will never run out of stories. We are married, Allie. He is my husband.'

'I have your rocking-horse. I got it from your father's. Don't you want it? For a planter. Or in case some children come to visit. You could put it on a porch. Do you have a porch?'

'I don't need it now.'

'Don't you want anything from us? Don't you want to even know we're here?'

'Meet me at the corner of Forty-eighth and Randolph tomorrow at noon. I'll come and get it from you there.'

'What's going on, Baby Kate? Why can't I come to your house?'

'Meet me there. It's a Wal-Mart. I'll be by the main door.'

'Of course I will. At twelve then.' I was there at eleven-thirty. Pacing up and down the sidewalk in my Red Cross shoes. At ten to twelve he came and took the horse from me.

'She had to work,' he said. 'She said to tell you she tried to call. You'd already left.'

'Is she all right, Franke? Are you all right? Do you have everything you need?'

'We're doing fine. I'm teaching her to cook. We're doing good. Yes, we are.' He drove off in her car. He was wearing a white visor, a white shirt with long sleeves. I don't believe the world I lived to see.

Perhaps I will go and visit him in the jail. He could say he didn't mean to do it. If it was an accident I could watch the evening news again, could care about my fellow man. Black people. We brought them here. Someone did. Not me.

The crowd has thinned. The girl on the Fuji rides off down the street. The man climbs back into his van. The whining girl goes in to bed. The chaplain gets out of his car carrying a child's car-seat and stows it in the trunk. Saint John wipes his hands on his T-shirt. The white house floats above the street. 'Is this a bad neighborhood?' a woman says. 'I have to know. I just moved here.'

'I don't know,' I tell her. 'I'm sorry. I just don't know.'

The American Novel

A new series of introductory critical guides to the great works of American fiction

Each book contains a long introduction giving details of the novel's composition, its publication history, as well as a survey of major critical trends and opinions from first publication to the present. This is followed by chapters discussing various aspects of the text.

The first titles in the series:

New Essays on *The Great Gatsby*
Edited by MATTHEW J. BRUCCOLI

128 pp.	0 521 26589 4	**Hard covers £20.00 net**
	0 521 31963 3	**Paperback £6.95 net**

New Essays on *Huckleberry Finn*
Edited by LOUIS J. BUDD

144 pp.	0 521 26729 3	**Hard covers £20.00 net**
	0 521 31836 X	**Paperback £6.95 net**

New Essays on *The Scarlet Letter*
Edited by MICHAEL J. COLACURCIO

176 pp.	0 521 26676 9	**Hard covers £20.00 net**
	0 521 31998 6	**Paperback £6.95 net**

The Library of America

'The texts and general presentation are superb ... This is going to be the American Pleiade. The publication of these volumes represents an opportunity which anyone or any institution remotely interested in American literature would be foolish if not positively remiss to miss.'   *The Times Higher Education Supplement*

The works of America's greatest authors – novelists, poets, essayists, dramatists, historians – are at last being collected in a uniform series of attractive hard cover editions. 24 titles are already available: the series will eventually grow to a hundred or more volumes.

Each volume *c. 1000-1500 pp.*   **£30.00 net**

For details of titles published please contact the Publicity Department.

▇ Cambridge University Press
The Edinburgh Building, Shaftesbury Road, Cambridge CB2 2RU, England

ROBERT OLMSTEAD
THE CONTAS GIRL

In the season between fall and winter, Harley and Dunfee hunted deer. They went back into the woods where they had a shack. There they drank beer, talked dirty and shot deer if any happened to wander by the front porch. They were reputable hunters.

This year Harley had gone round to pick up Dunfee. Dunfee had taken up with the Contas girl and now was trying to get shed of her so he could leave. Harley waited in the truck. His face was knotted with burn scars from the time when he had smashed a road flare with a brick. It had exploded and the sulfur burned off half his face. He had grown up in a house without any mirrors. His father had removed them all while Harley's head was still wrapped in bandages. He often wore a baseball cap with the bill skewed low over half his face. Sometimes he wore sunglasses and kept his collar turned up.

Harley owned his truck. It didn't track down the road in the direction it was pointed. It always headed for the ditch. Its frame had twisted and buckled up between the box and the cab. This made the headlights bank down toward the road at night and everything you put in the back rolled out. One time Dunfee and Harley were in Brattleboro, Vermont, trying to drink their way through town. By two in the morning they were still in the same bar they began in, so they decided to give up. Harley drove, and Dunfee stretched out in the back. He wanted to look up at the sky as it rushed above him. When Harley hit the gas pedal in front of the Howard Johnson's Restaurant, Dunfee started sliding and finally dropped out of the truck on the bridge that spans the river. He lay there between Vermont and New Hampshire, the stars above him caught in the green steel girders arching over his head.

Harley didn't know he'd lost Dunfee until he got home and looked in the back of the pick-up. He was too tired to go back and find him, but he did take the time to make a tailgate from a sheet of plywood he had lying around so it wouldn't happen again.

It was morning, but the sun had not come up on the Contas's property yet. From where Harley sat, he could see the Contas girl's father. He was beating a goat over the head with a stick. It seemed to Harley like the kind of work one wanted to get an early start on. The goat would shake its head and then the old man would smack it right between the horns. Three little children sat on the front porch watching. They sat in bucket seats. They were quiet. Harley wondered if the old man was trying to teach them something.

A branch was sticking out from the front of Harley's truck. When he had driven up the road, he had run over it, and it had wedged underneath. It looked like an old woman's hand reaching out with the palm down.

Dunfee was inside the house. He had been here most of the summer. He was packing his belongings in a paper bag. The Contas girl was looking out the window at her father hitting the goat. She said she thought he was starting to look tired. He was taking a breather between hits. Then he'd bring the stick down as if he was chopping wood, each time a little slower than the time before. She lay down on the bed and asked Dunfee when he would be back.

'Harley's waiting in the truck,' he said.

'Harley doesn't have a face,' she said.

'And you don't have any brains.'

The Contas girl laughed. She rolled on to her back and stuck one leg straight in the air. Her ankle was caked with laundry soap. Underneath, poison ivy blisters were starting to dry. The rest of the leg was pretty, though. Dunfee looked at it. He saw how it went all the way to her ass. He knew Harley was waiting in the truck. Dunfee touched her. He knew he didn't plan on coming back here again, but probably would.

Harley and Dunfee had gone to school with the Contas girl. The three of them had become friends because they all lived near each other. They were older now and better friends. Mostly because no one else had stayed around. They'd gone off to other places to live. Twice the Contas girl had gone off for a year at a time. She went off to have babies. Harley and Dunfee didn't think much about it. They figured it was her business. Other people spoke about it though. Dunfee got in a fight once because of something said about her by one of the other boys. He didn't talk to her for a long time after that.

Harley didn't fight much. Most people left him alone. They didn't say much around him because they didn't know what he would do. He was always there for Dunfee though. He backed him up so no one would take a sucker punch. Harley was a big boy. His face was always secret.

When Dunfee fought, he went into a rage. He'd come flying through the air, all black shoes and red hairy knuckles that were just scabbing over from the last fight. He didn't fight any more though. He didn't have to.

The sun finally came up on the Contas's property. It got hot inside the truck. Harley got out to stretch his legs. He was happy to be unemployed. He pulled up his collar and rested his elbows on the hood of his truck. He had enough money to get him through the winter. His house wasn't much, but it was paid for. He lived in a tee pee once and that wasn't so bad.

Mostly, he was happy that it was hunting season. He liked to be alone in the woods with Dunfee. When they were boys, they took more than their share. They stayed out of school the whole season. For a fee, they began shooting deer for other people to tag. They never collected the money, though, so everyone thought Harley and Dunfee were giving them a break. People bragged about how much they had paid because they thought that everyone else was paying. They told their friends that Harley and Dunfee were expensive, but they were worth it.

Harley and Dunfee talked about becoming guides. It was something neither of them had ever tried. They didn't pursue it though. They didn't like the idea of showing the woods to outsiders.

Harley went away to school and Dunfee worked only when he had to make ends meet. The last few years, though, they did as little as they needed to. They got by.

The old man was slowing down. The goat seemed to be enjoying it. Harley tried to pull the branch out from under his truck. It wouldn't come. He got down on his knees to see where it was caught. There was a patch of anti-freeze on the ground. It was still dripping from the core. He couldn't figure out how the branch had punctured it.

Beside the road there was a plastic gallon jug. The kids were watching him. He cut the top off with his hunting knife and set it under the radiator. Anti-freeze was expensive.

Harley looked at his watch and then took it off. He put it in the glove box and slapped the door shut. He thought about asking the old man if he wanted him to take over for a while, give him a break. Harley went over and offered him a smoke. The old man took it. Harley had one too.

'Don't have a spare pack on you, do you?' The old man was looking at the goat. He was sizing it up as if he had more work to do on it before it would be finished. 'I'm so tired,' he said, 'it seems like I've been tired all my life.'

Harley pulled up his collar. He held his hand up to his face the way someone would for a moment, but then he left it there. He finished his smoke and wanted to say something to the old man but he didn't know what. He went over to where the kids were sitting on the porch. Their heads were together. He expected them to start singing Christmas carols or maybe an old Supremes tune. There was an extra bucket seat. It was out of a Ford Mustang. Harley sat down and lit another cigarette. The old man started hitting the goat again. This time he used a four-foot piece of inch-and-a-half black plastic water pipe.

'How come he's doing that?' Harley asked the kid sitting closest to him.

'He got his shoe wet yesterday. It made him mad.'

Harley butted out his cigarette and lit another one. He struck the match off the bottom of his front teeth. The kids watched him do it.

Inside the house, Dunfee and the Contas girl made love. They did it in a friendly sort of way. Dunfee had to be careful. He let her tell him what to do, because she often had pains inside her. It had to be done just right or he'd hurt her. When he made a mistake, her eyes would roll back in her head and she would lie there as if she had been stabbed. Sometimes she'd make him stop altogether.

The first time, Dunfee was drunk. It was late at night and neither of them had intended for it to happen. He and the Contas girl had driven over to the college to see Harley, but they couldn't find him. They were on the athletic field, lying in a pile of foam rubber that the pole vaulters used to land in. Afterwards, the Contas girl started to bleed. Dunfee balled up his T-shirt and gave it to her. She clutched it between her legs and closed her eyes. She didn't cry. She only lay there in the moonlight, the smell of mowed grass all around them.

Dunfee prayed that the bleeding would stop and finally it did. He swore to himself he would marry her, go to church and give up his

116

drink, but he never did any of these things. It took him a while to forget the promises he made, but he managed to do so.

Every time the old man hit the goat, the sound echoed from the end of the pipe. The goat cocked his head to listen. The old man missed and fell over. The pipe skittered off the goat's right horn and down the side of its face. The old man stood up and held his back.

'There goes his back again,' said one of the kids.

The old man walked into the house, holding his back up as if he were trying to carry a bag of groceries behind him. Harley went to the truck and got a six-pack off the front seat. He went inside too. He had never been in the Contas's house before.

He stopped inside the front door. There was an aquarium on a stand against the wall. A brown trout took up most of the room in the tank. It looked white in the light that came up from behind it. Air bubbles rose up under it and spread out around its head to the surface. Harley wanted to reach in and stroke its back, but he knew he shouldn't. He pulled back a set of drapes and went into the living-room. He could see the backs of the kids' heads. They were sitting on the sofa watching television. It was a console set with the front smashed in. Wire mesh was tacked over the opening. Snakes were inside, lying quietly among the wires, tubes and broken glass.

A plastic box was on top of the set. White mice were inside. Some were running around inside a wheel, while others wormed their way in and out of tunnels. The kids didn't say anything. They stared at the snakes that weren't moving.

'How come you guys aren't in school?' Harley said.

The kids still didn't speak, so he let it go. He figured it was none of his business. He went into the kitchen. The old man was sitting at the table. He was surrounded by chain-saw parts. He was eating a sandwich and having a glass of water. Harley saw three different kinds of casings. He wondered if the old man was trying to come up with one saw from the parts of the three different ones.

The old man finished his sandwich and his water and then had a beer. He drank it down without stopping and then opened another to sip on. Harley had one too. From the other room, they could hear the Contas girl telling Dunfee what to do.

The old man told the kids to turn on the radio. It was a news station. There was a lot of snow in Montana, a lot more than usual. A man in Texas wanted to raise the Titanic, maybe move it to San Antonio. It sounded to Harley like a good idea.

The old man grabbed his head. 'You don't have any Nyquil on you, do you?'

Harley didn't say anything. He drank his beer and fiddled with a carburetor. He tried to concentrate on it but it didn't make any sense to him.

'So what do you do for a living, Mr Contas?' Harley asked.

'Move pianos. Work's been slow.'

The old man finished his sandwich. He bummed a smoke off Harley. Harley gave it to him and then left the pack on the table. He set it on an Oregon bar. The roller head was burned out. It was purple and black from overheating.

The kids took the box of mice off the console set and put a twelve-inch portable on top. They rigged the rabbit ears with tin foil and then plugged it in. A spark whipped out from the wall and the kids laughed. The one who was holding the cord grabbed his hand. He laughed too.

It was quiet in the other room. Dunfee and the Contas girl lay on the bed. The air was damp and warm. Her eyes were closed. She held a finger to her lips. She held it there a long time. Dunfee felt foolish. He always felt foolish after he finished making love to the Contas girl. He felt a little piece had been given up of its own will. It had gone away and become something else. The Contas girl got up after a while and walked around the room. She walked as if she were trying out her legs. She walked slowly, one step after another, remembering as she went.

She stood by the window.

'Harley's still here you know.'

Dunfee sat up. He wondered why she didn't get pregnant, but then stopped thinking about it. He put his feet on the floor and his elbows on his knees.

Harley was on the other side of the drape that separated the Contas girl's room from the kitchen.

From where he sat, he could hear her say, 'I can feel you seeping out of me.'

He looked at the old man. He didn't seem to hear. His gums were white, with bread pasted to them. Harley wasn't sure if he had heard the remark himself. He set the carburetor down and looked at his hands. He drank some more beer. He made himself hear again the words he thought she said.

After a time Dunfee and the Contas girl came out. She had on a dress that looked like a man's shirt. Harley caught himself wondering what color underpants she had on. She gave him a hug. He could feel her warmth coming through the dress. Dunfee nodded at him.

'There's a storm coming down the river,' she said. 'It should be here any minute.'

Dunfee made a stack of sandwiches. He handed them out to the kids. The Contas girl took one and so did the old man. They sat, eating their sandwiches and drinking beer. It was warm in the house. Harley looked at her. He tried to remember when she had been ugly, but he couldn't. He tried to remember anything that was ugly, but couldn't do that either. The kids sat on the couch, watching the little television that was stacked on the console.

'I hear work's been slow,' Harley said to her.

'Keiper wants him to chop rowan, but he won't.'

Harley nodded at her, but didn't say anything. He picked up a muffler. 'You don't have any Stop Leak, do you?' he said to the old man. 'I popped a hole in my radiator.'

'Use an egg white,' the old man said. 'Pour it in there. When it gets hot, she'll swell up and plug the hole. I ran from here to Springfield with a baby grand on. Went through a half-dozen large, but I made it.'

He slumped back in his chair when he finished talking. He picked up his beer can with both hands and finished it off.

'You got any eggs then?'

'No. They're bad for the heart.'

Dunfee was sitting on the kitchen counter. Harley looked up at him but didn't say anything. Dunfee was watching the girl. Harley grabbed his collar and pulled it up tight to his cheek. The girl was looking out the window. She held her legs together. Her hands were folded on her lap. Dunfee jumped off the counter. He grabbed the last beer and shouted. 'So how's life?'

Harley smiled. Before he could speak, the girl said, 'It doesn't hurt so much any more,' and then everyone was quiet. No one moved.

She looked out the window.

'Whole days go by and I don't even think about it. I don't think about him or you or nothing,' she said.

She stood up and looked at the kids. She took stock of them. She pointed at each as if she were counting the hairs on their heads. The back of her dress had a red stain on it. It was an old stain, dry and almost black.

She sat back down and the power went off. It surged back once or twice and then was gone. The lights, the refrigerator, the television and the aquarium, everything was gone. Harley didn't mind. He sat up and stretched. The darkness was everywhere in the room, except some light that came in through the windows over the sink, but it wasn't much. He began to think about going to the woods with Dunfee. They were headed for the woods, that he knew.

Harley looked at the old man. His head was thrown back and his mouth was open to the ceiling. His bony chest barely moved inside his shirt.

Dunfee went to the Contas girl and told her not to cry. She told him she wasn't going to. They stood apart looking at each other. The kids came into the kitchen. They looked at everyone. They drained the empty beer cans into one and passed it among them. Harley could hear the old man sucking air into his lungs. Harley sent one of the kids out to his truck to get another six-pack. Dunfee and the Contas girl went back into her room.

The one who went for the beer came back. He gave it to Harley. They all sat down together like a family and watched Harley open a can of beer and begin to drink it. He let go of his collar and went around the table making up names for each one of the kids and then he toasted them. He gave a little speech for each name.

The kids smiled. The one he named Roy got up from the table and went to the drawer next to the stove. He took out a box of Ohio Red Tips and passed them out. The kids stood up around the table and began lighting the matches, snapping them off their front teeth and throwing them in beer cans.

Harley sat back and watched. He felt the tiredness that lovers feel after a fight. He thought about how good it was to be in the Contas girl's house, watching the tiny flares come from the kid's mouths, one after another.

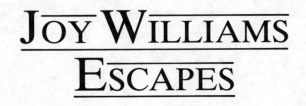

When I was very small, my father said, 'Lizzie, I want to tell you something about your grandfather. Just before he died, he was alive. Fifteen minutes before.'

I had never known my grandfather. This was the most extraordinary thing I had ever heard about him. Still, I said, No.

'"No!"' my father said. 'What do you mean, "No".' He laughed.

I shook my head.

'All right,' my father said, 'it was one minute before. I thought you were too little to know such things, but I see you're not. It was even less than a minute. It was one moment before.'

'Oh stop teasing her,' my mother said to my father.

'He's just teasing you, Lizzie,' my mother said.

In warm weather once we drove up into the mountains, my mother, my father and I, and stayed for several days at a resort lodge on a lake. In the afternoons, horse races took place in the lodge. The horses were blocks of wood with numbers painted on them, moved from one end of the room to the other by ladies in ball gowns. There was a long pier that led out into the lake and at the end of the pier was a night club that had a twenty-foot-tall champagne glass on the roof. At night, someone would pull a switch and neon bubbles would spring out from the lit glass into the black air. I very much wanted such a glass on the roof of our own house and I wanted to be the one who, every night, would turn on the switch. My mother always said about this, 'We'll see.'

I saw an odd thing once, there in the mountains. I saw my father, pretending to be lame. This was in the midst of strangers in the gift shop of the lodge. The shop sold hand-carved canes, among many other things, and when I came in to buy bubble-gum in the shape of cigarettes, to which I was devoted, I saw my father, hobbling painfully down the aisle, leaning heavily on a dully-gleaming, yellow cane, his shoulders hunched, one leg turned out at a curious angle. My handsome, healthy father, his face drawn in dreams. He looked at me. And then he looked away as though he did not know me.

My mother was a drinker. Because my father left us, I assumed he was not a drinker, but this may not have been the case. My mother loved me and was always kind to me. We spent a great deal of time together, my mother and I. This was before I knew how to read. I suspected there was a trick to reading, but I did not know the trick. Written words were something between me and a place I could not go. My mother went back and forth to that place all the time, but couldn't explain to me exactly what it was like there. I imagined it to be a different place.

As a very young child, my mother had seen the magician Houdini. Houdini had made an elephant disappear. He had also made an orange tree grow from a seed right on the stage. Bright oranges hung from the tree and he had picked them and thrown them out into the audience. People could eat the oranges or take them home, whatever they wanted.

How did he make the elephant disappear, I asked.

'He disappeared in a puff of smoke,' my mother said. 'Houdini said that even the elephant didn't know how it was done.'

Was it a baby elephant, I asked.

My mother sipped her drink. She said that Houdini was more than a magician, he was an escape artist. She said that he could escape from handcuffs and chains and ropes.

'They put him in straitjackets and locked him in trunks and threw him in swimming pools and rivers and oceans and he escaped,' my mother said. 'He escaped from water-filled vaults. He escaped from coffins.'

I said that I wanted to see Houdini.

'Oh, Houdini's dead, Lizzie,' my mother said. 'He died a long time ago. A man punched him in the stomach three times and he died.'

Dead. I asked if he couldn't get out of being dead.

'He met his match there,' my mother said.

She said that he turned a bowl of flowers into a pony who cantered around the stage.

'He sawed a lady in half too, Lizzie. Oh, how I wanted to be that lady, sawed in half and then made whole again!'

My mother spoke happily, laughing. We sat at the kitchen table and my mother was drinking from a small glass which rested snugly in her hand. It was my favorite glass too but she never let me drink from it. There were all kinds of glasses in our cupboard but this was the one we both liked. This was in Maine. Outside, in the yard, was our car which was an old blue convertible.

124

Was there blood, I asked.

'No, Lizzie, no. He was a magician!'

Did she cry that lady, I wanted to know.

'I don't think so,' my mother said. 'Maybe he hypnotized her first.'

It was winter. My father had never ridden in the blue convertible which my mother had bought after he had gone. The car was old then, and was rusted here and there. Beneath the rubber mat on my side, the passenger side, part of the floor had rusted through completely. When we went anywhere in the car, I would sometimes lift up the mat so I could see the road rushing past beneath us and feel the cold round air as it came up through the hole. I would pretend that the coldness was trying to speak to me, in the same way that words written down tried to speak. The air wanted to tell me something, but I didn't care about it, that's what I thought. Outside, the car stood in the snow.

I had a dream about the car. My mother and I were alone together as we always were, linked in our hopeless and uncomprehending love of one another, and we were driving to a house. It seemed to be our destination but we only arrived to move on. We drove again, always returning to the house which we would circle and leave, only to arrive at it again. As we drove, the inside of the car grew hair. The hair was grey and it grew and grew. I never told my mother about this dream just as I had never told her about my father leaning on the cane. I was a secretive person. In that way, I was like my mother.

I wanted to know more about Houdini. Was Houdini in love, did Houdini love someone, I asked.

'Rosabelle,' my mother said. 'He loved his wife, Rosabelle.'

I went and got a glass and poured some ginger ale in it and I sipped my ginger ale slowly in the way that I had seen my mother sip her drink many, many times. Even then, I had the gestures down. I sat opposite her, very still and quiet, pretending.

But then I wanted to know was there magic in the way he loved her. Could he make her disappear. Could he make both of them disappear was the way I put my question.

'Rosabelle,' my mother said. 'No one knew anything about Rosabelle except that Houdini loved her. He never turned their love into loneliness which would have been beneath him of course.'

We ate our supper and after supper my mother would have another little bit to drink. Then she would read articles from the newspaper aloud to me.

'My goodness,' she said, 'what a strange story. A hunter shot a bear who was carrying a woman's pocket book in its mouth.'

Oh, oh, I cried. I looked at the newspaper and struck it with my fingers. My mother read on, a little oblivious to me. The woman had lost her purse years before on a camping trip. Everything was still inside it, her wallet and her compact and her keys.

Oh, I cried. I thought this was terrible. I was frightened, thinking of my mother's pocket book, the way she carried it always, and the poor bear too.

Why did the bear want to carry a pocket book, I asked.

My mother looked up from the words in the newspaper. It was as though she had come back into the room I was in.

'Why, Lizzie,' she said.

The poor bear, I said.

'Oh, the bear is all right,' my mother said. 'The bear got away.'

I did not believe this was the case. She herself said the bear had been shot.

'The bear escaped,' my mother said. 'It says so right here,' and she ran her finger along a line of words. 'It ran back into the woods to its home.' She stood up and came around the table and kissed me. She smelled then like the glass that was always in the sink in the morning, and the smell reminds me still of daring and deception, hopes and little lies.

I shut my eyes and in that way I felt I could not hear my mother. I saw the bear holding the pocket book, walking through the woods with it, feeling fine in a different way and pretty too, then stopping to find something in it, wanting something, moving its big paw through the pocket book's small things.

'Lizzie,' my mother called to me. My mother did not know where I was, which alarmed me. I opened my eyes.

'Don't cry, Lizzie,' my mother said. She looked as though she were about to cry too. This was the way it often was at night, late in the kitchen with my mother.

My mother returned to the newspaper and began to turn the pages. She called my attention to the drawing of a man holding a hat with stars sprinkling out of it. It was an advertisement for a magician who would be performing not far away. We decided we would see him. My mother knew just the seats she wanted for us, good seats, on the aisle close to the stage. We might be called up on the stage, she said, to be part of the performance. Magicians often used people from the audience, particularly children. I might even be given a rabbit.

I wanted a rabbit.

I put my hands on the table and I could see the rabbit between them. He was solid white in the front and solid black in the back as though he were made up of two rabbits. There are rabbits like that. I saw him there, before me on the table, a nice rabbit.

My mother went to the phone and ordered two tickets, and not many days after that we were in our car driving to Portland for the matinee performance. I very much liked the word matinee. Matin*ee*, matin*ee*, I said. There was a broad hump on the floor between our seats and it was here my mother put her little glass, the glass often full, never, it seemed, more than half empty. We chatted together and I thought we must have appeared interesting to others as we passed by in our convertible in winter. My mother spoke about happiness. She told me that the happiness that comes out of nowhere, out of nothing, is the very best kind. We paid no attention to the coldness which was speaking in the way that it had, but enjoyed the sun which beat through the windshield upon our pale hands.

My mother said that Houdini had black eyes and that white doves flew from his fingertips. She said that he escaped from a block of ice.

Did he look like my father, Houdini, I asked. Did he have a moustache.

'Your father didn't have a moustache,' my mother said, laughing. 'Oh, I wish I could be more like you.'

Later, she said, 'Maybe he didn't escape from a block of ice, I'm not sure about that. Maybe he wanted to, but he never did.'

We stopped for lunch somewhere, a dark little restaurant along the road. My mother had cocktails and I myself drank something cold and sweet. The restaurant was not very nice. It smelled of smoke and dampness as though once it had burned down, and it was so noisy that I could not hear my mother very well. My mother looked like a woman in a bar, pretty and disturbed, hunched forward saying, 'Who do you think I look like? Will you remember me?' She was saying all matter of things. We lingered there, and then my mother asked the time of someone and seemed surprised. My mother was always surprised by time. Outside, there were woods of green fir trees whose lowest branches swept the ground, and as we were getting back into the car I believed I saw something moving far back in the darkness of the woods beyond the slick, snowy square of the parking lot. It was the bear, I thought. Hurry, hurry, I thought. The hunter is playing with his children. He is making them something to play in as my father had once made a small playhouse for me. He is not the hunter yet. But in my heart I knew the bear was gone and the shape was just the shadow of something else in the afternoon.

M y mother drove very fast but the performance had already begun when we arrived. My mother's face was damp and her good blouse had a spot on it. She went into the ladies' room and when she returned the spot was larger, but it was water now and not what it had been before. The usher assured us that we had not missed much. The usher said that the magician was not very good, that he talked and talked, he told a lot of jokes and then when you were bored and distracted, something would happen, something would have changed. The usher smiled at my mother. He seemed to like her, even know her in some way. He was a small man, like an old boy, balding. I did not care for him. He led us to our seats, but there were people sitting in them and there was a small disturbance as the strangers rearranged themselves. We were both expectant, my mother and I, and we watched the magician intently. My mother's lips were parted, and her eyes were bright. On the stage were a group of children about my age, each with a hand on a small cage the magician was holding. In the cage was a tiny bird. The magician would ask the children to jostle the cage occasionally and the bird would flutter against the bars so that everyone would see it was a real thing with bones and breath and feelings too. Each child announced that they had a firm grip on the bars. Then the magician put a cloth over the cage, gave a quick tug and cage and bird vanished. I was not surprised. It seemed just the kind of thing that was going to happen. I decided to withhold my applause when I saw that my mother's hands too were in her lap. There were several more tricks of the magician's invention, certainly nothing I would have asked him to do. Large constructions of many parts and colors were wheeled onto the stage. There were doors everywhere which the magician opened and slammed shut. Things came and went, all to the accompaniment of loud music. I was confused and grew hot. My mother too moved restlessly in the next seat. Then there was an intermission and we returned to the lobby.

'This man is a far, far cry from the great Houdini,' my mother said.

What were his intentions exactly, I asked.

He had taken a watch from a man in the audience and smashed it for all to see with a hammer. Then the watch, unharmed, had reappeared behind the man's ear.

'A happy memory can be a very misleading thing,' my mother said. 'Would you like to go home?'

I did not really want to leave. I wanted to see it through. I held the glossy program in my hand and turned the pages. I stared hard at the print beneath the pictures and imagined all sorts of promises being made.

'Yes, we want to see how it's done, don't we, you and I,' my mother said. 'We want to get to the bottom of it.'

I guessed we did.

'All right, Lizzie,' my mother said, 'but I have to get something out of the car. I'll be right back.'

I waited for her in a corner of the lobby. Some children looked at me and I looked back. I had a package of gum cigarettes in my pocket and I extracted one carefully and placed the end in my mouth. I held the elbow of my right arm with my left hand and smoked the cigarette for a long time and then I folded it up in my mouth and I chewed it for a while. My mother had not yet returned when the performance began again. She was having a little drink, I knew, and she was where she went when she drank without me, somewhere in herself. It was not the place where words could take you but another place even. I stood alone in the lobby for a while, looking out into the street. On the sidewalk outside the theatre sand had been scattered, and the sand ate through the ice in ugly holes. I saw no one like my mother passing by. She was wearing a red coat. Once she had said to me, 'You've fallen out of love with me, haven't you?' and I knew she was thinking I was someone else, but this had happened only once.

I heard the music from the stage and I finally returned to our seats. There were not as many people in the audience as before. On stage with the magician was a woman in a bathing suit and high-heeled shoes holding a chain-saw. The magician demonstrated that the saw was real by cutting up several pieces of wood with it. There was the smell of torn wood for everyone to smell and sawdust on the floor for all to see. Then a table was wheeled out and the lady lay down on it in her bathing suit which was in two pieces. Her stomach was very white. The magician talked and waved the saw around. I suspected he was planning to cut the woman in half and I was eager to see this. I hadn't the slightest fear about this at all. I did wonder if he would be able to put her together again or if he would cut her in half only. The magician said that what was about to happen was too dreadful to be seen directly, that he did not want anyone to faint from the sight, so he brought out a small screen and placed it in front of the lady so that we could no longer see her white stomach, although everyone could still see her face and her shoes. The screen seemed unnecessary to me and I would have preferred to have been seated on the other side of it. Several people in the audience screamed. The lady who was about to be sawed in half began to chew on her lip and her face looked worried.

It was then that my mother appeared on the stage. She was crouched over a little, for she didn't have her balance back from having climbed up there. She looked large and strange in her red coat. The coat, which I knew very well, seemed the strangest thing. Someone screamed again, but more uncertainly. My mother moved towards the magician, smiling and speaking and gesturing with her hands, and the magician said, No, I can't of course, you should know better than this, this is a performance, you can't just appear like this, please sit down...

My mother said, But you don't understand I'm willing, though I know the hazards and it's not that I believe you, no one would believe you for a moment but you can trust me, that's right, your faith in me would be perfectly placed because I'm not part of this, that's why I can be trusted because I don't know how it's done...

Someone near me said, Is she kidding, that woman, what's her plan, she comes out of nowhere and wants to be cut in half...

Lady... the magician said, and I thought a dog might appear for I knew a dog named Lady who had a collection of colored balls.

My mother said, Most of us don't understand I know and it's just as well because the things we understand that's it for them, that's just the way we are...

She probably thought she was still in that place in herself, but everything she said was the words coming from her mouth. Her lipstick was gone. Did she think she was in disguise, I wondered.

But why not, my mother said, to go and come back, that's what we want, that's why we're here and why can't we expect something to be done you can't expect us every day we get tired of showing up every day you can't get away with this forever then it was different but you should be thinking about the children... She moved a little in a crooked fashion, speaking.

My God, said a voice, that woman's drunk. Sit down, please! someone said loudly.

My mother started to cry then and she stumbled and pushed her arms out before her as though she were pushing away someone who was trying to hold her, but no one was trying to hold her. The orchestra began to play and people began to clap. The usher ran out onto the stage and took my mother's hand. All this happened in an instant. He said something to her, he held her hand and she did not resist his holding it, then slowly the two of them moved down the few steps that led to the stage and up the aisle until they stopped beside me for the usher knew I was my mother's child. I followed them, of course, although in my mind I continued to sit in my seat. Everyone watched us leave. They did not notice that I remained there among them, watching too.

We went directly out of the theatre and into the streets, my mother weeping on the little usher's arm. The shoulders of his jacket were of cardboard and there was gold braid looped around them. We were being taken away to be murdered which seemed reasonable to me. The usher's ears were large and he had a bump on his neck above the collar of his shirt. As we walked he said little soft things to my mother which gradually seemed to be comforting her. I hated him. It was not easy to walk together along the frozen sidewalks of the city. There was a belt on my mother's coat and I hung on to that as we moved unevenly along.

Look, I've pulled myself through, he said. You can pull yourself through. He was speaking to my mother.

We went into a coffee shop and sat down in a booth.

'You can collect yourself in here,' he said. 'You can sit here as long as you want and drink coffee and no one will make you leave.' He asked me if I wanted a donut. I would not speak to him. If he addressed me again, I thought, I would bite him. On the wall over the counter were pictures of sandwiches and pies. I did not want to be there and I did not take off either my mittens or my coat. The little usher went up to the counter and brought back coffee for my mother and a donut on a plate for me.

Oh, my mother said, what have I done, and she swung her head from side to side.

I could tell right away about you, the usher said. You've got to pull yourself together. It took jumping off a bridge for me and breaking both legs before I got turned around. You don't want to let it go that far.

My mother looked at him. I can't imagine, my mother said.

Outside, a child passed by, walking with her sled. She looked behind her often and you could tell she was admiring the way the sled followed her so quickly on its runners.

You're a mother, the usher said to my mother, you've got to pull yourself through.

His kindness made me feel he had tied us up with rope. At last he left us and my mother laid her head down upon the table and fell asleep. I had never seen my mother sleeping and I watched her as she must once have watched me, the same way everyone watches a sleeping thing, not knowing how it would turn out or when. Then slowly I began to eat the donut with my mittened hands. The sour hair of the wool mingled with the tasteless crumbs and this utterly absorbed my attention. I pretended someone was feeding me.

As it happened, my mother was not able to pull herself through, but this was later. At the time, it was not so near the end and when my mother woke we found the car and left Portland, my mother saying my name. Lizzie, she said. Lizzie. I felt as though I must be with her somewhere and that she knew that too, but not in that old blue convertible travelling home in the dark, the soft, stained roof ballooning up in the way I knew it looked from the outside. I got out of it, but it took me years.

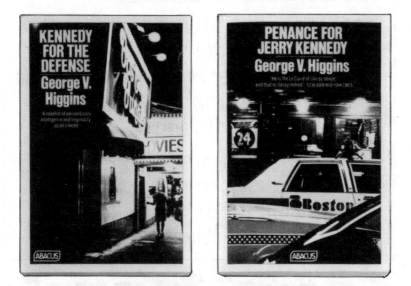

LOUISE ERDRICH
KNIVES

He is fine-boned, slick, agreeable, and dressed to kill in his sharp black suit, winey vest, knotted brown tie. His hair is oiled. His lips are fevered and red as two buds. For a long while he stands there, eyeing me, before he opens his mouth.

'You're not pretty,' are the first words he speaks.

And I, who have never bit off my words even to a customer, am surprised into a wounded silence, although I don't look in the mirror for pleasure, but only to take stock of the night's damage.

I work for Mary, who learned the butcher's trade and keeps a rundown shop on the edge of Argus, a town in which I've found no hope of marriage. I get along with men. I work right beside them in the cutting room and keep a long tally of the card debts they owe me. But this is not romance. In the novels I read at night, I experience with no satisfaction the veiled look, the guarded approach, the hungers I've come to live with in my thirties. I get heavier each year that no one sweeps me off my feet, so that now I outweigh most men. And perhaps I am too much like them, too strong and imposing when I square my shoulders, and used to taking control.

I am standing on a stool, changing the prices I chalk above the counter each week on a piece of slate. Blutwurst. Swedish sausage. Center-cut chops. Steak. I keep writing and do not give him the satisfaction of an answer. He stands below me, waiting. He has the patience of a cat with women. When I finish, there is nothing left for me to do but climb down.

'But pretty's not the only thing,' the man continues smoothly, as though all my silence has not come between.

I cut him off. 'Tell me what you want,' I say. 'I'm closing shop.'

'I bet you never thought I'd come back,' he says. He steps close to the glass counter full of meats. I can see, through the false, bright glare inside the case, his dumbell-lifting chest. His sharp, thick hands. Even above the white pepper and sawdust of the shop, I can smell the wildroot, tobacco, penetrating breath-mint.

'I never saw you the first time,' I tell him. 'I'm closing.'

'Look here,' he says, 'Mary...'

'I'm not Mary.'

He goes rigid, puts his hand to the back of his skull, pats the hair in place thoughtfully.

'Who are you then?'

'Celestine,' I say, 'as if it's any of your business.'

I have to ring out the register, secure the doors, set the alarm on the safe before I can walk home. Around that time of early evening the light floods through the thick block-glass windows, a golden light that softens the shelves and barrels. Dusk is always my time, that special air of shifting shapes, and it occurs to me that, even though he says I am not pretty, perhaps in the dusk I am impossible to resist. Perhaps there is something about me, like he says.

'Adare. Karl Adare.'

He introduces himself without my asking. He crosses his arms on the counter, leans over, and deliberately smiles at my reaction. His teeth are small, shiny, mother-of-pearl.

'This is something,' I say. 'Mary's brother.'

'She ever talk about me?'

'No,' I have to answer, 'and she's out on a delivery right now. She won't be back for a couple of hours.'

'But you're here.'

I guess my mouth drops a little. Me knowing who he is has only slightly diverted what seems like his firm intentions, which are what? I can't read him. I turn away from him and make myself busy with the till, but I am fumbling. I turn to look at Karl. His eyes are burning holes and he tries to look right through me if he can. This is, indeed, the way men behave in the world of romance. Except that he is slightly smaller than me, and also Mary's brother. And then there is his irritating refrain.

'Pretty's not everything,' he says to me again. 'You're built...' He stops, trying to hide his confusion. But his neck reddens and I think maybe he is no more experienced at this than I.

'If you curled the ends at least,' he says, attempting to recover, 'if you cut your hair. Or maybe it's the apron.'

I always wear a long white butcher's apron, starched and swaddled around my middle with thick straps. Right now, I take it off, whip it around me, and toss it on the radiator. I decide I will best him at his game, as I have studied it in private, have thought it out.

'All right,' I say, walking around the counter. 'Here I am.' Because of the market visit I am wearing a navy-blue dress edged in white. I have a bow at my waist, black shoes, and a silver necklace. I have always thought I looked impressive in this outfit, not to be taken lightly. Sure enough, his eyes widen. He looks stricken and suddenly uncertain of the next move, which I see is mine to make.

'Follow me,' I say, 'I'll put a pot of coffee on the stove.'

It is Mary's stove, of course, but she will not be back for several hours. He does not follow me directly, but lights a cigarette. He smokes the heavy kind, not my brand anymore. The smoke curls from his lips.

'You married?' he asks.

'No,' I say. He drops the cigarette on the floor, crushes it out with his foot, and then picks it up and says, 'Where shall I put this?'

I point at an ashtray in the hall, and he drops the butt in. Then, as we walk back to Mary's kitchen, I see that he is carrying a black case I have not noticed before. We are at the door of the kitchen. It is dark. I have my hand on the light switch and am going to turn on the fluorescent ring, when he comes up behind me, puts his hands on my shoulders, and kisses the back of my neck.

'Get away from me,' I say, not expecting this so soon. First the glances, the adoration, the many conversations must happen.

'How come?' he asks. 'This is what you want.'

His voice shakes. Neither one of us is in control. I shrug his hands off.

'What I want.' I repeat this stupidly. Love stories always end here. I never had a mother to tell me what came next. He steps in front of me and hugs me to himself, draws my face down to his face. I am supposed to taste a burning sweetness on his lips, but his mouth is hard as metal.

I lunge from his grip, but he comes right with me. I lose my balance. He is fighting me for the upper hand, straining down with all his might, but I am more than equal to his weightlifting arms and thrashing legs. I could throw him to the side, I know, but I grow curious. There is the smell of corn mash, something Mary has dropped that morning. That's what I notice even when it happens and we are together, rolling over, clasped, bumping into the legs of the table. I move by instinct, lurching under him. We're held in my mind as in a glass, and I see my own face, amused, embarrassed, and relieved. It is not so complicated, not even as painful, as I feared, and it doesn't last long either. He sighs when it is over, his breath hot and hollow in my ear.

Louise Erdrich

'I don't believe this happened,' he says to himself.

That is, oddly, when I lash out against his presence. He is so heavy that I think I might scream in his face. I push a chest, a dead weight, and then I heave him over so he sprawls in the dark away from me, so I can breathe. We smooth our clothing and hair back so carefully, in the dark, that when we finally turn the light on and blink at the place where we find ourselves, it is as though nothing has happened.

We are standing up, looking anyplace but at each other.

'How about that coffee?' he says.

I turn to the stove.

And then, when I turn around again with the coffee-pot, I see that he is unlatching a complicated series of brass fittings that unfold his suitcase into a large stand-up display. He is absorbed, one-minded, not too different from the way he was down on the floor. The case is lined in scarlet velvet. Knives gleam in the plush. Each rests in a fitted compartment, the tips capped so as not to pierce the cloth, the bone handles tied with small strips of pigskin leather.

I sit down. I ask what he is doing but he does not answer, only turns and eyes me significantly. He holds out a knife and a small rectangle of dark wood.

'You can slice,' he begins, 'through wood, even plaster, with our serrated edge. Or...' he produces a pale dinner roll from his pocket, 'the softest bread.' He proceeds to demonstrate, sawing the end off the block of balsa wood with little difficulty, then delicately wiggling the knife through the roll so it falls apart in transparent, perfect ovals.

'You could never butter those,' I hear myself say, 'they'd fall apart.'

'It's just as good with soft-skinned vegetables,' he says to the air. 'Fruits. Fish fillets.'

He is testing the edge of the knife. 'Feel,' he says, holding the blade toward me. I ignore him. One thing I know is knives and his are cheap-john, not worth half the price of the fancy case. He keeps on with his demonstration, slicing bits of cloth, a very ripe tomato, and a box of ice cream from Mary's freezer. He shows each knife, one after the other, explaining its usefulness. He shows me the knife sharpener and sharpens all Mary's knives on its wheels. The last thing he does is take out a pair of utility shears. He snips the air with them as he speaks.

140

'Got a penny?' he asks.

Mary keeps her small change in a glass jar on the window-sill. I take out a penny and lay it on the table. And then, in the kitchen glare, Karl takes his scissors and cuts the penny into a spiral.

So, I think, this is what happens after the burning kiss, when the music roars. Imagine. The lovers are trapped together in a deserted mansion. His lips descend. She touches his magnificent thews.

'Cut anything,' he says, putting the spiral beside my hand. He begins another. I watch the tension in his fingers, the slow frown of enjoyment. He puts another perfect spiral beside the first. And then, since he looks as though he might keep on going, cutting all the pennies in the jar, I decide that I now have seen what love is about.

'Pack up and go,' I tell him.

But he only smiles and bites his lip, concentrating on the penny that uncoils in his hands. He will not budge. I can sit here watching the man and his knives, or call the police. But neither of these seems like a suitable ending.

'I'll take it,' I say, pointing at the smallest knife.

In one motion he unlatches a vegetable parer from its velvet niche and sets it between us on the table. I dump a dollar in change from the penny-ante jar. He snaps the case shut. I handle my knife. It is razor sharp, good for cutting the eyes from potatoes. But he is gone by the time I have formed the next thought.

In my stories, they return as a matter of course. So does Karl. There is something about me he has to follow. He doesn't know what it is and I can't tell him either, but not two weeks go by before he breezes back into town, still without ever having seen his sister. I see my brother Russell all the time. I live with him. Russell looks outside one morning and sees Adare straddling the chubstone walk to our house.

'It's a noodle,' says Russell. I glance out the window over his shoulder, and see Karl.

'I've got business with him,' I say.

'Answer the door then,' Russell says. 'I'll get lost.' He walks out the back door with his tools.

The bell rings twice. I open the front door and lean out.

'I can't use any,' I say.

The smile falls off his face. He is confused a moment, then

shocked. I see that he has come to my house by accident. Maybe he thought that he would never see me again. His face is what decides me that he has another think coming. I am standing there in layers of flimsy clothing with a hammer in my hand. I can tell it makes him nervous when I ask him in, but he thinks so much of himself that he can't back down. I pull a chair out, still dangling the hammer, and he sits. I go into the kitchen and fetch him a glass of the lemonade I have been smashing the ice for. I half-expect him to sneak out, but when I return he is still sitting there, the suitcase humbly at his feet, an oily black fedora on his knees.

'So, so,' I say, taking a chair beside him.

He has no answer to my comment. As he sips on the lemonade, however, he glances around, and seems slowly to recover his salesman's confidence.

'How's the paring knife holding out?' he asks.

I just laugh. 'The blade snapped off the handle,' I say. 'Your knives are duck-bait.'

He keeps his composure somehow, and slowly takes in the living-room with his stare. When my ceramics, books, typewriter, pillows and ashtrays are all added up, he turns to the suitcase with a squint.

'You live here by yourself?' he asks.

'With my brother.'

'Oh.'

I fill his lemonade glass again from my pitcher. It is time, now, for Karl to break down with his confession that I am a slow-burning fuse in his loins. A hair trigger. I am a name he cannot silence. A dream that never burst.

'Oh well...' he says.

'What's that supposed to mean?' I ask.

'Nothing.'

We sit there for a while collecting dust until the silence and absence of Russell from the house grows very evident. And then, putting down our glasses, we walk up the stairs. At the door to my room, I take the hat from his hand. I hang it on my doorknob and beckon him in. And this time, I have been there before. I've had two weeks to figure out the missing areas of books. He is shocked by what I've learned. It is like his mind darkens. Where before there was shuffling and silence, now there are cries. Where before we were hidden, now the shocking glare. I pull the blinds up. What we do is well worth a second look, even if there are only the squirrels in the box-elders. He falls right off the bed once, shaking the whole house. And when he gets up he is spent, in pain because of an aching back. He just lays there.

'You could stay on for supper,' I finally offer, because he doesn't seem likely to go.

'I will.' And then he is looking at me with his eyes in a different way, as if he cannot figure the sum of me. As if I am too much for him to compass. I get nervous.

'I'll fix the soup now,' I say.

'Don't go.' His hand is on my arm, the polished fingernails clutching. I cannot help but look down and compare it with my own. I have the hands of a woman who has handled too many knives, deep-nicked and marked with lines, toughened from spice and brine, gouged, even missing a tip and nail.

'I'll go if I want,' I say. 'Don't I live here?'

And I get up, throwing a house-coat and sweater over myself. I go downstairs and start a dinner on the stove. Presently, I hear him come down, feel him behind me in the doorway, those black eyes in a skin white as veal.

'Pull up a chair,' I say. He settles himself heavily and drinks down the highball I give him. When I cook, what goes into my soup is what's there. Expect the unexpected, Russell always says. Butter beans and barley. A bowl of fried rice. Frozen oxtails. All this goes into my pot.

'Godalmighty,' says Russell, stepping through the door. 'You still here?' There is never any doubt Russell is my brother. We have the same slanting eyes and wide mouth, the same long head and glaring white teeth. We could be twins, but for his scars and that I am a paler version of him.

'Adare,' says the salesman, holding out his perfect hand. 'Karl Adare. Representative at Large.'

'What's that?' Russell ignores the hand and rummages beneath the sink for a beer. He makes it himself from a recipe that he learned in the army. Whenever he opens that cupboard I stand back, because sometimes the brew explodes on contact with air. Our cellar is also full of beer. In the deepest of summer, on close, hot nights, we sometimes hear the bottles go smashing into the dirt.

'So,' says Russell, 'you're the one who sold Celestine here the bum knife.'

'That's right,' Karl says, taking a fast drink.

'You unload many?'

'No.'

'I'm not surprised,' Russell says.

Karl looks at me, trying to gauge what I've told. But because he doesn't understand the first thing about me, he draws blank. There is nothing to read on my face. I ladle the soup on his plate and sit down across the table. I say to Russell, 'He's got a suitcase full.'

'Let's see it then.'

Russell always likes to look at tools. So again the case comes out, folding into a display. While we eat Russell keeps up a running examination of every detail a knife could own. He tries them out on bits of paper, on his own pants and fingers. And all the while, whenever Karl can manage to catch my eye, he gives a mournful look of pleading, as if I am forcing this performance with the knives. As if the apple in Russell's fingers is Karl's own heart getting peeled. It is uncomfortable. In the love magazines, when passion holds sway, men don't fall down and roll on the floor and lay there like dead. But Karl does that. Right that very evening, in fact, not long after the dinner when I tell him he must go, he suddenly hits the floor like a toppled statue.

'What's that!' I jump up, clutching Russell's arm, for we are still in the kitchen. Having drunk several bottles in the mellow dusk, Russell isn't clear in the head. Karl has drunk more. We look down. He is slumped beneath the table where he's fallen, passed out, so pale and still I fetch a mirror to his pencil-moustache and am not satisfied until his breath leaves a faint silver cloud.

The next morning, the next morning after that, and still the next morning Karl is here in the house. He pretends to take ill at first, creeping close to me that first night in order to avoid deadly chills. The same the night after, and the night after that, until things begin to get too predictable for my taste.

Sitting at the table in his underwear is something Karl starts doing once he feels at home. He never makes himself useful. He never sells any knives. Every day when I leave for work the last thing I see is him killing time, talking to himself like the leaves in the trees. Every night when I come home there he is, taking up space like one more piece of furniture. Only now, he's got himself clothed. Right away, when I enter the door, he rises like a sleepwalker and comes forward to embrace me and lead me upstairs.

'I don't like what's going on here,' says Russell after two weeks of hanging around on the outskirts of this affair. 'I'll take off until you get tired of the noodle.'

So Russell goes. Whenever things heat up at home he stays up on the reservation with Eli, his half-brother, in an old house that is papered with calendars of naked women. They fish for crappies or trap muskrats, and spend their Saturday nights half-drunk, paging through the long years on their wall. I don't like to have him go up there, but I'm not ready to say goodbye to Karl.

I get into a habit with Karl and don't look up for two months. Mary tells me what I do with her brother is my business, but I catch her eyeing me, her gaze a sharp yellow. I do not blame her. Karl has gone to her only once for dinner. It was supposed to be their grand reunion, but it fell flat. They blamed each other. They argued. Mary hit him with a can of oysters. She threw it from behind and left a goose egg, or so Karl says. Mary never tells me her side, but after that night things change at work. She talks around me, delivers messages through others. I even hear through one of the men that she says I've turned against her.

Meanwhile, love wears on me. Mary or no Mary, I am tired of coming home to Karl's heavy breathing and even his touch has begun to oppress me.

'Maybe we ought to end this while we're still in love,' I say to him one morning.

He just looks at me.

'You want me to pop the question?'

'No.'

'Yes you do,' he says, edging around the table.

I leave the house. The next morning, when I tell him to leave again, he proposes marriage. But this time I have a threat to make.

'I'm calling the state asylum,' I say. 'You're berserk.'

He leans over and spins his finger around his ear.

'Commit me then,' he says, 'I'm crazy with love.'

Something in all this has made me realize that Karl has read as many books as I, that his fantasies always stopped before the woman came home worn out from cutting beef into steaks with an electric saw.

'It's not just you,' I tell him. 'I don't want to get married. With you around I get no sleep. I'm tired all the time. All day I'm giving wrong change and I don't have any dreams. I'm the kind of person that likes having dreams. Now I have to see you every morning when I wake up and I forget if I dreamed anything or even slept at all, because right away you're on me with your hot breath.'

He stands up and pushes his chest, hard, against mine, and runs his hands down my back and puts his mouth on my mouth. I don't have a damn thing to defend myself with. I push him down on the chair and sit, eager, in his lap. But all the while, I am aware that I am living on Karl's borrowed terms.

They might as well cart me off in a wet sheet too, I think.

'I'm like some kind of animal,' I say, when it is over.

'What kind?' he asks, lazy. We are laying on the kitchen floor.

'A big stupid heifer.'

He doesn't hear what I say though. I get up. I smooth my clothes down and drive off to the shop. But all day, as I wait on customers and tend fire in the smoke room, as I order from suppliers and slice the head cheese and peg up and down the cribbage board, I am setting my mind hard against the situation.

'I'm going home,' I say to Mary, when work is done, 'and getting rid of him.'

We are standing in the back entry alone; all the men are gone. I know she is going to say something strange.

'I had an insight,' she says. 'If you do, he'll take his life.'

I look at the furnace in the corner, not at her, and I think that I hear a false note in her voice.

'He's not going to kill himself,' I tell her. 'He's not the type. And you,' I am angry now, 'you don't know what you want. At the same time you're jealous of Karl and me, you don't want us apart. You're confused.'

She takes her apron off and hangs it on a hook. If she wasn't so

proud, so good at hardening her heart, she might have said what kind
of time this had been for her alone.

But she turns and sets her teeth.

'Call me up when it's over,' she says, 'and we'll drive out to The
Brunch Bar.'

This is a restaurant where we like to go on busy nights when there
is no time for cooking. I know her saying this has taken effort, so I feel
sorry.

'Give me one hour, then I'll call you,' I say.

As usual, when I get home, Karl is sitting at the kitchen table.
The first thing I do is fetch his sample case from the couch where he
parks it, handy for when the customers start pouring in. I carry it into
the kitchen, put it down, and kick it across the linoleum. The leather
screeches but the knives make no sound inside their velvet.

'What do you think I'm trying to tell you?' I ask.

He is sitting before the day's dirty dishes, half-full ashtrays, and
crumbs of bread. He wears his suit pants, the dark red vest, and a shirt
that belongs to Russell. If I have any hesitations, the shirt erases
them.

'Get out,' I say.

But he only shrugs and smiles.

'I can't go yet,' he says. 'It's time for the matinee.'

I step closer, not close enough so he can grab me, just to where
there is no chance he can escape my gaze. He bends down. He lights a
match off the sole of his shoe and starts blowing harsh smoke into the
air. My mind is shaking from the strain, but my expression is still
firm. It isn't until he smokes his Lucky to the nub, and speaks, that I
falter.

'Don't chuck me. I'm the father,' he says.

I hold my eyes trained on his forehead, not having really heard or
understood what he said. He laughs. He puts his hands up like a bank
clerk in a hold-up and then I give him the once-over, take him in as if
he was a stranger. He is better looking than I am, with the dark eyes,
red lips and pale complexion of a movie actor. His drinking has not
told on him, not his smoking either. His teeth have stayed pearly and
white although his fingers are stained rubbery orange from the
curling smoke.

'I give up! You're the stupidest woman I ever met.' He puts his arms down, lights another cigarette from the first. 'Here you're knocked up,' he says suddenly, 'and you don't even know it.'

I suppose I look stupid, knowing at that instant what he says is true.

'You're going to have my baby,' he says in a calmer voice, before I can recover my sense.

'You don't know.'

I grab his suitcase and heave it past him through the screen-door. It tears right through the rotten mesh and thumps hard on the porch. He is silent for a long time, letting this act sink in.

'You don't love me,' he says.

'I don't love you,' I answer.

'What about my baby?'

'There's not a baby.'

And now he starts moving. He backs away from me towards the door, but he cannot go through it.

'Get going,' I say.

'Not yet.' His voice is desperate.

'What now?'

'A souvenir. I don't have anything to remember you.' If he cries, I know I'll break down, so I grab the object closest to my hand, a book I've had sitting on the top of the refrigerator. I won it somewhere and never opened the cover. I hold it out to him.

'Here,' I say.

He takes the book, and then there is no other excuse. He edges down the steps and finally off at a slow walk through the grass, down the road. I stand there a long time, watching him from the door, before he shrinks into the distance and is gone. And then, once I feel certain he has walked all the way to Argus, maybe hopped a bus, or hitched down Highway 30 south, I lay my head down on the table and let my mind go.

The first thing I do once I am better, is to dial Mary's number.

'I got rid of him,' I say into the phone.

'Give me ten minutes,' she says, 'I'll come and get you.'

'Just wait,' I say. 'I have to have some time off.'

'What for?'

'I went and got myself into the family way.'

She says nothing. I listen to the silence on her end before I finally hear her take the phone from her ear, and put it down.

In the love books a baby never comes of it all, so again I am not
prepared. I do not expect the weakness or the swelling ankles.
The tales of burning love never mention how I lie awake, alone
in the heat of an August night, and panic. I know the child feels me
thinking. It turns over and over, so furiously that I know it must be
wound in its cord. I fear that something has gone wrong with it. The
mind is not right, just like the father's. Or it will look like the sick
sheep I had to club. A million probable, terrible things will go wrong.
And then, as I am lying there worrying into the dark, bottles start
going off under the house. Russell's brew is exploding and all night,
with the baby turning, I keep dreaming and waking to the sound of
glass flying through the earth.

John Updike
Getting the
Words Out

John Updike

'**U**pdike,' the *Jerusalem Post* of November 10, 1978, told
its readers, 'has the slight slurp of a speech impediment,
the sort of thing once affected by cavalry subalterns.'
I liked to imagine, all evidence to the contrary, that my stutter was
unnoticeable, that only I was conscious of it. Conscious, that is, of a
kind of window pane suddenly inserted in front of my face while
I was talking, or of a barrier thrust into my throat. My first memory
of the sensation is associated with our Shillington neighbor Eddie
Pritchard, a somewhat larger boy than I whom I was trying, on the
sidewalk in front of our houses, to scream into submission. I think
he was calling me 'Ostrich', a nickname I did not think I deserved,
and a fear of being mistook or misunderstood accompanies the
impediment ever since. There seems so much about me to explain—
all of it subsumable under the heading of, 'I am not an ostrich'—
that when freshly encountering, say, a bored and hurried electrician
over the telephone, I tend to seize up. If the electrician has already
been to the house, the seizing up is less dramatic, and if I encounter
not his voice but that of his maternal and amused sounding
secretary, I become quite vocal, indeed something of a minor
virtuoso of the spoken language. For there is no doubt that I have
lots of words inside me; it's just that at moments, like rush-hour
traffic at the mouth of a tunnel, they jam and I can't get them out.

It tends to happen when I feel myself in a false position. My
worst recent public collapse that I can bear to remember came at a
May meeting of the august American Academy and Institute of
Arts and Letters, when I tried to read a number of award citations—
cagey and intricate, as award citations tend to be—that I had not
written. I could scarcely get through the words. Similarly, many
years before, one spring evening, on the stage of the Shillington
High School auditorium, I—I, who played the father in our class
plays, who was on the debating team, who gave droll chalk talks
with aplomb even in other county high schools—could scarcely get
out a few formal words of announcement, in my capacity as class
president. I did not, at heart, feel I deserved to be class president
(whereas I did somehow deserve to give the chalk talks), and in
acknowledgement of my false position my throat jammed. In most
people there is a settled place they speak from; in me it remains
unsettled, unfinished. Viewing myself on taped television, I see the

repulsive symptoms of an approaching stammer take possession of my face—an electronically rapid flutter of the eyelashes, a distortion of the mouth as of a stiff leather purse being cinched, a terrified hardening of the upper lip, a fatal tensing and lifting of the voice. And through it all a detestable coyness and craven willingness to please, to assure my talk-show host and his millions of viewers that I am not, appearances to the contrary, an ostrich.

Stuttering is popularly associated with fear and its hyper-excitement, and of course I was afraid of Eddie Pritchard, afraid of being miscast by him into a role, perhaps for life, that I did not wish to play. I am afraid of the audiences I discomfit and embarrass, to my own embarrassment and discomfiture. And yet some audiences can be as comforting, with their giant collective sighs and embracing laughter, as an ideal mother—southern college audiences, particularly. Unlike audiences recruited from the tough old American Northeast, they hold nary a wise guy or doubting Thomas or mocking cackle in a thousand, just hosts of attentive and comely faces, lightly sweating and drawing forth from my chest my best and true music, the effortless cello throb of eloquence. One could babble on forever, there at the lectern with its little warm light, and the pitcher of assuaging water, and the microphone cowled in black sponge and alertly uptilted like the screened face of a miniature fencer. Reading words I have written, giving my own answers, I have no fear of any basic misapprehension; the audience has voluntarily assembled to view and audit an image within which I am comfortable. The larger the audience, the better; the larger it becomes, the simpler its range of responses, the more teddy bear-like and unthreatening it grows. But an electrician answering the phone, or a uniformed guard at the entrance to a building, or a stranger at a cocktail party, do not know who I am, and I apparently doubt that my body and manner and voice will explain it to them. Who I am seems impossibly complicated, unobvious and difficult. Some falsity of impersonation, some burden of disguise or deceit seems to be part of my personality, an untrustworthy part that can collapse at odd or uncomfortable moments into a stutter. This burden was present even in Shillington, perhaps as my strong desire, even as I strove to blend in and recognized each day spent there as a kind of Paradise, eventually to get out.

John Updike

If fear—fear, that is, of an unpredictable or complex response that might wrench aside my rather delicately constructed disguise—activates the defect in my speech, then anger, nature's adrenal answer to fear, tends to cancel it. A frontal attack clarifies the mind and stiffens the tongue. Testifying once on my own behalf in a lawsuit, I never thought to stutter; I spoke loudly and carefully, my tone observing no distinction between falsehood and truth. I laid on words as one lays on paint. And I remember with pleasure a reading given long ago, in the fraught and seething sixties, at some newly founded two-year community college in Dallas, where the audience, instead of presenting the respectful and hopeful white faces I was accustomed to, consisted of a few young blacks sprinkled in bored postures throughout the arc of plush, mostly empty auditorium seats. Black hostility was expected then and even to be approved of, and my studiously composed souvenirs of a small-town life, whether rhymed or unrhymed, did seem rather off the point; nevertheless, I had contracted to make this appearance, my gorge rose to the challenge, and I gave (to my own ears) one of my better, firmer readings.

No, it is not confrontation but some wish to avoid it, some hasty wish to please, that betrays my flow of speech. The stammering comes on, too, amid people of whom I am fond, and wish very much to amuse—perhaps to butter over some fundamental misapprehension that I suspect exists within our relationship. My excessive and tongue-tripping anxiousness to please feels traceable to my original family, the family of four discontented, harried, and (in three of the four) highly verbal adults into which I was born. As I remember the Shillington house, I was usually down on the floor, drawing or reading, or even under the dining room table, trying to disassociate myself from the many patterns of conflict, emanating from my mother, that filled the air above my head. Darts of anger rayed from her head like that crown of spikes on the Statue of Liberty; a red V, during those war years, would appear, with eerie appositeness, in the middle of her forehead. Her anger was aimed at me rather rarely. I was chastised for coming home late—not so much for being careless or wilful about time but for allowing myself to be the weak-minded victim of

154

the other, stronger-minded boy, my retentive playmate—and, on one odd occasion, for cutting my own hair, because the forehead lock kept getting in my way as I bent to some complicated mirrored tracing toy.

My mother was fanatic about haircuts; the full weight of her under-utilized intelligence and sensitivity fell on my head when I returned from the barber's, where each chair was manned, to her fine eye, by a different scissoring style, a different proclivity to error. One of the many unsatisfactory theories about stuttering ties it to parental over-correction of the three-to-five-year-old child's flawed and fledgling speech; I don't remember ever having my speech corrected, but certainly the haircuts with which I returned from Artie Hoyer's barber's shop were subject to an overwhelming critique. As my mother looked me over, my exposed ears would grow hot and I would hold my breath. My stuttering feels related to the bizarre complexity and vulnerability of the human head, that knob of hair and rubbery sensory organs, that tender bud our twig puts out to interact with the air and mist and psychic waves of others. Other people—their eyes, their desires, their voiced and unvoiced opinions, their harbored secrets—make an atmosphere too oppressively rich, too busy for me. My sensation, when I stutter, is sometimes as if I have, with the afflicted sentence, carefully picked and plotted my way out of a room full of obstacles, and, having almost attained (stealthily, cunningly) the door, I trip, calling painful attention to myself and spilling all the beans.

Where these beans have already been partially spilled, the pressure of perfectionism is less. My speech eases where I feel already somewhat known and forgiven, as for example, with:

1. people from Shillington
2. people from Ipswich
3. literary people—agents and editors, especially
4. people who want something from me
5. women—but not children, at least children from whom I have secrets. With my own children, after I left them, I developed a sharp stutter that had not been there before. I stutter, then, when I am 'in the wrong', as, for example, with:

1. people from metropolises
2. people of evident refinement or distinction
3. law enforcement officers
4. Israeli journalists
5. men.

So: what to do? As Gerald Jonas pointed out in 'Stuttering: the Disorder of many Theories' (1977), the foremost experts on stuttering, to a dismaying extent, are inveterate stutterers who, for all their expertise, still stutter. The defect arises, it would seem, from self-consciousness—a failure to let the intricate muscular events of speech be subconscious. Between the thought and the word falls a shadow, a cleavage; stuttering, like suicide and insomnia and stoicism, demonstrates the duality of our existence, the ability of the body and soul to say no to one another. And yet self-consciousness (which does nothing for, say, acne but make it agonizing) can be something of a cure here: concentrating on not stuttering, we do stutter less. My flattering father would tell me I had too many thoughts in my head, and that I should speak slower. This did help. Consciously keeping my voice in the lower half of its register also helps; other stutterers, I notice, tend to have high, forced voices, riding a thin hysterical edge. When they manage to speak, it is louder or faster than normal. Stuttering, perhaps, is a kind of recoil at the thrust of your own voice, an expression of alarm and shame at sounding like yourself, at *being* yourself, at taking up space and air. A well-known principle of speech therapy is that any mechanism which displaces your customary voice—singing, having a sore throat, affecting a funny accent—eliminates the stoppage; the captive tongue is released into *Maskenfreiheit,* the freedom conferred by masks. The paralysis of stuttering stems from the dead center of one's being, a doubt there. Being tired increases the doubt, and—contrary to what one might suppose—so does having had too much to drink: speaking is a physical act and susceptible to the same things that impair the co-ordination of other physical acts. Stuttering, I have come to believe, is a simple matter of breath: we arrive at the spasm when in truth we are out of breath, when in our haste and anxiety we have forgotten to breathe; and taking a breath, or concentrating on keeping the breath flowing, erases the problem as easily as mist swiped from a window pane. Could that have been me, a moment ago, hung up on a mere word? Ridiculous!

But breathing, too, is not necessarily easy. It is one of those physical acts on the edge of thought; it can be conscious or unconscious. These semi-conscious acts are troublesome: start to think about blinking, and it is hard to stop, and hard not to feel squeamish about your entire optical apparatus; consider your walking, and you tend to stiffen and stumble. Though I was never diagnosed, as a child, as having asthma, I was generally 'snuffly' with colds in the winter and hay fever in the warm months. The precariousness of breathing was borne in upon me when, in one unfortunate moment, I leaped toward my father's arms while he was treading water in a swimming pool and found myself sinking in an unbreatheable molten green while my own bubbles rose up in my vision like ornaments on this terrible tree of my strangling. I was plucked out soon enough, back into the immense air, and I gasped and coughed the water from my lungs; but the sensation lingered enough to make me dread water—its sting of chlorine, its coldness.

My claustrophobia I drew from a radio play that, sometime in the early forties, I heard over the little wooden round-topped Philco that sat on a table next to the red wing chair, its arms stained by the many peanut-butter-and-cracker sandwiches I consumed there, in what we called 'the side parlor'. Here stood the upright piano, with the brass tiger on top, and here we gathered, in a rare family circle, to listen to broadcasts of Joe Louis's fights and, Sunday nights, to the line-up of the half-hour Jack Benny, Phil Harris and Alice Faye, and Edgar Bergen and Charlie McCarthy shows. But I was alone in auditing a radio play that told, as I remember it, of two prisoners planning to escape from jail. One was a large man, and one was small. Their plan involved crawling through ducts and pipes; the larger man insisted the smaller go first, and in the end we discover why: the big prisoner gets stuck. The sounds, as he communicated his hopeless immobility there at some turning in the tight and implacable darkness, were conveyed as vividly as only the art of radio could, with no visual distractions to soften the horror. His gasping voice echoed in the pipes, urging his brother on, and the smaller man presumably did crawl and squeeze his way to freedom;

but my attention stayed behind, with the stuck fat man and his living entombment.

The fear of being buried alive is not, of course, in itself peculiar or unusual. Poe has made the phobia familiar to generations of American school children, and the unquiet grave is a staple of horror movies. Cremation owes some of its popularity, no doubt, to its elimination of the possibility of waking in a satin-lined box six feet underground, in an utter darkness smelling of formaldehyde and wilted flowers. Our lives begin with a slither through a tight place, and end, according to Tolstoy's version in 'The Death of Ivan Ilyich', with being pushed deeper and deeper into a black sack. The cause of natural death is generally one form of constriction or another; we all will be buried alive in those last seconds, lying immobilized like the Frau Consul in *Buddenbrooks*: 'Her lips were drawn inward, and opened and closed with a snap at every tortured effort to breathe, while the sunken eyes roved back and forth or rested with an envious look on those who stood about her bed, up and dressed and able to breathe.' We move and have our lives within a very narrow stratum of chemical conditions, on a blue-skinned island of a planet from which there is no escape, save for the legendary few who have enjoyed space travel or bodily ascension. Our physical lives depend upon an interior maze of chemical process and osmosis and of pumping, oozing tubular flow whose contemplation itself can induce claustrophobia (though I found the intravenous adventures of *Fantastic Voyage*, with Raquel Welch along, less terrifying than the conventionally submarine *Das Boot*). My nameless radio play dramatized the precarious squirming that, in our constricted carnal circumstances, is the alternative to death, and it sharpened my awareness of how narrow are those passageways by which the ego communicates with the world.

The throat: how strange that there is not more erotic emphasis upon it. For here, through this compound, pulsing pillar, our life makes its leap into spirit, and in the other direction gulps in what it needs of the material world. Choking figured among my childhood traumas. The first time that I remember, I was sledding, high on Chestnut Street, which slanted sharply up to Cedar Top and whose bottom block, after a snowstorm, was strewn with cinders—a thrifty method, amid Depression simplicities, of creating a civic playground. I had put a fresh cough-drop in my mouth, and in the excitement of sitting upright on a Flexible Flyer behind another child and preparing for the cheek-stinging ride down into the scraping, sparking patch of cinders that halted us short of Philadelphia Avenue, I swallowed it. *Swallowed it.* I felt it slide irretrievably into the slippery downhill at the back of my oral cavity and lodge halfway down my throat. The distinction between oesophagus and trachea was hazy in my mind, and I thought that if the cough-drop stayed long in my throat I would suffocate and die. I ran home—dragging, in memory, the sled behind me, and carrying a huge lump of panic in my chest—down Chestnut Street, the four steep blocks of it, and then down Philadelphia Avenue, gagging at the obstacle in my throat. In my memory I arrive at my big white house and here, strangely, the season changes, for it is summer, and I am in shorts, and Al Richards, one of my father's fellow teachers, is standing under the leafed-out grape arbor with him. Al sizes me up, swiftly grabs me by the bare legs and holds me upside-down down, while my father pounds my back. My throat convulses once more, and the cough-drop lies on the ground inches from my eyes, puddling what has become, again, snow. I can see it exactly—it is a golden, oblong honey-flavored Luden's, which were made right in Reading, in a huge factory that scented one whole side of the city with menthol. *I will live* is my thought. I will live to see many other sights, few of them more welcome than this, the cough-drop no longer in my throat but lying there half-melted in the snow. Though it would (I now believe) have dwindled and slipped down of its own, I credited Al Richards—a short, dynamic former baseball player with quaint, centrally parted hair and a son my own age—with saving my life, and could never, even in high school where he became my social studies teacher, look at him without love, as the embodiment of the benign forces in Shillington that protected and preserved me for something beyond.

A parallel incident occurred nearly thirty years later, after I had developed, in my ripe maturity, asthma. I was staying with my family in the old stone farmhouse my parents had bought after the war. The place was crowded by the eight of us. My parents, when we visited in the summer, betook themselves to the barn, and slept on a mattress on an old hay wagon, surrounded by bundled newspapers, pigeon droppings, antique, rusted farm tools and horse-feed bags full of empty cat food cans. This comical hardship—the sort of thing my father, costumed like a Beckett character, seemed to relish—added by way of empathy to the congestion in my mind and chest; at the height of the pollen season, in an overburdened house besieged at the back door by the hordes of stray cats that my mother had taken to feeding, I was playing the triple familial role of son, husband and father, and the demands from each side sliced my inner freedom thinner and thinner. As my four children—seaside New Englanders unaccustomed to the jungly outdoors of rural Pennsylvania, where cornfields receded to the horizon and wild grapevines strangled the hemlocks and poison ivy grew to the size of wistaria—huddled around the television set and its fuzzy images from Philadelphia, they were terrorized by an old dog my parents had, a collie with a blind and droopy eye, a crooked inquisitive way of holding his head, and a bad habit of suddenly snapping. Several of my children had already been nipped. Dog hair was on all the furniture and ghosts of the past in every conversation. Furthermore, this particular afternoon, the Houcks were coming to visit, adding yet more presences to my overcrowded inner theatre.

Karl and Caroline Houck, like my parents, had gone to Ursinus college, courted there, married, settled in Berk County, and been blessed with one cherished child. They figured in our oldest snapshots and in my earliest memories; my very first memory, indeed, is of looking down into a play-pen in a house of theirs (I think) in Reading and smelling the oilcloth and seeing these toys that were not mine but, quite mysteriously, someone else's, someone not there. As is the way with one's parents' friends, their very pleasantness and affection for me seemed to constitute one more demand, a debt incurred in a world I had never made. As the time of their visit approached, my breathing grew shallower and shallower; repeated gulps of isoproterenol and epinephrine from my constant pocket companion, the Medihaler, failed to bring relief, that delicious opening of the bronchial tree which is to asthmatics a small dawn, a rebirth into the normal world. I thought the house might be the problem and moved outside to the lawn.

There, on a little walk of spaced sandstones we had made in those first hard-working years here on this farm where I had never wanted to be, a few feet from the privet bush my grandmother had transplanted from the Shillington yard when we moved and that she had defended with her life when a bull escaped from our rented meadow and in his bafflement gored the little round green round thing with his horns, giving it a splayed shape it still bore—there, I tried one more hit from the Medihaler, and found no space in my lungs.

An asthma attack feels like two walls drawn closer and closer, until they are pressed together. My back hurt. I could not stand up straight and, looking down at the flourishing grass between the sandstones, thought: *This is the last thing I'll see. This is death.* The breathless blackness within me was overlaying the visual world, consisting of this patch of my mother's grass, with a thin gray film, and the space between the two walls I was struggling to pry apart felt hardly wide enough for a razor blade. My children and parents had come out on the back porch to watch, and a rictus twitched my face as I thought how comic this performance must seem, this wrestle with invisible demons, out here where my grandmother had battled the bull on behalf of the privet bush. I felt immensely angry at my own body and at everybody. Like a child blind in his tantrum I thought, *Serve them right*, and waited to die, standing hunched and gasping, of suffocation.

It was at this point that the Houcks arrived. Karl was a doctor, a Reading bone surgeon. Like Al Richards long ago, he acted swiftly and calmly. He had me get into his Mercedes and drove me the eleven or so miles to the Reading hospital, where I had been born. During the drive I sat hunched in the front seat, studying the fancy dashboard and trying to be droll, with what breath I could muster, about my incapacity. He talked, but not too much. He was a surgeon, not an internist: a wiry, moustached man who loved to play tennis and whose strong hands could force thigh bones back into alignment. His manner could be brusque but he belonged to that dying breed that still called me 'Johnny', and I thought, as I perched there cupping my almost useless lungs within me, how pleasant his voice was—a deliberate, self-assured baritone, with a well-combed fringe of Pennsylvania accent, a kind of brush on the consonants that stood straight upright.

My breathing slightly eased; encapsulated inside his speeding Mercedes, I was relieved of some psychological pressure. The hospital was in a tony, spacious area of West Reading which also, comfortingly, held the local art museum and many expensive, spacious homes. I breathe easier, it would seem, in an atmosphere of money. We arrived and walked across the parking lot in the milky, Pennsylvania sunshine; without much delay I was sat on the edge of a high hospital bed and given a shot of adrenalin and was born again. Though cataleptics on the edge of a fit must be allowed the exclusive religious ecstasies that Dostoevsky described, something should be said for the rush of bliss that floods an asthmatic whose bronchial muscles have unclenched. Of course: air. In, out: this is how people do it. How simple. As with stuttering, it is difficult to believe there had ever been a problem. I thanked the young doctor who had injected me; I thanked Karl. Full of adrenalin, one trembles, as if violently scoured to admit the passage of oxygen. There was another shot of adrenalin before I was dismissed, and an appointment made for the next day, with a third doctor who smilingly told me that Medihalers can be over-used, so that their condensed mist clogs the bronchial passageways, and that I had made a wise decision in leaving allergen-rich Berks County. Both facts were not unknown to me, but in the beggarly physical condition to which I had been reduced I was grateful for all admonitions and encouragements.

My asthma, or at least my consciousness of it, had begun in this manner: as part of my attempt to lead an adult life in Ipswich, Massachusetts, I let myself be persuaded to buy some life insurance, and the routine medical examination found my lungs 'slightly emphysematous'. The adjective was new to me; I looked up 'emphysema' in the dictionary and then in medical reference books, and could only conclude that, young as I was, still in my twenties, I had death in my lungs; the pockets of tissue whereby inhaled air oxygenated my blood were bloated and slack, and could only get worse. These alveoli wink out one by one, like brain cells, irrevocably. 'Unfortunately,' the encyclopaedia said, 'treatment is often ineffective when the condition is advanced, and prevention of further injury is all that the physician can hope to accomplish.' Though my friendly family practitioner, sensing my panic, ran me through a battery of tests whose conclusion was that my lungs were, in his considerate phrase, 'not significantly emphysematous', he did hear wheezes through his stethoscope, and I did have the barrel chest, the spread ribcage, of the chronic asthmatic. Though I was judged a good enough health risk to be allowed to pay insurance premiums, the message had been delivered: I was mortal. I carried within me fatal imperfections. My efforts to quit smoking cigarettes became more serious, and my efforts to live what life I had left became slightly more reckless.

In my memory there is a grayness to that period of my life in Ipswich, a certain terror out of which I struggled to write those last, fragmentary stories in *Pigeon Feathers* which I think of, in retrospect, as my best, perhaps because the words were attained through such an oppressive blanket of funk. The sky in memory is gray. Shortly after the insurance report, I was playing basketball and looked up at the naked, netless hoop: gray sky outside it, gray sky inside it. As I waited, on a raw, rainy, fall day, for the opposing touch-football team to kick off, there would come sailing through the air the realization that in a few decades we would all be dead. I remember squatting in our cellar making my daughter a doll's house, under the close sky of the cobwebby ceiling, and the hammer going numb in my hand as I saw not only my life but hers, so recently begun, as a futile misadventure, a leap out of the dark and back. The rust and rot of material things, in that town of ancient wooden houses, spoke the same lesson; our house dated from 1687 and its foundation walls were unmortared fieldstones heaped up by men long reduced to bones, and the cellar felt crowded by semi-forgotten objects that rose to my eyes encrusted with time as if with oxide-ruddy earth.

These remembered gray moments, in which my spirit could scarcely breathe, are scattered over a period of years; to give myself brightness and air I read Karl Barth and fell in love with other men's wives. Kierkegaard had got me through the two years in New York; the previous year in Oxford I associate with Chesterton and Maritain and C.S.Lewis and gazing for reassurance at the fat, uniform spines of the collected Aquinas at Blackwell's great book store. Ipswich belongs to Barth. The other women—I would see them in bright party dresses, or in bathing suits down at the beach, and in my head they would have their seasons of budding, of flamboyant bloom, and of wilt, all while my ageing, emphysematous body remained uxorious and dutiful.

Dreams come true; without that possibility, nature would not incite us to have them. In brief: I tried to break out of my marriage, and failed, and began to have trouble breathing. A door had opened, and shut. My timidity and conscience slammed it shut. My wife and children were my captors, but I could not blame them; they had done nothing, after all, but come, years before, when I called. When young I had wanted a wife who would be beautiful, and motherly, and (unlike my own mother) quiet, and she materialized. We wanted children, and they obediently came, healthy and lovable and two of each sex. Now, through no fault of their own, they composed a household whose walls seemed to be shrinking around me, squeezing my chest.

No first attack stands in my memory; the squeezing, the panic crept in and were suddenly there. Like my Barth-reading and my poetry-writing (for I was never more of a poet than in this angst-besmogged period) the breathlessness would tend to come on in the evening. We didn't know what it was—pure inner demons, or an ingenious psychosomatic mechanism to make my wife feel guilty about being still married to me, or what. I remember sitting on the wide old floor-boards in front of one of our many fireplaces, before I had been prescribed any medication, trying to settle my struggling lungs with a cigarette and contemplation of a log fire; my wife observed hopefully that my difficulties seemed to be going with the smoke up the chimney. The children watched in silence. I stood, and tried to suppress my panic, my inner clenching, for their sake. The anxiety surrounding me made breathing yet harder; it reduced my space. On another evening, my wife returned from her Monday-night singing group with a merry clutch of friends, and one of them, a doctor (doctors seem to have been as ubiquitous in my life as teachers), looked down to where I lay gasping on the floor (since dramatizing my condition seemed the next best thing to curing it) and drily observed that this syndrome was usually confined to teen-age girls and that when they fainted their breathing went back to normal.

I never fainted. But I had many bad nights, my head up on two pillows and my breath, I felt, travelling in and out of me by a very small aperture, a little gap between the cotton skin of the pillow and the dark that filled the room. Without my Medihaler, I felt lost and naked; once, in the middle of the second fairway of a golf course, I had to walk off and drive home and get the thing. After that, I kept one in my golf bag. I kept another in the glove compartment of my car, and several more in drawers around the house. And so for some years I enjoyed the illusion of chemical-induced security, until that moment in Pennsylvania, just before Dr Houck arrived, when in a terminal paroxysm I stared down at the lawn (each grassy blade of grass distinct and a venomous midsummer green), marked the limits of this particular palliative.

The final answer turned out to be cats. Cat dander, and to a lesser extent that of our dogs as well, was giving me asthma. When the children were small we had acquired Pansy and Willy, a sister and brother, though she was a calico and he taffy-colored. We saw Pansy through a number of litters before getting her 'fixed', and welcomed Willy home after a number of bloody fights before performing the same kindness for him. Even so, Willy had suffered eyeball injuries, and there was a long and clumsy series of ministrations, with drops and a purple spray, before his worse eye was at last, in Boston, removed by a team of experts. They rarely had a chance to operate on cats and were grateful to try. How these animals in our midst suffer, for our edification! How poor Willy would wriggle when we tried to hold him still for his dose of purple eye-spray! *Pfft*. It was meant, I believe, for cows, and must have stung fearfully. Nevertheless, both cats lived to a ripe age. They outlived my tenancy with my family, in fact.

They used to sleep on my pillow, and my doctor's advice, when I would go to him with my wheezing lungs and panicky bronchi, was invariably, 'Get rid of the cats.' But how could we get rid of two such venerable members of our family, who from kittenhood had enriched our conjoined lives with lessons in birth and murder, flirtatiousness and fortitude, who had endured and tamed a succession of bouncy puppies and brought us gifts of half-chewed field mice many a dewy morning? We tried keeping the cats outdoors and in the cellar, but of course they were too old and stubborn to change habits, and sneaked back in to their cosy nests on the furniture. As I contemplated the problem, it seemed easier to get rid of me. My children sensed the crisis; I painfully remember my younger son, age fifteen in those last months when I lived with him, angrily throwing, tears of exasperation in his eyes, Willy down the cellar stairs. But in the end, rather than discomfit the cats, I discomfited the human beings of my family and moved to Boston. This was twelve years after my first attempt to break out. In that dozen of years, my children had grown to their full sizes if not quite adulthood, and my wife, that mysterious partner of my life, had developed, my hopeful impression was, some resources of her own. Ten years before, in the Soviet Union, a picturesque elderly artist had given us a drawing of two overlapping heads with the third eye shared between them; he said it was of us. It was true: we saw many things the same way, and never had much trouble understanding one another. We rarely needed, it seemed, to talk, and under this quietness resentments and secret lives came to flourish. Had we each had two eyes, we might have made a better couple. But she saw, with me, that it was impossible to drown or give away Willy and Pansy, and that it was possible, at last, that I go.

Two respiratory developments succeeded my move to Boston: my asthma got better, and I began to stutter, especially with my own children. Their cheerful unblaming voices over the phone, the apparition of their healthy, round pale faces, put a stopper in my throat. Stuttering had not been a problem for years. Suddenly I was afraid, again, of being misunderstood, of being mistaken for somebody else. I doubted my worthiness to mar the air with my voice.

Yet I was not unhappy in my bachelor room; twenty years of the free-lance writer's life had habituated me to solitude and the solitary organization of a day's hours and a desk's drawers. The psychiatrist I was seeing remarked upon the similarity of my single life, my dishevelled, between-marriages life, and the part-time life I had led for years in my Ipswich office. I continued, amid the distractions of guilt and needy phone calls and the necessity to do my own laundry and feed myself, to get the words out—to get them out in the specialized sense I had developed, the sense of words to be printed, as smooth in their arrangement and flow as repeated revision could make them, words lifted free of the fearful imperfection and impermanence of the words we all, haltingly, stumblingly, speak.

I did not like it when my first books met the criticism that I wrote all too well but had nothing to say: I, who seemed to myself full of things to say, who had all of Shillington to say, Shillington and Pennsylvania and the whole immense mass of middling, hidden, troubled America to say, and who had seen and heard things in my two childhood homes, as my parent's giant faces revolved and spoke, that would take a lifetime to sort out, particularize and extol with the proper dark beauty. *In the beauty of the lilies Christ was born across the sea*—this odd and uplifting line from among the many odd lines of 'The Battle Hymn of the Republic' seemed to summarize what I had to say about America, to offer itself as the title of a continental *magnum opus* of which all my books, no matter how many, would be mere instalments, mere starts at the singing of this great, roughly rectangular country severed from Christ by the breadth of the sea. What I doubted was not the grandeur and plenitude of my topic but my ability to find the words to express it; every day, I groped for the exact term I knew was there but could not find, pawed through the thesaurus in search of it and through the dictionary in search of its correct spelling. My English language had been early bent by the Germanic locutions of my environment, and, as my prose came to be edited, I had to arbitrate between how I in my head heard a sentence go and how, evidently, it should correctly go. My own style seemed to be a groping and elemental attempt to approximate the complexity of envisioned phenomena, and it surprised me to have it called luxuriant and self-indulgent; self-indulgent, surely, is exactly what it wasn't—*other*-indulgent, rather. My models were the styles of Proust and Henry Green as I read them (one in translation): styles of tender exploration that tried to wrap themselves around the things, the tints and voices and perfumes, of the apprehended real. In this entwining and gently relentless effort there is no hiding that the effort is being made in language: all professorial or critical talk of inconspicuous or invisible language struck me as vapid and quite mistaken, for surely language, printed language, is what we all know we are reading and writing, and this knowledge is what we breathe as we go along.

The notion of writing a novel presented itself to me, and still does, as *making a book*; I have trouble distinguishing between the functions of a publisher and those of a printer. The printer, in my primitive sense of the literary enterprise, is the solid fellow, my only real partner, and everyone else an intermediary between him and myself. My confused yearnings merged the notions of print, Heaven and Manhattan—a map of which looks like a type tray. To get into print was to be saved. And to this moment a day when I have produced nothing printable, when I have not gotten any words out, is a day lost and damned as I feel it.

Perhaps I need not be too apologetic about my crass approach. The great temple of fiction has no front portal; we all come in through some side door. Fiction, which can be anything, is for those whose interest has not crystallized short of ontology. Coming so relatively late to the novel, I find I still feel, after completing a dozen of them, virginal, still excited and slightly frightened by the form's potency. My assets, in tackling this grand form, I take to be the affectionate knowledge of middle-class (not upper-middle-class) American life acquired in Shillington, a certain indignation and independence also acquired there, and a cartoonist's ability to compose within a prescribed space. Carleton Boyer, my high-school art teacher, once gave me an underlined 'excellent' in composition; it struck me as an authentic artistic compliment, one of the few I have received. My debits include many varieties of ignorance, from a bone-deep, only-child uncertainty as to the human grapple to a certain invincible innocence about literature. After Big Little books, I read books of humor by Thurber and Benchley and Wodehouse and Frank Sullivan and E.B.White and mystery novels by Ellery Queen and Erle Stanley Gardner and John Dickson Carr and Agatha Christie and Ngaio Marsh. This diet pretty well took me up to Harvard, where I read what they told me, and was much the better for it. But certain kinds of novels, especially nineteenth-century novels, should be read in adolescence, on those dreamily endless solitary afternoons that in later life become so mysteriously short and full of appointments, and if they are not, one will never catch up.

But the books I did read—bought, in the case of the humorists, with pennies I saved, and borrowed, in the case of the mysteries, from the Reading Public Library or the lending library in Whitner's Department Store—communicated magic enough. The library, one of Carnegie's stately granite benefactions, sat next to Schoeffer's Bakery, where one could buy warm and wickedly sweet 'bear claws' for a dime, and Whitner's basement held the nicest cafeteria-restaurant in downtown Reading; so a heartening association of books with things delicious was inculcated. The sturdy transparent wrappers that Whitner's added to the publisher's gaudy jackets also implied something precious, like orchid corsages in their plastic boxes. My middle-brow and resolutely contemporary diet of boyhood reading had the advantage of being thoroughly escapist, so my sense of a book was of a space one gratefully escaped into, rather than of a burden of wisdom that bent one lower to the ground; the firm implicit contracts that the humorist and the mystery-writer draw up with their readers (*I will make you laugh; I will concoct a murderous puzzle and then explain it all*) remained with me even when, belatedly, I encountered the exhilarating, bourgeois-baiting lawlessness of modernisms. I had known there was something of the sort, out there beyond Berks County, for in my teens I would make an abrupt foray like reading *The Wasteland* at a table in the public library, or ploughing through my mother's copy of *Requiem for a Nun*, or doing a high-school paper on James Joyce, of whom my English teacher seemed never to have heard. But basically I was a cultural bumpkin in love not with writing but with print, the straight lines and serifs of it, the industrial polish and transcendence of it.

What did I wish to transcend? Somehow, my beloved Shillington: the assumption was in the air, like the high humidity and the eye-irritating pollen, that I should get out. I was, along with my parents and grandparents and the cherry trees in the backyard and the horse-chestnut trees out front and the robins and squirrels and fireflies, *in* something, somewhat like the trapped victims of the mine and cave disasters that frequently figured in the news of those dingy, coal-burning decades. How that Pennsylvania anthracite did roar when it cascaded down the truck chute into our cellar! These intruded inky strata that fascinated my childish self, these comic strips and cartoon captions, were veins of a lighter sort, that led to a bigger, glossier part of the cave called America. Looking back upon my transitions from Shillington to Plowville, from Plowville to

Harvard, from Harvard to New York, from New York to New England, I seem to witness a wriggling feat of spelunking little less alarming than the prison escape in that terrifying radio play. Yet of course at each stage, even in the narrowest passage, there was air to breathe, daily comforts and amusements, and the blessed animal cushion of unforeseeing that pads our adventure 'here below' (as Grandfather Hoyer used to say). That obstacle in my throat when I tried to scream a detailed refutation at Eddie Pritchard was something to 'get around', and though it still crops up, this suffocating tightness in my throat, I have managed to manoeuvre several millions of words around it.

RICHARD RAYNER
LOS ANGELES
WITHOUT A MAP

I lay by the pool in the heat. The clock on the Dunes gave the temperature as 117 degrees and the time as 12.03, when the man with the green Hawaiian shirt announced himself.

'Hi. Name's Mal.'

I pulled myself up on to my elbows. Mal was small and tanned and wide as a lorry. He looked a little like the actor Jan Michael Vincent. He wore a red baseball cap that said SCREW YOU.

'Wanna hear something beautiful?' He didn't wait for a reply. 'I'm thirty-five years old and I'm a bond salesman from Dayton, Ohio.' He pronounced Ohio like it was Oh-*one beat*-hi-*at least three beats*-oh. 'I pull down over a hundred grand per. And you know what? I'm coming blood. I'm actually *coming* blood. Every time I have an orgasm blood comes shooting out my dick.'

My eyes blinked against the sun. Mal stood over me, staring, expecting some confidence in return. I gurgled nervously. 'Listen fella,' he said, smiling, his teeth white and perfectly shaped. 'Only woman'd give me a blow job be a goddam vampire.'

Las Vegas. It boiled, it came at me, it was full of men like Mal. And then there was Barbara Ann. I saw her step to the edge of the board and dive. She surfaced and trod water and lifted her face towards the sun. Barbara Ann hadn't spoken to me for thirty-six hours.

I was having difficulties making the fantasy come to life. The fantasy was a movie called 'California Beach Girl'. It starred her and me, and was supposed to be reaching a hard-core, technicolor climax right now in an air-conditioned room on the twenty-fifth floor of the Dunes Hotel, high above the Nevada desert. Instead I was prostrate in 117-degree heat, dripping sweat, listening to Mal. This was not my script. This was definitely not my script.

There was an explosion at the hotel end of the pool.

'A gun,' I said.

'Like hell it is,' said Mal. Everything stopped. The only sound was the boom of the PA, announcing Keno winners. Barbara Ann had opened her eyes and a beefy lifeguard was swooping down from his high-chair to investigate when it happened again: CRACK.

'Some crazy bastard's throwing bottles,' said Mal. He was right. Another was on its way, which carried further and smashed on the edge of the diving board. Glass pock-marked the water and splintered on the hot, poolside concrete.

'I see him,' said Mal. I saw a figure way up on the thirtieth or fortieth floor. Its arm waved, once and then again and again, sending down more and more missiles in a long and terrifying arc.

'Gotta be a kid,' said Mal. 'Only a kid would do that.' C-RACK . . . C-RACK . . . C-RACK. People were running for cover and there was glass all over, twinkling in the sun. A woman screamed as a splinter pierced her Bikini flesh. Blood petalled the concrete.

'Just look at that. Boy, what a mess,' said Mal.

C-RACK. There were more bottles, and panic set in. Some were screaming, others had pulled on shoes and dived into the pool. An old man stood paralysed, not knowing whether to stand still and duck the bottles or run and take his chances with the glass. I looked round for Barbara Ann.

The PA stopped announcing Keno winners and issued the droning sounds of Kenny Rogers singing 'The Gambler'. Mal threw his arm around my shoulder and said: 'God, I love this song. Don't you?' I began to laugh. All in all the story of Barbara Ann and me in Las Vegas was not working out as planned.

It had been a boring year. At home my girlfriend and I had been arguing for months. At the office things were monotonous. In November my friend Todd called from Beirut: he had been kidnapped and held hostage. The kidnappers had been teenagers, who brandished AK47s and walked stiffly with pistols thrust down the waistbands of their Levis. They had snatched him from a restaurant in the Moslem sector, bundled him into the back of a Mercedes and driven across the city, firing shots into the air as they sped through check-points. One of them had pressed a gun barrel to Todd's temple and assured him he would find his brains in his lap if he moved a muscle. Another had asked him if he liked the films of Clint Eastwood. They had robbed him, then released him. Todd wanted to hear all about my life. He asked me to describe the taste of a pint of Bass.

Todd and I met in Crete during the Spring. We were in a bar in a small fishing port on the south coast. It was gloomy, almost deserted. The stereo thumped out 'Smoke on the Water' by Deep

Purple and the walls were covered with faded LP sleeves from the early 1970s and the bodies of crushed insects. It was here that I first saw Barbara Ann.

She sat on a stool at the counter, laughing. She wore jeans and a T-shirt. She had slender, tanned arms and large brown eyes. She was unbelievably beautiful. She was also in a stupor, and gazed into a glass of ouzo.

'Why aren't *you* drunk?,' she asked.

She was twenty-two, came from Buffalo and now lived in Los Angeles, waitressing and picking up modelling work whenever she could. 'I just kinda hang out,' she said. 'I might become an actress. Or the next Madonna.'

We met the next day. It was warm and sunny and we went to look at a ruined villa. A pair of stone lions stood guard. Barbara Ann was unimpressed and sat on a bench, plunging herself deeper into her bomber jacket. 'Just a bunch of rocks,' she said.

'The book says Theseus might have stayed here.'

She popped her gum but said nothing. When we left she took the gum from her mouth and stuck it in the eye of one of the lions.

'I don't think she's real at all,' Todd said later. 'She walked straight out of a surfing movie.' She had a boyfriend called Patterson who rented a house in the hills above Hollywood and was trying to sell movie scripts. They were engaged. She told me all this when we met that evening in a bar. The stereo played 'Benny and the Jets'. It was late.

'Don't worry,' she said suddenly. 'Really.'

I couldn't see who she was talking to.

'He's a nice guy,' she continued. 'I can feel it.' She was staring at the dance floor, but there was no one on it. 'You saw *that*?' she asked. 'But I was drunk. Oh, my God. I can't believe you saw that.' She nodded. 'Yeah. I'll be careful.'

I was feeling a little confused. She was quiet for a moment and then turned to me: 'What do you think of him?'

'Who?'

'My father.'

'Your father? But there was no one there.'

'Oh,' she said, and then was silent. 'He died when I was seven. Real sudden. He was a great man, but it's OK. He comes and talks to me, tells me what I'm doing right, what I'm doing wrong. When I need him he's always there.' She smiled and kissed me hard on the lips. 'Do you want to come to my room?'

Back in London, I stopped going to work and haunted the underground, riding the loop on the Circle Line, exploring easterly offshoots of the Central. I called Todd in Beirut. Sirens screamed in the background. I told him I couldn't stop thinking about Barbara Ann. He told me I was losing my marbles. I hung up, collected my passport and took the tube to Heathrow. At Terminal Three I saw that a flight to Auckland, New Zealand, was leaving in two hours. It was a flight to Auckland, New Zealand, via Los Angeles. I was a hysterical adolescent. But I was a hysterical adolescent with a credit card and there was a seat available.

I was on the plane to California, on the lam from everything that was real, playing at adventure, taking a 10,000 mile trip on impulse and thinking: what an interesting movie I'm making. I remembered Auden's remark that any marriage, happy or unhappy, is infinitely more interesting than any romance, however passionate. I had something like a marriage at home. It was hard work. Auden, it seemed to me, didn't know shit.

At a nearby table two men were talking up a movie deal. One was tanned and relaxed, with a beard like Castro's. The other had a desperate manner, purple lips and a terrible face. He looked as if he was unaccustomed to daylight, and was in need of help urgently.

'Last weekend I saw Spielberg on the beach at Malibu,' the man with the purple lips was saying. 'I've got a house there, ya know. He was with his kid. Max. You know Max? Great kid. Anyway, when Steven left I went and sat in the hollow he'd made in the sand. I sat there and I thought, What was going on in your mind, Steven? What was going on in your beautiful mind?'

His bearded companion nodded. He was lighting a cigar the size of an Exocet. It was ablaze, and he drew on it contentedly, puffing smoke into the face of the man with the purple lips.

'One thing the Cubans do real good,' he said. 'This is a stoker. Torpedo-shaped. *Gangster style.*'

'This place is too much,' I said. It was. It was gaudy and faded and the colour of left-over mustard.

'Just a lot of men who want to party.'

'With you?'

'One guy pays me 500 bucks to swim naked in his pool. He sings opera while I swim, and he never touches me. Holly-WEIRD. He's a producer and his brain is gone. Pure ozone.'

I was in shock. I had arrived and I had found her. But Barbara Ann was wearing *ears*. She was also wearing five-inch green stilettos, and she towered above me. Her breasts were supported by a corset of green satin and a white pom-pom waggled on her backside. Bunny Barbara.

She kneeled beside me. 'You're crazy, you know that? Why didn't you tell me you were coming?' She pulled my head down and kissed me. My arm was round her and I felt the sweat between her shoulder blades.

'How did you find me?'

'I called the house. Someone said you were working at the Playboy Club. Was that Patterson?'

'Patterson's in Boston,' she said.

Everything was going to be alright. But Barbara Ann didn't stop work until four, and her friend Connie had been invited to a water sports party up in Coldwater Canyon. She said, 'You and Connie'll get along great. She's from London, England.' She pointed Connie out. Connie was the white bunny, and her hair had been soaked in peroxide. She had large breasts and looked like Diana Dors on mescalin. My mind raced: *a water sports party*?

Connie drove a white Cadillac Eldorado, a convertible with fins sharking from the rear. As I clambered in, she said, 'We'll 'ave to make a detour. I've gotta pick up vese two geezers.' Her cockney accent was so exaggerated I laughed. *Come on,* I was about to say, but happened to glance at Barbara Ann.

'Isn't Connie great?' she whispered.

'Absolutely.'

Connie drove erratically—'I always get the brake and the gas mixed up,' she said—and the Eldorado lurched and pitched all the way to Marina del Rey. Barbara Ann sang along to the radio while I fought off sleep in the back. Connie pulled up in front of a wood-framed house in baby blue. She honked the horn and waited. Nothing happened. She honked again. Roxy Music were on the radio. 'And it's drowning the sound of my tears,' crooned Barbara Ann.

Connie lifted her cowboy-booted foot and kicked the horn. 'Where are they?'

'Lighten up,' said Barbara Ann.

'Jack and Hooter,' Connie screamed.

Finally the baby-blue front door swept open and Jack and Hooter emerged, shouting 'CONN-IE' and squirting cans of shaving foam. A gob landed on my lap.

'Just look at those guys,' said Barbara Ann. I *was* looking. I couldn't help it. Jack and Hooter were wearing gorilla suits.

The house was high in the canyon, overlooking a neat garden with tennis court and swimming pool. The hosts were a minor movie star and her boyfriend, former kick-boxing champion of Sweden, now also an actor. She was tiny, blonde and improbably beautiful. He was tall, blond and just improbable. Even his eyebrows were intensely muscular. She was in the pool with a margarita in one hand, trying to organize a game of water polo. So much for the water sports.

'C'mon Benny,' she said. 'You've got to play.' She turned to me. 'Make Benny play. He was in the swim team at USC.'

I said I thought Benny should definitely play.

'There,' she said triumphantly.

A triangular hulk of bronzed muscle stepped forward and poked me in the throat, hard, with its finger. 'Penis breath,' it said. This was Benny. He leaped into the pool and sank.

'Benny's bombed out of his brain,' said Barbara Ann. 'He'll drown.' We walked towards the tennis court where the Swede, legs crammed into red and white running shoes, had stripped off his clothes and was taking all comers.

'Bring your money,' he shouted in his clipped accent. 'Bring all your money. One game. I give odds of five to one.' Two challengers had been swiftly dismissed from the court when one of the gorillas ambled forward, waving five twenty dollar bills. Everyone laughed. The Swede took the game easily, his penis bobbing in the night air, but the real win was the gorilla's. Afterwards he had a woman on either arm and he gave them proprietorial, simian hugs.

'Are you Jack or Hooter?' I asked.

'I think I'm Hooter but I'm not sure,' he said.

'You know,' Barbara Ann whispered, 'people's characters really change once they get inside a gorilla suit.'

I looked around. There were lots of women, all tanned and beautiful, California Girls even if they weren't girls from California, just like Barbara Ann.

'Can't we go somewhere?' I asked her.

'Sure,' she said. 'Connie wants to go to the beach with Jack and Hooter. Doesn't that sound neat?'

Around midnight the Eldorado nosed on to the ocean front a mile or so north of Santa Monica and we walked on the beach. Jack, or it could have been Hooter, ran headlong, beating his chest, into the roaring, dark Pacific surf, and disappeared. Afterwards his waterlogged gorilla suit was so heavy we had to carry him back to the car.

'Just think about it man,' he said. 'This is it. This is where America ends. It's something else.'

It was after three when we got to the hotel, an imitation French chateau in beige concrete some place on Sunset. Barbara Ann told me it was here John Belushi died, strung out on booze and cocaine. The desk clerk was a regimental gay: close-cropped hair, lumber-jack shirt, moustache. I asked if we could check in to the room where Belushi checked out. He shook his head sadly. 'You have to book that room a month in advance,' he said. He sighed. 'Did you know that "Cocaine" is the name of a men's store in Acapulco? *Weird*.'

The room was on the third floor and through the window I saw a floodlit billboard, fifty feet high, advertising MAD MAX, BEYOND THUNDERDOME. Barbara Ann said she thought Mel Gibson was just the best.

We fucked. I was lost to her reaction, lost to the traffic sounds that drifted up occasionally from Sunset, lost to everything. I was in my movie at last.

Afterward I lay unable to sleep, Barbara Ann beside me, breathing regularly, head resting on the crook of her arm. It had happened. I had made it happen.

I got up to go to the bathroom. Barbara Ann's blue and gold LA Rams bag was on the chair, and I picked it up and took it with me.

The bathroom light shone bright off the white tile floor, straining my eyes. I opened the bag. Here was: comb, lipstick, a California driver's licence, eye-liner, an old black and white of a couple in their late twenties (parents?), a paperback called *Rich Is Better* and a plastic bag from Nieman-Marcus. Inside the plastic bag I found Barbara Ann's Bunny costume. I looked in the mirror. My face was tired and drawn.

I had to stretch the band to make the velvet ears fit. I pulled on the tights, which were elastic enough, and then the corset, which was snug across the chest. The green stilettos pinched less than I would have expected. I had never realized Barbara Ann had such big feet.

I went back into the bedroom and stood at the foot of the bed, watching Barbara Ann as she slept. Outside a police siren went *whoo-whoo-whoo*. I fingered the pom-pom on my arse: Bunny Richard.

Barbara Ann left early the next morning, saying Patterson was due back from Boston in a couple of hours, kissing me briefly and inviting me to dinner.

Patterson sat in front of the TV watching a basketball game, empty Coors cans scattered at his feet. He said nothing when I arrived. He said nothing when Barbara Ann said who I was. He was thin and bearded.

'He's so intense,' said Barbara Ann. She led me to the open window. Rosemary mingled with the smell of hot rubber and exhaust fumes. 'Why do guys get so wound up about sport?' She said the game was one in a series between the LA Lakers and the Boston Celtics. Patterson had a large bet on the Lakers.

'How large?'

'10,000 dollars on the game tonight. Another 20,000 dollars on the series.'

Patterson stared at the TV with furious concentration, willing the Lakers to victory, shouting 'Go, Magic, go.' Every time they scored he slammed his fist into his palm, and five minutes from the end he was beaming: the Lakers had it wrapped up, they were in clover. But the Celtics came late with a destructive surge and stole it in the final seconds.

Patterson said nothing. He gazed at the screen in disbelief. Then he screamed, picked up a Coors can and hurled it at the TV. He slumped down the sofa, put his head in his hands, and began to cry. 'My God,' he said. 'I feel as though my parents died.'

'Poor baby,' said Barbara Ann.

I helped Barbara Ann make a salad and hamburgers. Over dinner Patterson announced: 'I gotta make another bet. If the Lakers win the next game, I'll still be up. I gotta make another bet.'

'I thought you had to stay in LA next week,' said Barbara Ann.

'I do. You'll have to go to Vegas to make the bet for me. Take Richard with you.'

Barbara Ann was unsurprised. It was illegal, she explained, to make such a bet in the Los Angeles area.

Patterson turned to the back pages of the *LA Times*. 'Two nights, Flamingo, plus flight, 110 dollars. Two nights, Golden Nugget, plus flight *and* jacuzzi, 150 dollars. Two night, Dunes, plus flight, ninety-nine dollars. That sounds like the best deal,' he said, turning to me. 'Unless you want a jacuzzi.'

What movie was *he* making?

Somewhere between Burbank and Las Vegas Barbara Ann stopped talking to me. I didn't know why. During the flight I tried to touch her on the arm, but she flinched and struck me firmly in the centre of my forehead with a bottle of Jack Daniels. I presumed this was just a mood. A nun sat next to me on the other side, about forty years old with a robust, bucolic face. She told me her name was Sister Theresa, and I asked her why she was going to Las Vegas.

'God's work is everywhere,' she said, and stood up and beckoned me to follow. I walked behind her down the aisle until she found an empty window seat. She pointed at the desert below, an alien landscape, red and desolate and cratered and infinite. She said, 'Sometimes I imagine all the dead of the world rising up through the crust of this desert and coming down like a great plague on the City of Sinners.'

Barbara Ann and I were walking through the marbled lobby of Las Vegas airport when I saw Sister Theresa again. She was shovelling quarters into a slot machine, pumping the handle, muttering, 'Hit me. Hit me in the Name of the Lord.'

The cab was a Ford Galaxy, white, twenty years old, suspension shot. In the back Barbara Ann and I bounced like beach balls. The driver had small, delicate features, and his name was John. He wore Ray-Bans and a dirty white cowboy hat with a silver band.

'This is what I call *real* heat,' said John. That was what I called it too. My thin T-shirt felt like a horse blanket. Barbara Ann stared at the desert.

'You English?' John asked. 'I lived in London once. Met David Bowie.'

'No *shit*,' Barbara Ann said. I looked at my watch. This was the first time she'd spoken in three hours.

It shut up John, at least until we were bumping down the Strip and he pointed towards one of the hotels. 'Frank Sinatra tossed a table through a plate glass window on the top floor. Right there. Just 'cos a waitress spoke to him. It was like diamonds falling from the sky. The Mafia hushed it up.' He gave the steering wheel a sudden jerk to the left. The Galaxy went into a shuddering dive on to the Dunes forecourt and my head smacked against the roof. Barbara Ann asked if he was drunk.

'Hell, no,' said John. 'I used to drink and drive. Now I just do drugs.'

The room was circular. There was an emperor-sized circular water bed and on the ceiling a circular mirror. The carpet, curtains, walls, sofa and chairs were pink. Barbara Ann walked to the window and looked out over the Strip. I set down the bags.

'What's going on?' ·

'I'm going to sleep. And you're going downstairs. That's what's going on.'

181

'What's the matter?'

She turned round quickly. 'Go away, Richard,' she said.

She locked me out of the room and kept the chain on the door. By three in the morning I was in a low-stakes poker game at Caesar's Palace. The cocktail waitresses were dressed like Roman slaves. I called for scotch each time one walked by, losing money in a steady trickle, and then won the biggest pot of the night by accident, too drunk to see that in a hand of seven-card stud I had a five-card flush. There was silent amazement, followed by groans of disbelief. The old man playing opposite liked his pale lips and asked if this kind of play was not, in some way, illegal. The dealer said nothing and pushed a mountain of chips towards me. I sorted them into piles of blue and red. There was about 900 dollars. I tipped the dealer fifty.

News spread fast. I became a celebrity. I had lots of friends. There were prostitutes and buskers, but most people just wanted to meet someone who had been touched by luck. A middle-aged housewife said she had seen the same thing happen once in Reno and such a blessing came only from God. She asked me to make the sign of the Cross.

A man wearing a black suit bought me a bottle of champagne. 'The limey so bombed he couldn't see he had five hearts. That's what I call a real Las Vegas story,' he said. 'Lemme buy you a drink.'

His name was Tom and he said he was a musician. He was unshaven and his eyes were cracked with red. He looked like he had been run over. He lived in LA and came to Vegas each month. He liked watching the people. He said, 'It's the butt end of the American dream. The only town where I ever saw false teeth in a pawn shop window. And prosthetic devices. I've seen a guy trade his glass eye for one more roll.'

The crowd drifted away. When the champagne was finished, we found a table and drank bourbon. I told Tom about Barbara Ann. We agreed women were a pain in the heart, a pain in the head, a pain in the arse. Whereas we were real shit-kickers. 'Sex,' Tom said. 'It's a bitch.'

I was drunk when a whore approached us and asked if we wanted to party.

'What kind of party?' asked Tom.

'That depends on what you want and what you want to spend.' One of her front teeth was capped in gold.

'Suck and fuck,' Tom said.

'Your friend clean?'

'Clean? He's English.'

'200 dollars.'

'That's too much. 150 dollars.'

'OK. 150 dollars. Fantasy's extra.'

'My friend might want you to be someone else,' said Tom.

'That's fantasy,' she said. 'That's 200 dollars.'

The three of us took the elevator to the fifteenth floor. Tome opened the door and politely motioned me ahead. He turned on the light.

Both he and the whore had produced Saturday night specials and were waving them in my direction. I laughed, assuming it was a game. Tom pushed me onto the bed and demanded I hand over the money. He was very calm about it.

The whore leaned over me. She rubbed her gun up and down, up and down, against my crotch. My prick hardened. 'Easy come, easy go,' she said.

'This isn't happening,' I said.

'I hope they really feed that jerk's balls into the wringer,' said Mal, as the nine or ten security guards led away the bottle-thrower at gun-point. Things were calmer. Men in beige uniforms were sweeping away the glass. 'I hope they really kick that guy's ass through his brains.'

'At least they got the guy.'

'Whaddya mean?' Mal asked. I explained how I had been robbed, and how uninterested security had been. Mal was unimpressed. He said, 'You should carry a piece. I always do. Got my brother's .45 service automatic.' He formed his thumb and forefinger into a gun and *blammed* at imaginary poolside assailants. '*Make my day*,' he snarled.

Someone touched my shoulder. 'Can I speak to you?' It was Barbara Ann.

'Excuse me,' said Mal, politely tugging his baseball cap, and not bothering to move.

'I've made the bet,' she said. 'And I don't want to stay another day. I'm taking the four o'clock flight to LA. You can do what you like.'

There was a splash from the pool.

'What the fuck's happening, Barbara Ann?' Mal rocked gently to and fro on his heels, grin widening.

'I can't handle this,' she said. 'What's going on in your head, Richard? I never know. You're messing me up. I don't know what you want from me.'

Barbara Ann ran towards the hotel, Mal's gaze tracking her all the way. He let go a long, appreciative whistle. He said, 'I'll tell you something for free and that's this, buddy. If that were my muff, I know what *I'd* want from her.'

'Mal,' I said. 'You don't happen to have your gun here, do you?'

Patterson picked us up at LAX. In the sprawl of Los Angeles, I was a dinosaur, a non-driving Englishman. But I had always felt that not driving made me colourful. Patterson's smile informed me of the error.

We were in a tailback on the San Diego freeway, six lanes of traffic nose to bumper, inching forward into the valley. Barbara Ann sat in the front with Patterson, tapping her fingers in time to the radio. At the end of the song the DJ said: 'That was Tears for Fears with "Everybody Wants to Rule the World".'

'Not me,' said Barbara Ann. 'I just wanna go to the beach.' *California Girl:* I realized what it meant. I no longer gave her pleasure, and she had switched channels.

They dropped me on the deserted pavements of Sunset and I got caught in the middle while trying to cross. I was beached for about twenty-five minutes, traffic blasting by on either side and Mel Gibson looming over me, sawn-off shotgun slung casually over his shoulder. A blonde driving a sky-blue Corvette almost clipped my legs off at the knee, but I got away in time to see the basketball game. The Celtics lost.

ADAM MARS-JONES
SLIM

I don't use that word. I've heard it enough. So I've taken it out of circulation, just here, just at home. I say Slim instead, and Buddy understands. I have got Slim.

When Buddy pays a visit, I have to remind myself not to offer him a cushion. Most people don't need cushions, they're just naturally covered. So I keep all the cushions to myself, now that I've lost my upholstery.

Slim is what they call it in Uganda, and it's a perfectly sensible name. You lose more weight than you thought was possible. You lose more weight than you could carry. Not that you feel like carrying anything. So I'll say to Buddy on one of his visits, Did you see the local news? There was an item about newt conservation, and then there was an item about funding Slim research. But newts first. What's it like talking to someone who's outranked by a newt?

Buddy just looks sheepish, which is probably best in the circumstances. Buddy would rather I avoided distressing information. He thinks I shouldn't read the papers, shouldn't upset myself. Even the doctors say that. If there was anything I should know, I'd hear it from them first anyway. Maybe. Yes, very likely. But whenever they try to protect me, I hear the little wheels on the bottom of the screens they put round you in a ward when you're really bad, and I'll do without that while I can.

Buddy's very good. That sounds suitably grudging. He tries to fit in with me. He doesn't flinch if I talk about my chances of making Slimmer of the Year. He's learned to say *blackcurrants*. He said 'lesions' just the once, but I told him it wasn't a very vivid use of language, and if he wasn't a doctor he had no business with it. Blackcurrants is much better, that being what they look like, good-sized blackcurrants on the surface of the skin, not sticking out far enough to be picked. So now, if the subject comes up, he asks about my blackcurrants, asks if any more blackcurrants have showed up.

I do my bit of adjusting too. Instinctively I think of him as a social worker, but I know he's not that. He's a volunteer attached to the Trust, and he's got no qualifications, so he can't be all bad. What he does is called *buddying,* and he's a buddy. And apparently in Trustspeak I'm a string of letters, which I don't remember except the first one's P and stands for person. Apparently they have to remind themselves. But I've decided if he can say Slim and blackcurrants to oblige me, I can meet him halfway and call him Buddy. Illness is making me quite the internationalist: an African infection and some dated American slang.

Buddy may not be qualified, but he's had his little bit of training. I remember him telling me, early on, that to understand what was happening to me perhaps I should think of having fifty years added to my age, or suddenly having Third World expectations instead of First. I suppose I've tried thinking that way. But now whenever I see those charity ads in the papers, the ones that tell you how for a few pounds you could adopt someone in India or the Philippines, I think that maybe I've been adopted by an African family, that poor as they are they are sending me what they can spare from their tainted food, their poisoned water, their little lifespans.

Except that I'm not young by African standards. Pushing forty, I'd be an elder of the tribe, pretty much, and the chances of my parents still being alive would be slight. So I should be grateful for their being around. They've followed me step by step, and now I suppose I take that for granted. But I didn't always. Before I first told them about myself, I pinched the family album, pinched it and had it photocopied. It cost me a fortune, and I don't know what I thought I wanted with a family album and no family, if it came to that. But at the time I thought, no sense in taking chances. Maybe if they'd lived nearer London, if I'd seen them more regularly, it wouldn't have seemed such a big risk. I don't know.

My African family doesn't have the money for photographs. My African family may never even have seen a photograph.

I've been careful not to mention my adoption fantasy to Buddy. No point in worrying him. And touch wood, I haven't cried while he's been around. That's partly because I've learned to set time aside for such an important function. I've learned that there is a yoga of tears. There are the clever tears that release a lot in a little time, and the stupid tears that just shake you and don't let you go. Once your shoulders get in on the act, you're sunk. The trick is to keep them out of it. Otherwise you end up wailing all day. Those kind of tears are very more-ish. Bet you can't cry just one, just ten, just twenty. But if I keep my shoulders still I can reach a much deeper level of tears. It's like a lumbar puncture. I can draw out this fluid which is a fantastic concentrate of misery. And then just stop and be calm.

I used to cry to opera, Puccini mostly. Don't laugh. I thought the best soundtrack was tunes, tunes and more tunes. But now I cry mainly to a record I never used to listen to much, and don't particularly remember buying: *Southern Soul Belles,* on the Charly label. I find records far more trouble to put on than my opera cassettes, but *Southern Soul Belles* is worth it. It has a very garish cover, a graphic of a sixties soul singer with a purple face, for some reason, so that she looks like an aubergine with a beehive hairdo. The trouble with the Puccini was that you could hear the voices, but never the lungs. On *Southern Soul Belles* you hear the lungs. When Doris Allen sings 'A Shell of a Woman', you know that she could just open her mouth and blast any man out of the door. Shell she may be, breathless she ain't. There's a picture of her on the back cover. She's fat and sassy. She could spare all the weight I've lost. Just shrug it off. Her lungs must be real bellows of meat, not like the pair of wrinkled socks I seem to get my air through these days.

I treat myself to *Southern Soul Belles* every day or so. I've learned to economize. Illness has no entry qualifications. Did I say that already? But being ill—if you're going to be serious about it—demands a technique. The other day I found I was writing a cheque. I could hardly lift the pen, it wasn't a good day, not like today. But I was writing everything out in full. No numerals, no abbreviations. Twenty-one pounds and thirty-four pence only. Only! I almost laughed when I saw that *only*. I realized that ever since my first cheque book, when I was sixteen, I've always written my cheques out in full, as if all the crooked bank-clerks in the world were waiting for their chance to defraud me. Never again. It's the minimum from now on. If I could have right now all the energy I've wasted writing every word on my cheques, I could have some normal days, normal weeks.

One of the things I'm supposed to be doing these days is creative visualization, you know, where you imagine your white corpuscles strapping on their armour to repel invaders. Buddy doesn't nag, but I can tell he's disappointed. I don't seem to be able to do it. I get as far as imagining my white corpuscles as a sort of cloud of healthiness, like a milkshake in the dark flow of my blood, but if I try to visualize them any more concretely I think of Raquel Welch, in *Fantastic Voyage*. That's the film where they shrink a submarine full of doctors and inject it into a dying man's bloodstream. He's the President or something. And at one point Raquel Welch gets attacked and almost killed by white corpuscles, they're like strips of plastic—when I think of it, they *are* strips of plastic—that stick to her wetsuit until she can't breathe. The others have to snap them off one by one when they get her back to the submarine. It's touch and go. So I don't think creative visualization will work for me. It's not a very promising therapeutic tool, if every time I try to imagine my body's defences I think of their trying to kill Raquel Welch. I still can't persuade myself the corpuscles are the good guys.

One thing I find I can visualize is a ration book. That's how I make sure I don't get overtired. Over-overtired. I suppose my mother had a ration book before I was born. I don't think I've ever seen one. But I imagine a booklet with coupons in it for you to tear out, only instead of an allowance for the week of butter or cheese or sugar, my coupons say One Hour of Social Life, One Shopping Expedition, One Short Walk. I hoard them, and I spend them wisely. I tear them out slowly, separating the perforations one by one.

In a way, though, it's not that I don't have energy, it's just the wrong kind. My head may be muzzy but my body is fizzing. I suppose that's the steroids. But I feel like an electric razor that's been plugged into the wrong socket, I'm buzzing and buzzing but I'm not doing any work. It's so odd having sat at home all day, when your body tells you you've been dancing all night in a night-club, just drinking enough lager to keep the sweat coming, and you're about to drive home with all the windows down, smelling your own sweat. And sleep.

I can't work. That should be pretty clear. But I've been lucky. I'm on extended sick leave for a while yet, and everybody's been very good. I said I had cancer, which I do and I don't, I mean I do but that isn't the problem, and while I was saying *cancer* I thought, All the time my Gran was ill we never once said *cancer,* but now cancer is a soft word I am hiding behind and I feel almost guilty to be sparing myself. Suddenly *cancer* had the sound of 'interesting condition' or 'unmentionables'. I was curling up in the word's soft shade, soothed gratefully by cancer's lullaby. Cancer. What a relief. Cancer. Oh that's all right. Cancer. That I can live with.

Sometimes I'm asleep when Buddy visits. Sleep is the one thing that keeps its value. He presses the buzzer on the entry-phone, and if I haven't answered in about ten seconds he buzzes again. I know the entry-phone is a bit ramshackle and you can't hear from the doorway whether it's working or not, but when Buddy buzzes twice it drives me frantic. I don't need to be reminded that I'm not living at a very dynamic tempo right now. I'll tick him off one of these days, tear off a coupon and splurge some energy.

Then Buddy comes pounding up the stairs. Sometimes he

smells of chlorine and his hair's still damp from swimming, but I suppose it's a bit much to ask him to slow down, to dry off properly and use cologne before he comes to see me, just so I don't feel bruised by his health. I'll bet his white corpuscles don't need a pep talk. Crack troops, no doubt about it. I'll bet he drinks Carling Black Label.

I watch too much television. Television isn't on the ration.

Buddy's breaking in new shoes, which creak. Why would anyone crucify his feet in the name of style—assuming liver-coloured Doc Martens are stylish in some way—when comfortable training shoes are readily available almost everywhere? It's a great mystery.

Buddy likes to hug. I don't. I mean, it's perfectly pleasant, it just doesn't remind me of anything. It was never my style. I'm sure the point is to relieve my flesh of taboo, and the Trust probably gives classes in it. But when Buddy bends over me, I just wait for him to be done, as if he was a cloud and I was waiting for him to pass over the sun. Then we carry on, and I'm sure he feels better for it.

He's still got a bruise above the crook of his elbow, from his Hepatitis B jab. I really surprised myself over that. I wasn't very rational. He wasn't sure whether to have it done or not, and I almost screamed at him *Do it! Get it done!* If I'd had a needle handy I'd have injected him myself, and I don't think getting my own back was my only motive. I remember Hep B. That was when illness came up and asked me what I was doing for the rest of my life. That was before there was even a vaccine.

The back of his neck is something I tend to notice when Buddy visits. It always looks freshly shaved. He must have a haircut every week or so, every couple of weeks anyway. As if he would feel neglected unless he was being groomed at regular intervals. Neglect is what I dream of. I long for the doctors to find me boring, to give me one almighty pill and say Next please. But my case history seems to be unputdownable.

A real thriller.

My grooming standards are way below Buddy's, but perhaps they always were. There's not a lot I can do about that now. If the Princess of Wales was coming to pay me a visit, if she was coming to lay her cool hand on my forehead, stifling her natural desire to say Oh Yuk—I'm with you there, Di—I might even trim my fingernails. But not for Buddy. Fingernails are funny. They're the only part of my body that seems to be flourishing under the new regime. They grow like mad. But the Princess of Wales isn't coming any time soon, to me or to anyone like me. I happen to know that now, now as we speak, she's opening a new ward in a newt hospital. A new *wing*.

I think I'm entitled to a home help. I believe that's one of the perks. But I'd rather go on as I am. Buddy told me a story about a man he visited for the Trust—I'm sure he's recovered by now, ha ha—whose mother was jealous of his home help. Just for that, she said, Just for Slim?

I couldn't believe it. I'm still not sure I believe it. But then Buddy explained that the mother was eighty-five, and when her son started saying, Sometimes I feel better but I never feel well, she must have thought, What else have I been saying all these years, fat lot of attention you gave me.

I think Buddy was making again the valuable point that getting Slim only involves being exiled from the young, the well, the real.

B uddy is always offering to wash up, but I'm happier when I don't let him. He doesn't do a great deal to help me, in practical terms, anyway. Tessa next door changes my sheets and does my washing, and Susannah still expects to hear my dreams, even the grim ones. It was Susannah who first suggested Buddy. She felt I was cutting myself off from real kin, that even if I was saying the same unanswerable things, Buddy would return a different echo. I even suppose she's right. I've earned my friends, but Buddy I seem to have inherited, though God knows from who, and whether he served them well.

I sometimes talk to Buddy as if he was the whole Trust gathered in one person. I'll say, My father says you're not reaching him. Why are your collection-boxes massed in London? Why do you insist on appealing to an in-crowd?

But then I let him off the hook and say, Mind you, my mother thinks that anyone collecting for Slim research in Eastbourne or Leamington would get a few swift strokes from a rubber-tipped cane, if nothing worse. And my father chooses to give me love and money direct.

Cutting out the middleman, says Buddy. He smiles. He doesn't have a Trust collecting box, of course. I'm not sure I've ever seen one. In fact, on this visit he's brought me a package. It's in a plastic bag, and it seems to be a foil container with a cardboard lid, and foil crimped down around it. I'm very much afraid it's food.

I've fed Buddy once or twice, used a shopping voucher and prepared a simple but exhausting lunch. Those times it has seemed to me that Buddy eats suspiciously little. I mean, he eats more than I do, he couldn't not. And I'm not the best judge of healthy habits. But somehow I expect an earthier appetite. It's certainly true that a little company at table can make me eat more than I usually do, without even noticing, while any sort of greed will inevitably sicken my stomach. So does that mean Buddy is obeying another mysterious Trust directive, and suppressing his true eating self? Perhaps he filled up with food before he came, or perhaps he's going to dive round the corner the moment he leaves, and into a burger bar. Before he leaves I open my mouth to say, Here's some money for your real lunch, but I manage to close it in time.

And now he's returning my hospitality. Go on, he says. Open it. You don't have to eat it now. It'll keep good for a few days. Not that it contains any preservatives.

He has written a few deprecating comments about his cooking on the lid of the container. There's no wishing it away. I edge up the rim of the foil and see inside a startlingly pure green. On the green lies a row of small cigars.

Fresh lamb sausages, he explains, with mint and parsley, on a bed of green pea purée. An old family recipe, that appeared quite by chance in last week's *Radio Times*.

I lower my nose over the container and breathe in the smell, trying to think that it is a bouquet of flowers that I must express thanks for, from someone I like and want nothing to do with, rather than a plateful of food that will stiffen in the fridge unless I am stupid enough to eat it, in which case I will most likely be sick.

Thanks. Can you put it in the fridge for me?

But Buddy has more to say about his choice of recipe. They're skinless, he says. I thought that would be easiest for you.

He's right, of course, with my teeth the way they are now. But I'm sure I haven't complained, I'm sure I haven't moaned to him. Perhaps my habit of dipping biscuits in my tea—not to be looked for in a man of my class—is a dead giveaway to a seasoned Trust volunteer. Next time I feel the need to dunk a digestive I'll be more discreet. I'll do my dunking behind closed doors.

The doctors are trying to save my teeth at the moment, and the last time I went to pick up some prescriptions they were being altogether too merry, it seemed to me, about the dosage that would do the trick. 200 mg, one of them was saying, that sounds about right. And the other one said, Yeeeees, in a kind of drawl, as if it wasn't worth the trouble to look it up.

Buddy is still expecting something from me. Thanks, I say again. That looks very nice. Yum yum.

Kid gloves are better than surgical gloves. Perhaps I should say that to him. That would give him some job satisfaction. I'm sure that's important.

Buddy puts his present in the fridge and heads for the door. He stops with his hand on the handle and asks me if there's anything I want, says if I think of anything I should phone him, any time. He always does this on his way out, and I suppose he's apologizing for being well and for being free to go and for being free to help or not as he chooses. There is nothing I want.

He clatters down the stairs. I remind myself that he clattered up them, so there is no reason to think he is moving as fast as he can and is planning to put a lot of space between me and him, now that his tour of duty is over.

I could check, of course, if I move to the window. I could settle my mind. I could see whether he skips along the road to the Tube, or whether he's too drained to do more than shamble. Maybe a trouble shared is a trouble doubled.

I try to resist the temptation to go to the window, but these days it's not often that I have an impulse that I can satisfy without asking myself whether I can afford what it will cost me. So I give in.

Buddy is moving methodically down the street, not rushing but not dawdling either, planting his feet with care like a man walking into a wind. I know that when I tear out and spend one of my shopping coupons and go out onto that street, I look like a man walking into a wind tunnel. I can see it in the way people look at me.

I look down on Buddy as he walks to the Tube. In the open air the mystique of his health dissipates, as he merges with other ordinarily healthy people. No-one in the street seems to be looking at him, but I follow him with my eyes. There is something dogged about him that I resent as well as admire, a dull determination to go on and on, as if he was an ambulance-chaser condemned always to follow on foot, watching as the blue lights fade in the distance.

MARY BENSON
A TRUE AFRIKANER

Visiting the Nevada desert with a friend in the autumn of 1974, I realized it was time to write a letter to Bram Fischer. It was eight years since I had seen him, eight years in which we had only occasionally been able to exchange letters: 500 words the limit, with no mention of politics or world affairs. But how, I wondered aloud, could I write about all the beauty of this desert to a man in a prison cell?

It was Bram who had opened my eyes to the beauty of barren landscapes, as we drove through the winter veld of the southern Transvaal. But now, to describe this space and freedom to a prisoner, to a man walled in, who saw only a scrap of sky from the exercise yard?

I began to shape the letter, counting the words, and the next morning I settled in the shade of cottonwood trees and wrote to him: Abram Fischer, an Afrikaner—grandson of a Prime Minister of the Orange River Colony—a distinguished lawyer and communist, in prison on Potgieter Street, Pretoria. The prison had been a part of my childhood, for we lived in the house next door and went for walks past its façade, watched by eyes peering through iron-barred windows. Its turreted walls, rising beyond our trees, were the background of snapshots in the family album. I tried to imagine him there, in a modern high-security section designed for the handful of South Africa's white political prisoners. Could he glimpse anything of the night sky from his little window?

Perhaps the Nevada desert would have reminded him of the veld. South Africans have an expression, *'n ware Afrikaner,* a true Afrikaner. In the sense that 'true' means typical, Bram was a true Afrikaner in his passion for the veld; for me he was *'n ware Afrikaner* in a more profound way.

I met him during the first great treason trial in 1959, in which 156 people of all races had been arrested. He was among counsel for the defence. What first struck me was his courtesy: it never faltered even when some remark by the prosecutor or an action by the police angered him, hardening the expression in his blue eyes. Not physically impressive—short, ruddy-faced with silver hair—he was nonetheless an immensely captivating man. I got to know him better when, unexpectedly, he was granted a passport to come to London in

October 1964—unexpected because he had just been arrested in Johannesburg and, with twelve others, had been charged with membership of the illegal Communist Party. He was in London to lead an appeal on behalf of the Bayer Company before the Privy Council. He had assured the South African authorities that he would return there to stand trial.

His short visit was both celebratory and arduous, seeing old friends and new, packing in visits to the theatre between serious discussions. He seldom spoke of himself; he was concerned rather to convey precisely what was happening under the ninety-day detention law. It was a terrible time in South Africa: through solitary confinement and torture the State—as Bram put it—was trying to break the forces striving for basic human rights. Militant opponents of the government had been intimidated, imprisoned or driven into exile. Innumerable political trials were taking place throughout the country. To Hugh Caradon, British Ambassador to the United Nations, Bram described the effects of police torture: a young Indian, Suliman Salojee, had somehow managed to smuggle a message to his wife from solitary confinement. 'Pray for me,' he had said. Bram could barely contain his wrath and grief as he explained that Salojee was not a religious man; a day or two later, while being interrogated, he had fallen seven storeys to his death from Security Police headquarters.

Influential politicians were profoundly impressed by Bram's calm courage. They tried to persuade him to remain in Britain rather than return home to almost certain imprisonment. 'But I gave my word,' he told them. From the bar of the Privy Council, Abram Fischer Q.C. went to the dock in a Johannesburg Magistrate's court.

The chief State witnesses in the trial were Gerald Ludi, a police spy who had been a member of a Communist Party cell, and Piet Beyleveld, who had been a friend of Bram's—an Afrikaner, long a leading member of the Party. Both agreed that the activities of the Party centred largely on propaganda about injustices. The very issues about which the English language press and the Liberal and Progressive parties legally protested became illegal when the Communist Party protested. But Ludi also declared that the Communists aimed to overthrow the government by violent revolution. Beyleveld contradicted this: revolution, he contended, did not mean violence but change. The Party had condemned acts of terrorism and insisted there must be no bloodshed.

'For years, Piet Beyleveld and I were comrades,' Bram told me. 'I do not believe that when he comes into court, when he looks me in the eyes, he will be able to give evidence against us.' But Beyleveld went into court, he stood in the witness box, and he did not look Bram in the eyes. When asked by the defence why he was giving evidence, he said he had agreed after persistent questioning by the Security Police; there had been no ill-treatment. Questioned further, he gave a startlingly accurate account of Bram's nature and influence. Fischer, he said, was well-known as a champion of the oppressed, with political views that had never been concealed; a man widely respected in all parts of the community. He himself, he added, still revered Fischer.

I could imagine the distress this admission must have caused Bram, who seemed to feel no bitterness against his old friend, only anger at the system which manipulated such an easy betrayal. The defence counsel must have been astounded. 'I was interested to hear you say that,' he remarked to Beyleveld, and then asked, 'I don't like to put this in my client's presence, but he is a man who carries something of an aura of a saint-like quality, does he not?'

'I agree,' was Beyleveld's reply.

After Christmas, when the trial had reconvened, I met Bram in a coffee-bar. His gaze was unusually intense, but I put this down to our activity over the previous days: I had encouraged him to write an article expressing his views about the crisis in the country, which would be suitable for the London *Observer*. Coming from him it was a seditious, illegal document, and he was worried lest I be incriminated as a fellow-conspirator. Throughout the adjournment he had been openly followed by Security Police, but he was sure that on this occasion he had given them the slip. He handed me the final copy of the piece. Then, gripping my hands, he asked me to be sure and come to court on Monday. Of course, I said. With a light kiss and a '*Totsiens*'—till I see you—he left me.

On Monday 25 January 1965 a friend who was staying with the Fischers stopped me as I approached the courtroom, drew me into an empty waiting-room and handed me a letter. 'Bram has gone underground,' she confided.

'I feel incredibly dishonest and have ever since our talk on Friday,' Bram wrote.

> This is so not because I am about to 'jump' my bail. The other side has never played according to the rules and has changed the rules whenever it has suited them. That is the least of my 'moral' worries. But throughout our talk I had to act to you and pretend I would see you on Monday and that was a singularly unpleasant experience.
>
> In some ways I suppose this would seem to be a crazy decision. Yet I feel it is up to someone among the whites to demonstrate a spirit of protest. It must be demonstrated that people can fight apartheid from within the country even though it may be dangerous. That is why I returned here from London. I have left the trial because I also want to demonstrate that no-one should meekly submit to our barbaric laws. I'm sure we shall meet again.

Everything seemed normal in the court. Police and officials, defence and prosecution teams were present, and the other twelve accused filed up from the cells below. Except no sign of Bram. The previous week I had nervously attended the trial for the first time; he had entered the court by a side-door and stood for a moment, looking directly at me in the public gallery. No greeting, only the acknowledgment of my presence. Now there was a rustling through the courtroom; the magistrate took his seat, leading counsel for the defence rose and announced that he had a letter from Number One Accused, Abram Fischer, and proceeded to read it. Bram had decided to absent himself from the trial. This act, he said, had not been prompted by fear of punishment—indeed, he realized his eventual punishment might be increased. He believed that white complacency in the face of the monstrous policy of apartheid made bloodshed inevitable. 'To try to avoid this,' he declared, 'becomes a supreme duty, particularly for an Afrikaner. If by my fight I can encourage even some people to think about, to understand and to abandon the policies they now so blindly follow, I shall not regret any punishment I may incur. I can no longer serve justice in the way I have attempted to do during the past thirty years.'

The Prosecutor called it 'the desperate act of a desperate man, and the action of a coward.' Conflicting views were vehemently expressed, in private and in public. Some felt it a futile gesture. Others were elated at a magnificent act of protest. Some felt 'let down' because he was 'the one man who could have united everyone.' Fischer, commented the editor of the Johannesburg *Sunday Times,* was 'a paragon, the model of gentleness and respectability' who, when young, 'had been regarded as a future Prime Minister or Chief Justice.' Now the tragedy was that he had become 'a hunted fugitive ostracised by society.'

Under the byline 'From a Special Correspondent in Johannesburg', Bram's article, which I had mailed to the London *Observer*, was headlined WORD FROM MISSING QC:

> The State thinks it has crushed the liberation movement, but it has not...If the struggle for freedom is smothered in one place or for the time being, it flares up again before long...
>
> World opinion has positive and constructive tasks to perform. It must prevent torture from being used again ... and should work for the release of our thousands of political prisoners; the wives and dependants of these prisoners must be cared for... But most important is the extension of human rights to all citizens. This is not Spain. It is 1965, not 1935 ... The United Nations can bring home to white South Africans the recognition that the maintenance of white supremacy is doomed.

Bram's message to the outside world, written with passionate urgency more than twenty years ago, has gained the weight of prophecy:

> A peaceful transition can be brought about if the Government agrees to negotiation with all sections of the people, and, in particular, with the non-white leaders at present jailed on Robben Island or in exile.

He concluded with a vision of a free South Africa: at last the country would fulfil its great potential internally, and in African and world affairs. When copies appeared for sale in Johannesburg, Bram's article had been neatly excised.

The South African press made only one brief reference to it, reporting that it had been cut out of copies on sale in shops. Since Fischer was on the banned list, he could not be quoted in South Africa.

Within days of his disappearance, the Johannesburg Bar Council—of which he had once been Chairman—applied to have his name struck from the roll of advocates. FIRST WORD COMES FROM BRAAM FISCHER (*sic*), the evening paper announced on 5 March. In protest against the Bar Council's action, he had written to lawyers, requesting legal opposition to the proposed expulsion.

Weeks passed. The English language press enjoyed taunting the police. BRAM FISCHER STILL FREE. The authorities said he might be disguised as a black-haired priest with dark glasses, or as an elderly invalid woman swathed in shawls. FISCHER COULD BE ANYWHERE FROM MALMESBURY TO MOSCOW.

In a sitting-room in Johannesburg, the curtains drawn against the night, two women sat beside me on a sofa. They had asked to see me urgently. I was warned that the room might be bugged. Gaps in their soft quickly-uttered sentences were filled by words they wrote on paper. They had seen Bram. He was known as Max. I watched the hand as it wrote, 'Max is depressed and isolated, will you visit him?'

'Of course,' I said, and wrote, 'When?'

'Tomorrow.'

The word took me aback. It gave me no time to prepare. Might not the police follow me? But how wonderful to see him again, how proud I felt to be asked. What were the implications of meeting a fugitive? I cared greatly for him. 'Yes,' I said.

A map was drawn, showing the street, the house, a nearby shopping centre and a discreet approach so as to ensure no police were following. 'Try to look as unlike yourself as possible,' was the final note.

Writing now of those events, in the detail made possible by the coded notes I kept, I can feel again the apprehension—and exhilaration—of being caught up in such a drama.

On a bright autumn day, my face obscured by heavy suntan make-up and an elaborate headscarf, I arrived at an ugly yellow-brick house with fancy iron railings. Head held high but with shaky knees, I walked up a long drive past an unkempt garden and tennis court. No one was visible in the neighbouring house. Pressing the doorbell, I heard its chime but no movement. I rang again and this time the door was opened by an African woman. There had been no mention of a servant. 'Is the master in?'

She motioned me through a bare hall to a large room furnished only with cane garden chairs and a table. I noticed an ashtray with pipe and matches. But Bram did not smoke. A sound made me swing round. A man was standing there, staring at me. Auburn-bearded, balding with receding auburn hair, his eyes blank behind rimless spectacles. Jesus—I had come to the wrong house. How could I explain and get out?

'Good God!' he said. It was the familiar voice, the warm, slightly accented voice. 'What are you doing here? How wonderful!'

Weird to embrace this strange-looking man—but the voice, the smile, were his. He was delighted and reassured by my failure to recognize him. 'You look like Lenin,' I teased. But he had not lost a mannerism of clearing his throat, nor a certain gesture with one hand.

He picked up the pipe. 'I've taken to smoking, it helps disguise my voice. And see how thin I've got. My walk,' he demonstrated. 'Not so bandy-legged.' I had heard his health was troublesome, but he said his high blood pressure was now under control. Seeing a doctor had been one of the tests of the disguise—a disguise accomplished by dieting, by shaving the crown of his head then dying his hair, eyebrows and beard to a colour natural to his reddish complexion.

The maid, Josephine, brought tea. As we talked, I began to realize just how cut-off he was, he who had led an immensely active professional and social life. I sensed how deeply he was missing family and friends. The time was up too soon. I would come again in a week, on Josephine's day off.

In the days that followed I marvelled that he was here, living in the heart of Johannesburg, within a mile or so of his old home. The police were scouring the country for him—a substantial reward had been offered for his capture. I thought of him, alone but for the maid, in that awful house. It was sickening that a man of such integrity should be forced to resort to subterfuge and lies.

'Get yourself a hat,' he had said. In the OK Bazaar I bought one, emerald-green to match a borrowed green-and-white suit: I had to look normal when I left my sister's flat, where I was staying, and arrive at Bram's house looking, I hoped, like a district nurse.

I was glad when he chose to have tea in the front garden rather than in the bleak, sparsely furnished house—he explained that he did not want to use his limited funds on unnecessary comforts. He enjoyed the informality of his new life, being able to wear sports shirts and flannels, and each week he grew more confident: a leading member of the Security Police had passed him in the street, a judge he knew well had stood beside him in a lift. Someone he had met for the first time had guessed he was in his thirties. But he wondered if he should go on with his hermit's existence, or join the local bowling club, become a new personality. He rehearsed me in preparation for possible encounters with the police. I was to say I had met 'Max' only recently, through friends. I found it hard to think of him as Max, although he was not quite Bram either.

On my second visit I had just handed him a cup of tea when footsteps crunched up the drive. I glimpsed a white man before I turned away saying to myself, 'Good heavens, no, his name is Max.' But Bram rose to intercept the stranger and lead him to the house. He had come about the electricity. I thought of how Bram could be caught over something quite trivial. Josephine was having problems over her pass-book—what if just coping with that led to his capture?

When we had relaxed again, Bram fed crumbs to sparrows in the dry grass. How different it had been three months earlier at his old home, when he had given a Sunday lunch party for family and a few close friends. He led me towards a cool corner by the front door. 'Look, Molly's special garden.' Small rare plants she had set in evergreen grass. 'It's a real monument to her,' he had said.

In 1961, when Bram was in Rhodesia on an important arbitration case, he had telephoned Molly every evening. I was staying with her and their son Paul at the time. After twenty-five years of marriage she had been like a girl preparing to meet her lover as she chose a new outfit for Bram's return. Then, in 1964, the night after he had concluded the defence of Nelson Mandela and the other men in the Rivonia trial, he and Molly set off for Cape Town to celebrate their daughter Ilse's twenty-first birthday. Crossing a bridge in the darkness Bram swerved to avoid a cow, and crashed into a stream.

Molly, trapped in the car, drowned.

Bram without Molly. The triumph of saving the Rivonia men from hanging had just been muted by the anguish of their life sentences—and now came this cruel, intolerable tragedy. There was no way I could try to console him.

In his letter telling me he was going underground Bram had concluded, 'It is very early in the morning and a glow is touching the garden that Molly and I tended for more than twenty-five years. I have wondered and wondered what she would advise in the present circumstances. I think she would have approved.'

BRAM SEEN CROSSING BECHUANALAND BORDER.

FISCHER SEEN IN DAR ES SALAAM.

How little he was understood. He had said he would not leave South Africa. 'Our place is *here*.' How often I heard him say that. And I had witnessed the extremes of his feelings: his fury when he heard that a comrade had fled the country—fury aroused not by the man's action but by the Security Police, who tortured and broke people and drove them to flight; his exuberance when I returned to Johannesburg despite fears that I might be arrested for lobbying at the United Nations. 'It was like the coming of a whole battalion,' he had said in welcome.

I did not want to know what Bram was doing or who he was seeing on the other days of the week. The ninety-day detention law had been suspended but it could be brought back at any moment; the less I knew, the better. Clearly, he was having to start from scratch.

Usually we met once a week. He loved to hear about friends. Alan Paton was in town and Bram wished he could see him. 'I'd give anything...' During the Rivonia trial he had visited Paton in Natal to ask if he would speak in favour of mitigation of sentence. He had hardly made the request before Paton agreed. 'But you've not heard all the facts,' Bram protested.

Paton replied, 'You told me that it's a matter of life and death.'

Judgement day in the trial of Bram's comrades: I waited in the main street of Benoni, a mining town. His Volkswagen approached, on time, and we headed for the southern border of the Transvaal. I was happy to be with him and relieved to escape the tension of the court.

We talked of his children, who were never far from his thoughts: Ruth and her husband were in London and, before going underground, Bram had sent his teenage son Paul to join them. Ilse was in Johannesburg. He worried about her having to cope with letting their old home. Packing before the move, Ilse had shown me family papers and mementoes removed from Bram's chambers.

Among the yellowed pages of letters which Ilse had shown me was one from Ouma Steyn, wife of the President of the Orange Free State, to Bram on his twenty-first birthday: '*As kind en as student was jy 'n voorbeeld vir almal, en ek weet dat jy nog 'n eervollig rol gaan speel in die geskiedenis van Suid Afrika.*' (As a child and as a student you were an example to everyone, and I know you will play an honourable role in the history of South Africa.) As Bram and I drove through the dried-out veld of the southern Transvaal, I said how moved I had been on reading Mrs Steyn's letter. 'What would Ouma say if she could see me now?' He tried to make a joke of it.

We began to talk of the Afrikaans language. Wanting to lighten his mood I recited a poem lodged in my brain since I had unwillingly learned it at school:

Dis donker, donker middernag
Nader kruip die Zulumag
Kruip swart adders om die laer...

(It's dark, dark midnight. The Zulu forces creep nearer. Black snakes creep around the laager.) 'It's so ugly and gutteral,' I protested.

'But it's a poetic language!' came his impassioned retort. 'Listen: *motreën*—moth rain—that soft rain. And *douvoordag*—dew before daybreak.' I had to concede that when he spoke those words, they sounded beautiful.

The Transkei homeland had recently chosen English as the first language in their schools and this, I thought, was good. 'Why *good*?' Bram asked. 'On the contrary, it's sad that my people, through their actions, are turning Africans against Afrikaans. Now it's the Transkei, ultimately all will be lost. In my ideal state we would try to preserve the language.'

When he spoke of his people, perplexity, anger and love clashed. Their historic Great Trek from the Cape early in the nineteenth century had been precipitated by the desire for freedom from British control. But they also wanted the freedom to own slaves, so were they freedom-fighters or oppressors? Bram thought one of their leaders, Piet Retief, had some fine ideas: 'His Manifesto in 1837 spoke of upholding the "just principle of liberty"—his followers would not molest others nor deprive them of property: they wanted peace and friendly intercourse with the African tribes.

'What made us rebels,' Bram said, 'was the Boer War.' His grandfather, a Member of Parliament at the age of twenty-five, had tried to moderate the Boer leader, President Kruger, while keeping at bay 'the wily old imperialist Milner'. When such efforts failed and war broke out in 1899, Bram's grandfather rallied people to the Boer cause, addressing endless meetings in dusty little dorps, coaching Hertzog, among the more extreme of their generals, in politics while keeping in touch with the moderates, Smuts and Botha. Listening to Bram talk about the war, I was struck by how real it seemed for him although he was born six years after it ended. His family had town and country houses and, like many Afrikaners, they were left with little but a few ornaments. British soldiers tore pages from their set of Dickens to stuff pillows.

When the British ceded power to white South Africans under the Act of Union, Bram's grandfather, as Minister of Lands, pushed through the 1913 Natives Land Act dispossessing Africans of their land, restricting four million of them to less than eight percent of the country. The million whites obtained access to more than ninety percent. 'Even up to 1926,' Bram said, 'Afrikaner Nationalism was a progressive force—against oppression, against big monopoly capital and *for* the working class, *for* the Jews. Why, in the early forties I had lunch with Verwoerd; he was trying to make up his mind whether to be a Nationalist or a Socialist!'

Bram laughed at that recollection, but the laugh turned to a sigh. 'Today in all South Africa Afrikaners are only about eight percent of the population, and who in the outside world backs them!' Perhaps, he mused, an oppressed people are always progressive until they get power; so, once Afrikaners attained it, their nationalism escalated into domination over the blacks, a domination to which it seemed there was no limit. It struck me that Bram's sacrifice of family, career and freedom had essentially been inspired by his Afrikaner heritage. He had implied as much in his letter to the magistrate in the trial: as an Afrikaner, he sought to make some reparation for the misdeeds of his people.

For me, sensing this as we drove on that day, there was also an intensely personal experience. Just as reading *Cry, the Beloved Country* had shattered my prejudice against the blacks, so now Bram had blown away the cobwebs of my childhood perception of Afrikaners as alien. Not our few Afrikaner friends, of course, who were Smuts supporters and spoke English, but 'Nats': my father used to joke that he'd left Ireland to escape a bunch of rebels, but at least in Ireland they had a sense of humour.

We reached our destination, Volksrust, and Bram drew up at the post office to mail letters to Helen Suzman and to Beyers Naude. He wanted to express his appreciation of their courage and tenacity in opposing apartheid, but it was also a way of demonstrating he was still in the country. However, such gestures soon staled. His letters to newspaper editors and other individuals, sent from each of the four provinces, had already been publicized. Besides, as a 'listed' communist his actual words could not be quoted. He wanted to support black political action, but it had been crushed through years of arrests and political trials. His success in evading capture seemed to me in itself the most potent form of protest.

'Molly and I often brought the children here.' He had turned off the main road to drive down a dirt track to a kloof. 'We were both so busy and picnics were the times we could all be together.' His pleasure in returning to those familiar spots gave me a sense of how desperately he missed Molly. Yet he was always the perfect host: the fire deftly made, the meat well-grilled, the drinks iced; the picnic was a festive occasion. He identified birds and trees and, after we had eaten, he shared a letter from his son Paul, proud of the literary style and amusing comments on life in London.

The sun, lighting the shaved area of his head, exposed white roots where the auburn hair began. 'Your hair,' I said, 'it's beginning to show.' Later, when we arrived in the suburbs, he drew up outside a chemist, where I bought the dye he used for his hair.

12 REDS ARE FOUND GUILTY. We stopped for an evening paper. His old friends, Eli Weinberg and Ivan Schermbrucker, had been sentenced to five years, the young communists to two. Five years. That was the sentence he would have been given.

Mary Benson

That winter I spent six weeks reporting on political trials in the Eastern Cape and exchanged postcards with 'Max'. Speculation about him continued in the press: 'Throughout South-West Africa police man roadblocks on all the main highways after tourists reported seeing Abram Fischer at the Etosha Pan. A Johannesburg professional man was detained at Warmbaths police station; he was mistaken for Abram Fischer Q.C.'

Bram had been underground for more than six months.

Back in Johannesburg, I found that he had moved. To my relief he was much more security-conscious than before and when we met on a corner one evening, he asked me to close my eyes until we had driven in the gate to the new house. It was semi-detached but he hardly saw his neighbours, a young couple. He no longer employed a maid. Inside was the same garden furniture; two garish paintings remained unhung in the nondescript sitting-room.

Warmed by an electric fire, we drank sherry to celebrate our reunion. He was eager to hear about my experiences. I told of the horror of trials held in obscure little village courts from which the families of the defendants were barred, of the trumped-up charges, of Security Police beatings and bribing and schooling of witnesses. He was not surprised to hear that magistrates—one after another—accepted blatantly parroted evidence. Hundreds of men and women who bravely resisted this terrorizing were being sentenced to years of imprisonment for such offences as attending a tea party to raise funds for the banned African National Congress or Pan Africanist Congress.

I had also attended a rehearsal of Athol Fugard's latest production, *Antigone*. Among men already imprisoned on Robben Island were actors from his black theatre group, Serpent Players. Since Fugard was denied a permit to enter New Brighton township, this rehearsal was surreptitiously held in a coloured kindergarten. The schoolmaster playing Haemon had particularly impressed me, but before opening night he too was arrested and no doubt would soon land up on the island. Nevertheless, the production had gone ahead as though the actors and Fugard were inspired by Antigone's words, 'I honoured those things to which honour truly belongs.'

And I also shared with Bram the moment when Govan Mbeki, whom Bram had defended in the Rivonia trial, arrived at the

courthouse in the village of Humansdorp. Handcuffed and flanked
by police and armed soldiers, he had been flown in from Robben
Island for a trial to give evidence for the defence. After a year of
labouring with Nelson Mandela and the other 'lifers' in a lime quarry,
he had aged considerably; it seemed to me that weariness had settled
on him like fine dust. But as I told Bram, his spirit was as strong as
ever : when the magistrate called on the press to withdraw, since it was
'not in the interests of the State' that we should report the evidence of
this 'important political prisoner', Govan stood in the witness box,
composed and radiating irony.

Later that evening when Bram drove me to a taxi-rank I
encouraged him with one further anecdote: a lawyer who regularly
visited prisoners awaiting trial told me that the first thing they asked
was, 'Is Bram still free?' When assured that he was, they were
jubilant.

A few weeks later, on an August day bathed in winter sunshine,
we drove along a road straight across the vast breathtaking
spaces of the Transvaal, the bare veld which previously I had
seen as boring. The glorious day suited our mood. During the past
weeks the *Rand Daily Mail* had published a series of articles on prison
conditions, and the Johannesburg *Sunday Times* had followed on
with revelations from a white prison warder. Police raided the
newspaper offices and interrogated the writers of the articles.
Laurence Gandar, editor of the *Mail,* had written increasingly
provocative editorials, but the Minister of Justice, Vorster, remained
uncharacteristically silent. Meanwhile, the Dutch government had
made a grant to the fund providing legal aid for political offenders
and assistance to their families.

'Do you think it's the flaring up of a new flame?' Bram asked,
elated. 'Or old ashes dying?' Before I could reply he exclaimed, 'I
believe it is a new flame! If now people could be brought together, a
whole new opposition working together...' I said that some such
activity might already be under way, although I believed the most
likely outcome was a penal reform committee of academics and
lawyers. But who was I to judge between a last spark and a phoenix?

As Bram turned off the main road in search of a picnic spot, I
described my meetings during 1964 with black leaders in Washington

and with Martin Luther King in London, when he had been on his way to receive the Nobel Peace Prize—the first signs, I thought, of a genuine black American interest in South Africa. Before long—now it was my turn for euphoria—the black vote would become crucial and, as the US Congress and the Government responded to that pressure, Britain would have to follow suit. Bram was sceptical. His outrage at the news from Vietnam was continually refuelled. Some months later however he said he had come round to the view that American blacks had a great potential role in the struggle.

The establishment of a non-racial government in South Africa was what really stirred his imagination. He could envisage the country becoming the industrial supplier for the entire continent. The conflict between white and black would then no longer endanger investments. But we both suspected that the short sight of Western investors and multinationals would prevent their support of economic pressures—taking a temporary loss now rather than losing everything in the future.

We picnicked under a cluster of thorn trees. From out of the bush came African women who knelt beside us, showing their handiwork. Bram bought grass mats and seed necklaces. The women quietly withdrew. There was always a slight melancholy when our time for packing-up came.

Bumping over the veld in search of the main road, we returned to our discussion, to Verwoerd's assertion that by 1978 the 'tide would be turned' and blacks would be drained from the cities, confined to Bantustans. Bram derided the idea. 'And by 1978,' he added, 'Verwoerd will no longer be Prime Minister. Others will reap the terrible whirlwind. We've done all we can to avoid that holocaust—has anyone done more? The last thing communists want is violence. But the Nationalists don't mind shedding blood. After Sharpeville Karel de Wet, a member of the Government, expressed regret that so few had been shot!'

He turned to me for a moment. 'Listen, Mary, the struggle here is not a communist one. The Africans' concern is for the liberation of their people and for a just way of life. They all say, we don't want violence, we hope it won't be inevitable.' He paused. 'No, it *is* the phoenix. I'll never believe we are dying ashes! We are glowing embers that will soon be part of a new flame.'

One evening at the end of August I brought him a gift, German poetry with translations, to mark his seven months of 'freedom'. It was a kind of milestone for me too—I had found that when you do something risky without being caught, each day is an extension of life that you truly value. We had separately seen a local production of *The Caucasian Chalk Circle.* Now I wanted to share with him Brecht's poem '*An die Nachgeborenen*' ('To Posterity') which I felt expressed the question Camus put, the most important of our age: How to cease to be victims without becoming executioners?

> We walked
> Through the wars of the classes, despairing
> When there was injustice only and no rebellion.
>
> And yet we know well:
> Even hatred of vileness
> Distorts a man's features.
> Even anger at injustice
> Makes hoarse his voice. Ah, we
> Who desired to prepare the soil for kindness
> Could not ourselves be kind.
>
> But you, when the times permit
> Men to be the helpers of men
> Remember us
> With indulgence.

Was repression inherent in Marxism or was it rather that successful revolutions deteriorated into repression? I had read somewhere the Levellers' appeal to the future Charles II: 'We have lost our way, we looked for Liberty; behold Slavery.' But before I could express such thoughts, Bram had responded by reading from Brecht's *Galileo*:

> On our old continent a rumour started: there are new continents! And since our ships have been sailing to them the word has gone round all the laughing continents that the vast dreaded ocean is just a little pond. And a great desire has arisen to fathom the causes of all things: why a stone falls when you drop it, and how it rises when you throw it in the air. Every day something new is

discovered... And because of that a great wind has arisen, lifting even the gold-embroidered coat-tails of princes and prelates, so that the fat legs and thin legs underneath are seen; legs like our legs. The heavens, it has turned out, are empty. And there is a gale of laughter over that.

'That's how it is,' Bram exclaimed. 'The great wind of socialism, do you see?' He put down the book and stood confronting me. 'Come over to us, Mary! Become a part of something great, be with the people!'

His appeal rang in me. I loved him and I admired him but I could not join him.

During the thirties I was a politically ignorant and racially prejudiced teenager in Pretoria; he was a Rhodes Scholar at Oxford, alive to the intellectual climate and to events in Europe. On student tours of the continent he witnessed Nazism and Fascism at first hand. The Italian invasion of Ethiopia, hunger strikes in England—these too had been part of the realities of his world. He had returned to South Africa to be confronted by the Greyshirts under Oswald Pirow, Minister of Justice. Only the Communist Party militantly opposed the spread of Fascism abroad and at home, regardless of the risks. Only communists were prepared to work alongside blacks and demand 'one man one vote'. Bram joined the Party, as did Molly, and when they became active in the forties, Stalin had been our great ally. During 1946, while I was in Germany working among displaced persons, many of whom had suffered under both Hitler and Stalin, Bram and other communists were assisting African miners in their momentous strike. He had seen the violent suppression of the union by the capitalist Chamber of Mines, aided by Smuts's army and police.

Our discussion that night, like those on other occasions, was amicable and animated, with a burst of exasperation now and then. Bram talked of the exploitation of one class by another. I had been with the Four Powers administration of Vienna at the end of the Second World War—'I saw the way the Russian officers treated their men!' I remonstrated. When Bram patiently explained dialectical materialism, my mind went blank. My arguments were vague. I was influenced then by the ideas of Camus, Lewis Mumford and Simone

Weil, and inspired by what I had seen of the human spirit, its capacity for transformation and transcendence.

Bram mentioned that he was studying the methods of the Portuguese Communist Party's underground: it was necessary, he said, to be ruthless even with your own family. But I knew he was quite incapable of ruthlessness: he was taking the considerable risk of regularly meeting his daughter, Ilse. To my surprise he added that he had been reading the Bible: how much love there was in it, and goodness; qualities inherent in communist ideals. (It later transpired that he used it as code in letters sent overseas.) In South Africa, he pointed out, communists had always tried to work with Christians—with Michael Scott, for instance, and Bishop Reeves. For him Marxism was the solution to the world's injustice. The future lay with socialism, and permeating his beliefs, his actions, his very nature was unquenchable optimism.

On a Sunday morning we drove to the north-west, through veld barren and strange under a sickly yellow sky. Again the weather matched the news. Vorster had at last reacted: splashed across the morning's front pages were reports of Security Police raids on the *Rand Daily Mail*; they had seized the passports of the editor and the chief political reporter and arrested those who had given information about prison conditions.

That October spring was heralded by snow in the mountains and cold rain in the city. On the Rand, one of the perpetually overcrowded trains of black workers crashed. Ninety-one passengers were killed. Survivors battered to death a white man coming to their aid.

FISCHER SEEN ON KAUNDA'S FARM.

FISCHER NOT HERE—KAUNDA.

On the wind that swept away the clouds came a host of yellow and white butterflies. Green shoots sprang in the veld. In a *kloof* below a high rocky *krans* Bram and I spread our rugs and cushions under blossoming trees. Kingfishers plunged towards a stream. We gathered wood for our *braaivleis* fire.

Lunch over, I read to Bram from the final chapter of my history of the African struggle. 'Laski once wrote, "The political criminals under a tyrant are the heroes of all free men."' I broke off. 'That's a good quote, hey?' He smiled his agreement. As I read on, shouts came from the woods on the opposite bank and from downstream.

'Your scarf!' he urged. The shouts sounded nearer and nearer. I quickly tied the scarf under my chin, and as helmeted heads appeared among bushes across the stream, Bram calmly offered me a banana. Voices now came from behind us. We turned to see soldiers in full battledress running towards us. This is it, I thought.

'*Gooie dag*!' called one brightly.

'*Dag,*' said Bram.

'*Dag,*' a second soldier and I said, as they trotted on by. We watched their booted feet begin to climb the almost vertical cliff. More shouts and more men running past. We were in the middle of army training manoeuvres!

With studied leisure we packed the picnic basket and rugs and drove up the track to the main road. There a jeep was parked. Three senior officers stared out at us and smilingly saluted as we waved back and speeded away.

A few days later came the inevitable but horrifying news that Vorster had brought back and doubled the ninety-day detention law. One hundred and eighty days of solitary confinement: you had no access to lawyers or courts while the Security Police interrogated you.

A man named Isaac Heymann was the first to be so detained. In prison he attempted suicide. I did not know him but was sure he was one of Bram's contacts. Bram's face was sombre when next we met. Yes, he confirmed, Heymann was a close friend. 'Do you know anyone who would put up a fugitive?' he went on to ask. I thought about it.

'No,' I said apologetically, ashamed that I did not want to expose myself or test my friends.

The net was closing in. He confided that he was having sleepless nights. He had assumed a new name, Peter West.

On 2 November came an event he had been dreading: the Judge President of the Transvaal, responding to the application from the Johannesburg Bar Council, ruled that Abram Fischer Q.C. should be struck from the roll of advocates. Bram was bitterly angry. 'Dishonest!' he burst out as soon as I joined him in his car. He had just read the evening paper. 'The Judge President called me dishonest and dishonourable!' He expressed his disillusion and anguish in a torrent of words. For thirty years he had worked hard to uphold the law, had done all a man could to struggle for justice: surely colleagues who had known him well should have the sense, the feeling and courage to understand his reasons for the drastic step he had taken in going underground. 'Why couldn't they let the Government do its own dirty work?' he cried out.

We drove to a suburban hotel. 'Let's have a gin and tonic to cheer ourselves up!' said Bram. We sat on the verandah under a rapidly darkening sky. There was only one other customer, a man at a nearby table. Was he observing us—the tall woman and the short, bearded man? Sensing my unease, Bram said, 'If anyone you know comes up, don't forget to introduce me as Peter West, from out of town.'

'Open your eyes.' We were back at his house. A jacaranda tree was in bloom, glowing phosphorescently in the light from the street. For the rest of the evening we hardly talked, just listened to music.

A few days later the woman who had been my contact with Bram was taken into detention: 180 days. When last I had seen her she said that on some days she felt well and was confident she could cope. But on days when she was feeling ill, she was not so sure. Women detainees were usually made to stand while interrogators questioned and threatened them, made to stand all through the day...

Would Bram want to put off our appointment for the coming evening? I telephoned his house from a shop. There was no reply. Knowing the number worried me but it was necessary in case of a change of plan.

Teams of interrogators worked in relays, night and day, banging on the table, 'Wake up!' Threatening to douse her with water...

Bram and I met, as arranged. In his house he took me through to a small room where a bed was ready. So this had been for the 'fugitive'. 'It was too late,' he said. And shut the door on the room.

She told her interrogators: 'You are like sadistic schoolboys pulling the legs and wings off a fly.'

Bram was distracted from his grave anxiety for what his friend might be going through only by the desperate need to get away from this house fast. He had found a suitable place, but the owner could not see him to conclude negotiations until the following Sunday.

Her interrogators kept mocking, 'You are going to land in

Weskoppies! We will crack you!' (Weskoppies is a Pretoria mental asylum.)

Bram wanted to post an important airmail letter. We drove to the post office. I watched him cross the road in front of a line of cars drawn up at the traffic lights.

Standing, standing, night and day... No food...

Next morning, the morning of Thursday 11 November, I telephoned Bram. He had asked me to arrange an appointment with a visitor from London and, although I had tried to dissuade him from so risky a venture, he had insisted. 'Your appointment on Saturday,' I told him, 'it's all right.' He was delighted.

That evening came news of Rhodesia's Unilateral Declaration of Independence. Surely, I thought, Britain would not stand for Ian Smith's rebellion. This crazy act must help our struggle. I felt suddenly exhilarated, but also sad that the Rhodesian whites could be so deliberately self-destructive. Bram must have seen the newspaper; we would discuss it when we met in a few days' time.

Early next morning an acquaintance called by to collect some photographs. She said, 'Bram Fischer's been caught!'

I did not believe it. There had been many false alarms—how he and I had laughed at them. I began to feel nauseated. She handed me a newspaper:

JO'BURG DRAMA: FISCHER IS ARRESTED

Security Police arrested a heavily-disguised Abram Fischer in a northern suburb of Johannesburg last night.

Brigadier van den Bergh said Fischer was in a car when police, who had been shadowing him, cut off his car and stopped him. The arrest took place very near his old home, and he handed himself over without any trouble.

For 290 days the police have searched far and wide for him in probably the biggest manhunt they have ever undertaken.

Die Transvaler had a picture of him beside the great bully Swanepoel, the most notorious of all the Security Police, whose fist clutched Bram's arm, while Bram's other hand adjusted the rimless spectacles as he stared into the photographer's flash.

A day of mourning. A day interminable, somehow to be survived. 'You've saved my sanity,' he had said when we parted on that last evening. 'Bless you.'

The semi-detached house was pictured in the press. It was called Mon Repos. A lorry stood outside, stacked with furniture—the garden chairs and table we had joked about. In the foreground was the mulberry tree from which we had picked leaves for a child's silkworms.

SURGERY CHANGED FISCHER'S FACE. A plastic surgeon, after studying pictures of Fischer, opined that it looked like the work of an expert—probably outside South Africa.

Die Transvaler assured readers that the police had been watching Fischer's house for a considerable time. Associates and friends who had visited the disguised fugitive would be 'snuffled out'. Clearly the Security Police hoped that we—whoever we were—would scatter and run. But if they had been watching the house, they would have known the telephone number and, overhearing our last conversation a few hours before Bram was captured, they would have waited to discover who he was due to meet on Saturday.

The corridors of the Magistrates Court clattered with uniformed police. Photographers' flash bulbs clicked busily—press or police? Ilse was absent but Ruth and Paul, back from London, were taken to see their father in the cells below the court. They returned, grinning at the list of practical things he had given them to do.

The courtroom bristled with Security Police. A handful of spectators, white on our side, black on theirs, sat in the public galleries. While we waited I counted the police milling round the dock. I had got to forty-nine when up the steps from the cells and into the dock came Bram.

As he stood there he turned once, calmly, deliberately, to look at us, and once to look at the black gallery. He had shaved off the beard and had reverted to his old, half-rimmed spectacles. I felt doubly bereaved.

It took but a few moments for the Magistrate to announce a remand; a glance from Bram at Ruth and Paul and he was gone. A prisoner, to be held behind bars and locked doors in a cell in Pretoria prison. I was never to see him again.

At his trial early in 1966, largely on the evidence of a black turncoat, Bram Fischer was found guilty of conspiring to commit sabotage with Nelson Mandela and the other men he had defended two years earlier in the Rivonia trial; guilty also of contravening the Suppression of Communism Act and of forging documents with assumed names. He made a statement from the dock in the course of which he said: 'There is a strong and ever-growing movement for freedom and for basic human rights amongst the non-white people of the country—that is, amongst four-fifths of the population. This movement is supported not only by the whole of Africa but by virtually the whole membership of the United Nations as well—both West and East.

'However complacent and indifferent white South Africa may be, this movement can never be stopped. In the end it must triumph. Above all, those of us who are Afrikaans and who have experienced our own successful struggle for full equality should know this.

'The sole questions for the future of all of us, therefore, are not whether the change will come but only whether the change can be brought about peacefully and without bloodshed, and what the position of the white man is going to be in the period immediately following on the establishment of democracy—after the years of cruel discrimination and oppression and humiliation which he has imposed on the non-white peoples of this country...

'It is true that apartheid has existed for many decades... What is not appreciated by my fellow Afrikaner, because he has cut himself off from all contact with non-whites, is that the extreme intensification of that policy over the past fifteen years is laid entirely at his door. He is now blamed as an Afrikaner for all the evils and humiliations of apartheid...

'All this bodes ill for our future. It has bred a deep-rooted hatred for Afrikaners, for our language, our political and racial outlook amongst all non-whites—yes, even amongst those who seek positions of authority by pretending to support apartheid. It is rapidly destroying amongst non-whites all belief in future co-operation with Afrikaners.

'To remove this barrier will demand all the wisdom, leadership and influence of those Congress leaders now sentenced and imprisoned for their political beliefs. It demands also that Afrikaners themselves should protest openly and clearly against discrimination. Surely, in such circumstances, there was an additional duty cast on me, that at least one Afrikaner should make this protest actively and positively even though as a result I faced fifteen charges instead of four.'

'It was to keep faith with all those dispossessed by apartheid that I broke my undertaking to the court, separated myself from my family, pretended I was someone else, and accepted the life of a fugitive. I owed it to the political prisoners, to the banished, to the silenced and those under house arrest, not to remain a spectator, but to act...

'All the conduct with which I have been charged has been directed towards maintaining contact and understanding between the races of this country. If one day it may help to establish a bridge across which white leaders and the real leaders of the non-whites can meet, to settle the destinies of all of us by negotiations and not by force of arms, I shall be able to bear with fortitude any sentence which this court may impose on me.'

He was sentenced to imprisonment for life.

The two women who had been his contacts were each sentenced to two years' imprisonment.

He had concluded by quoting President Kruger, the Boer leader—'prophetic words,' Bram said, 'when spoken in 1881,' and words which remained prophetic: '"With faith we lay our whole case bare to the world. Whether we win, whether we die, freedom shall rise over Africa as the sun out of the morning clouds."'

'I tried very hard,' Bram wrote to me, 'to reach my fellow Afrikaners, but that does not seem to have worked.'

I remember once saying to Bram that he was a source of strength. He was silent for a moment, then rounded on me as 'a silly ass!' He was really cross. 'It was Molly who gave strength,' he exclaimed. 'Molly, not I!'

During his fifth year in prison his son, aged twenty-three, died suddenly. One of Bram's brothers came to the prison to break the news. They stood, divided by a partition, two warders behind each of them. Bram was told that Paul had died that morning. Afterwards he was taken directly to his cell and locked in for the night. Not until the

221

next morning did his fellow-prisoners hear the news. He had been fourteen hours alone with the knowledge of Paul's death. He was not permitted to attend the funeral.

In 1968 I was allowed back to South Africa briefly to be with my dying father in Pretoria. I applied to visit Bram. The Commissioner of Prisons was a man of few words: 'Your request to visit A. Fischer cannot be acceded to.' But we were able to exchange occasional letters. He was not, however, allowed to receive my letter about Paul's death as his quota had already been filled; nor was his daughter allowed to tell him what I had said about how I had come to know and love Paul, with his passion for jazz and his mocking sense of humour.

The closest Bram could get to mentioning politics was a paragraph in his cheerful reply of 29 September 1974 to my letter from the desert:

> Striking was the contrast you created for me. Nevada/Berkeley/New England's misty coast... I'm sure Americans are extremely well-meaning, I've never met one who didn't appear so. Problem is, do they sufficiently understand what's going on, sufficiently to match up to their responsibilities in the next decade or two? I believe those responsibilities will be enormous, their performance may save or sacrifice millions of lives, by famine even.

For the most part he described his studies—he had passed Economics I and was reading 'Native Administration'—and the plants he was growing in the courtyard of their special section: gazanias and roses, Iceland poppies and freesias. He was experimenting with grafting guava and grenadilla; if it bore fruit he would name it guavadilla. He fed crumbs to sparrows, doves and rock-pigeons. 'Then we have a thrush coming after worms occasionally and can sometimes hear a Cape Robin before dawn.'

'Of course I remember the Trafalgar starlings,' he replied to an inquiry. 'When you see our host again, please give my regards.' This was a reference to an evening we spent with Hugh Caradon in his apartment overlooking the birds' shrill nightly invasion of Trafalgar

Square. 'Also remember picnics,' he added—his turn now to test my memory. 'The famous one where we watched youngsters practising crossing rivers, climbing crags.'

'Seven lines left,' he concluded, 'to serve for Xmas greetings, for I shall have to keep some months for family obligations. Celebrate happily.'

That Christmas he was in the Verwoerd Hospital, guarded by two warders. After a fall in prison, cancer had been discovered. Throughout his dreadful, slow dying he was said to be calm and cheerful, but exhausted. Despite the repeated appeals of family, friends and innumerable people from many countries, the Minister of Prisons and Justice refused to release him to the care of his family until he was incapable of appreciating their companionship.

Bram Fischer died on 8 May 1975. After the funeral, the authorities demanded that his ashes be returned to Pretoria prison.

'THIS IS A GREAT
LITERARY EVENT…
At last we have the
foremost novel of the
century in the form in which
the author wrote it…

JAMES JOYCE
ULYSSES
THE CORRECTED TEXT

Edited with an Afterword by Hans Walter Gabler

With a new Preface by Richard Ellmann

…Now the greatness –
the literary brilliance,
the humour, the
humanity – shine out.
REJOYCE!'
– Anthony Burgess

NAN RICHARDSON
AND GILLES PERESS
EYE FOR AN EYE

We are in Lisburn, attending a local version of the burning of Lundy. The Finaghy Boys Blues Band are here—marching up the high street with pipes and drums—as are the Apprentice Boys, with their bowlers, sashes and swords. The night is glazed with ice, and people tuck their heads round their front doors and then withdraw, having silently watched the passage of the small parade. On a scaffold in an empty parking lot, the wax effigy of Lundy hangs, dressed in a black suit and boots, waiting to be burned. It was Lundy who 'turned coat', opening the city gates when the city of Londonderry was under seige by the Catholic forces of King James in 1688. He was caught by a group of apprentices and burned at the stake.

The speeches begin, the onlookers in the car park stamping their feet and blowing into their cupped hands. A portly man in his late twenties speaks about Anglo-Irish sell-outs—his high-pitched rhetoric obviously inspired by Ian Paisley—and ends with a desperate, 'Wipe out the IRA scum!' He is followed by the president of the chapter, bearing a 'No Surrender' flag. He is elderly and his voice nearly inaudible, and, as he begins to tilt into the fire, someone stops him and leads him away. The reverend vice-president of the

The French photographer Gilles Peress has been working in Northern Ireland for seventeen years, and, more recently, was joined by Nan Richardson. The chronicle that follows is a selection of the work they have done together leading up to the Anglo-Irish Agreement. Gilles Peress and Nan Richardson are now covering the summer marches, and their account will be published in the next issue of *Granta*.

chapter intones a blessing: 'There will be no surrender. Oh, God of Jacob, God our refuge in these times of danger, hear us. I know His power is behind us, because we are the chosen people. But there are traitors in our midst today. There are teacheries all around us. *They* are encircling us! *They* were on this very spot but a few days ago. *They* came in and stole our cars to carry out their unholy activities!'

The boys and girls fidget in the cold. 'Everyone comes for the bonfire,' a boy confides. The children drift away, as the old men line up for the last march around the parking lot, attended by police at the front and rear.

Mark's house, off the Springfield Road. My friend rings the bell, just as I'm closing the iron gate behind me.

When Mark opens the door, he looks alarmed. 'You have a woman with you!' he says. We exchange uneasy glances. Once inside, Mark explains. Last week, the doorbell rang. A man asked to use the phone–few people in the Catholic areas have telephones. A dark-haired woman in a trench coat stood at the gate. He let the man in and suddenly a gun was against his side. The visitors explained carefully that they would be staying for two days, enough time to place a bomb in the wall of the house next door that bordered on the street, so that at the right moment, the armoured police Land Rover that routinely parks there could be blown up. They moved in and dug through the wall into the next building at night, when the paint shop on the ground floor was closed. The woman went out with Mark once to buy milk and cigarettes. Then they left, leaving behind ropes and wires.

Mark was in a panic. In the night he stole out and crossed the city to dump the paraphernalia left behind. No sooner had he deposited the bundle than he went back to retrieve it, worried that his fingerprints would be traceable. Finally, he wrapped the debris in plastic and buried it.

Two nights later, the intruders returned. The woman stood again at the gate, as a lookout, he assumed. They kept him and his elderly landlady in the kitchen while they adjusted the device and left with a warning to say nothing.

Mark is terrified by the proximity of the bomb, and the possibility that people will be killed. He thinks about how he could notify the authorities without seeming to be the informer. He hasn't yet considered that if the device explodes, and the wires are traced to his house, his failure to report it could be seen as collaboration and mean a jail sentence. We talk all night about what he can do. Even if he manages to convince the police that he knows nothing, he says, the old woman who owns the house cannot get the story straight. 'She is scared out of her wits,' he says in despair.

Five years later, the bomb has not gone off.

Kate is thirty-four. Her husband, a part-time member of the Ulster Defence Regiment, was shot eight years ago. She has three children: a seventeen-year-old son; a girl, fourteen; and a boy, fifteen, who is really Kate's brother, the youngest born of her aged parents. 'My grandad fought in the war. To keep this place British. He fought the Germans to keep us here – not so the Provies could take it away.'

'I don't believe you should be talking to children about hate. I'd pick up a gun and shoot them that killed my Michael if it would keep my son from doing it. But it's embedded in him. I've told him, I've talked to him, "For God's sake, Michael, forget about it. Your Da's dead. Nothing will bring him back." He'll say to me, "Mummy, whether it's twenty years or thirty, I'll get them, and I'll shoot them." How can you get that hate out of a child? His dad was shot sitting beside him on that sofa, watching TV.

'Ten years ago Michael did a television programme when he was seven. Ten years ago. The BBC came to make a film. Then the Troubles hadn't affected us in any way; we lived a normal life. They took three Catholic and three Protestant families. I says to Michael that the other boy's an RC, or as Michael knows them better a Fenian! And he says, "But he's a wee lad just like me!" Which is what they were trying to tell him, that Catholics didn't have two heads as the other wee boys thought. After this programme was done, a few months went by, and they'd have a weekend together. They came to our side of the barrier and played. But after what happened to his Da, Michael wouldn't go near the barrier unless he went there to hurt somebody. Hate was breeding hate. Michael had accepted the Catholic boy until that happened.

'The other night, I was in the house alone with the children. I heard this moaning, like, of someone being hurt, and I rushed out to see a gang gathered about, kicking and kicking this boy. I screamed at them, "Get the fuck out of here!" and they ran. I stood on the street, screaming for people to come out of their houses. You couldn't even tell what age he was, he had been beaten to a pulp. I've never seen a beating like to that. Two or three lights turned on and one man stuck his head out and said, "Well, it's just a Taig." I said, "I don't bloody well care who it is," and called the ambulance.'

Sunday at Divis. We are being trailed by children. The girls tug insistently at our sleeves, ask to be photographed, grab at the cameras, and somehow get all the information they want quickly: 'Where do you come from? Who is this for? Where are you staying? How long for?' And occasionally: 'Are you American-Irish?' They are rough, with us and with each other.

The boys show us their battle scars: a cut and discoloured eye, swollen closed; a wound, still bleeding, above the elbow; a scar on the hand of a five-year-old who had covered his face when a plastic bullet was fired at his head. Two skinheads start playing with two other boys, both brothers. The game gets tense and one boy jabs the jagged rim of a tin can against the throat of another. The snap of the camera shutter defuses the situation. He drops the tin and they all go off together to a fort built from the wreckage of the nearby apartments.

'Have any plastic bullets, rubber bullets?' the girls chorus. 'How much?' They are suddenly all business.

They explain how to make Molotov cocktails. Derrick, ten, says, 'You fill a milk bottle with the petrol, add some sugar or cornflakes to make it stick, stuff a rag in at the top for a wick. But one thing, you gotta be careful not to throw it too late or too soon. Count three,' he advises, 'then it'll burst when it hits 'em. If you put in soapy stuff, like Fairy Liquid, it helps to stick too.'

Do they know of anyone bribing kids to throw stones? I ask. The boy snorts cynically, 'If they were paying for it, the whole street would fucking be out. They'd be wasting their money. We do it for nothing. For the crack.'

His friend looks on, impassive. The side of his head is a liverish colour. 'Got hit by a rubber bullet,' he says, rolling up his sleeve to display an enormous bruise. 'Soldier got to me, up by Unity Flats. It's all gone blue and yellow now, though.' He shows it to the group. 'Got clubbed too,' he adds.

As we talk, they accomplish little acts of vandalism without thinking. They pick up metal rods, torn off the sides of the building, and fence with them, then use them to pry open metal cans which they set on fire, watching the flames spread to a mound of garbage. They steal bottles from a boy who is hoarding his collection for the evening's riot, and he screams at the pilferage. A blond punk in tartans and leather strolls by, flicking a silver chain like a whip, calling, 'Don't listen–it's all a lotta bunk!' Irene leans dreamily against a wall, adding her graffiti to the already defaced columns. 'Rude girls rule.'

'Walk me,' begs a small boy of an older one. 'These two fellas came up and asked us if we was Protestants, y'know, and I said yeah, so they took us into an entry and one took a Union Jack out of his pocket and told us to kiss it or else.'

'Didya?'

'Think we're daft? But there's more of them down the street, and I'm scared.'

'Come on then.' They trudge off down the street, hugging close to the shadows of the walls.

Susan, ten, brown-haired, lively, with an Aunt Rita in New York City, shows us 'the haunted stair where the Brits got blew up.' They call it the 'crying stair'. People avoid it and claim to see spirits on it. The doorway has a bar across it, a greyish, smoking carcass of a stove and piles of rubble. 'It's spooky. I wouldn't go near it,' Susan says, pulling us away. Suddenly a blond boy with a ruddy face appears, running. He points down the street, shouting, 'Go tell Nancy.'

Susan runs off, shouting, 'When the Brits come in, it's murder.' Along the way, she collars a small child and urges him to 'Go tell yer ma.' The Army foot patrol then appears, closing in from opposite sides of the complex, guns out, looking over their shoulders as they walk. Their appearance is greeted by a cacophony of noise, rubbish-bin lids are banged against the walls and railings, and the corridors are full of women and children running about, squealing, shouting, 'Hey, hey, IRA.'

Behind us the children are mouthing and miming frantically: 'Don't talk to them.'

28 December 1982: Patrick Elliot, nineteen, was shot dead by the soldiers of the British Army's Black Watch regiment as he left an Andersonstown Road chip shop which he was alleged to have robbed. 10 January 1983: police in an unmarked vehicle chased a stolen car along the Falls Road. Approaching an Army roadblock, the stolen car crashed through the barricade and hurtled on, while the Army opened fire. 30 January 1984: a car with six men was stopped at a check-point on the Springfield Road. Mark Marron, twenty-three, was shot dead when the patrolling soldier suddenly turned and fired into the waiting car.

Mark Marron's mother lives on Clonard Gardens near Cupar Street, surrounded by thirty feet of wire fencing. At the end of the street is a barricade, the 'peaceline', demarcated by a few rows of abandoned houses and a small door through which Protestants walk from their homes on the Shankill to work on the other side at Mackies Factory on the Springfield Road. Last week, the papers reported an incident involving the Marrons' youngest son, John: 'A punishment beating . . . paramilitary.' 'Hoods,' say people knowingly. There is talk in the district of vigilantes.

John Marron is thin and gangling, leaning on a cane, his right arm hanging uselessly at his side. 'It was half-nine and we had got a carry-out from the Chinese. I was sitting and drinking with my mate in a house on Cupar Street, watching TV. When we heard them trying to get in, busting the door, we tried to push a settee up against it, but there were six or seven of them, with masks on. They asked if we was Marron and McParland. We said, No, but one said, Yer lying. They took me into the hall and told me to get down on the floor and four of them stretched out my legs and arms and held them.'

'He couldn't get down fast enough and they kicked him,' his mother says.

'They did Jamie first and I could hear him yelling. Then they did me. The sticks had nails in them.'

I ask if he tried to call for help.

'Yeah, I yelled, but it was an empty house on one side and an old man, deaf, on the other. I was just thinking about the pain, about the sticks coming down on top of me.'

Did he know who they were?

'No. They bring them in from outside the district for a job like

238

this. I don't know why.'

His mother cuts in: 'Drinking and annoying people, that's all he done. Usually they'd beat you for stealing or breaking into houses. And then they just run off. You don't even meet your accusers. Hangmen, that's what they are. And to do it to the likes of this poor—well—just look at him.' She lowers her voice. 'In 1981 a plastic bullet paralysed him in the arm, the night that Bobby Sands died. It was on the corner of Canton Street. Someone from the district tipped them off. He's not the first—people have got worse for less. They come into the hospital and apologize for it afterwards when they get the wrong fella.

'My oldest son, Mark, was sixteen when they took him to the city cemetery and dropped breeze blocks on his legs and arms. And one of them that was doing it said he was Batman and jumped on him lying there. They cut his hair with a broken bottle, and tied him to a lamp-post and left.

Her second son, Paul, explains. 'In their areas, the Provisionals keep crime down, alright. If you rape someone, they take you out and knee-cap you. Same with rowdies, drunks and break-ins. They take you out to the city cemetery and put a hood on you and tie you upside down and question you. The way they look at it, they wouldn't come after you if you didn't deserve it. The IRA are self-proclaimed police. They'd get you just because you gave one of them a kicking in school, because you belted one of their members, see.'

I ask him to explain the joy in joy-riding. He laughs. 'People do it, I don't know, to get a chase out of it, to get the police up. People go to the Protestant areas to lift cars. They pack six kids into a car and drive up and down the Falls, trying to get the attention of the police, then turn into the side streets with them flying after. They used just to try to block you off. Now they shoot. They know they're just shooting at Taigs.

'I was in the car when my brother Mark was shot. I'd been in stolen cars before, and I didn't want to go. But, well, I said I'd just ride up the road to the house, and they could drop me. We got to the check-point and slowed, then stopped, to let this soldier walk by. Then the soldier turned and shot point-blank into the car. He wasn't shooting to wound. He aimed right at the driver's seat, and the guy who was driving ducked, and the bullet went right through the

headrest and hit Mark who was in the back. Right in front of the police station. We hadn't broken the check-point or nothing. The soldier came right up to the window after that, and then dropped his rifle and ran–he knew he'd done wrong–the others, the other soldiers, had to chase him down. We all abandoned the car. Left Mark there. Nobody else wanted to sit there and let them shoot them.'

He is silent for a moment. 'Another time,' he continues, 'we stole a car and it took eight rounds while we were actually driving it, but no one was shot. We ended up some place in the country and blew it up. A few friends of mine were killed later. They were fired on with Sterlings, the little machine guns, you know? Rocky, he was driving. They knew he was a hood–they had already shot him before–and they stopped him and told him to get out of the car. But they started firing at him before he even got out. And kept firing even though he had bullets in him.'

Belfast. There was a sound of glass breaking all over the city and a roar. Nine bomb blasts went off simultaneously in Belfast and five other cities: Newry on the border; Armagh; Londonderry; Portadown, the industrial city; and Lisburn, the Protestant northern enclave.

We drive slowly around the square. The damage is awesome – one million pounds of rubble, created in an instant with all nine bombs timed within seconds, synchronized to explode when no one was around. No one hurt, no one killed. Just a warning. The preliminary to a massive campaign? A reminder that behind the political solution is another one? The soldiers and police are visibly nervous, scanning the streets for snipers, odd parcels, lurking dangers, and questioning people in the cars that circle for a third time to stare. In a week or two, if nothing happens, the city will begin to relax. But tonight it all seems ominous. All night they will be at work, scraping the glass from the deserted streets.

241

T he village of Augnaskea. The hearse travels slowly up the narrow road. The bells toll, and we follow the many people streaming across the cow pasture. Beside the grey stone church, there are priests waiting with their hands folded. Loud-speakers hang from the trees and poles nearby. The stewards, with white armbands, form a human wall to restrain the crowd, linking arms against the crush.

There is the sour-sweet sound of a piper and the whirring of the low-flying helicopters overhead photographing the crowd. Some-where along the two-mile walk up this path of furze and fuchsia bushes there are soldiers, but they remain unseen.

The Mass begins, barely audible. I stand at the top of the hill, and spot a photographer moving among the tombstones, quietly, deftly skirting the mourners, and then disappearing among them. When the Mass ends, there is a sudden and agitated movement, as everyone presses in tightly to see, and to protect, the outlawed symbolic ceremony of the gun salute over the coffin. The guard of honour lifts its rifles into the air, and fires a volley that echoes across the round hills of the South Armagh border country. I see the photographer again, crouching before the guard of honour. The leader comes up to him and says something; the photographer nods and turns away.

A march passes through Newry in silence, black flags aloft, guarded on all sides by police. In the wasteland beside the A-1, the travellers—gypsies and tinkers—stand watching. Most of their children have scrambled down the ravine for a closer look. They are thin and wiry and their faces are very dirty, and the youngest clutch at the skirts of the women who have gathered atop the rough hillside. The women are stalwart and muscled, and stand with their arms akimbo.

'You hear a lot of rubbish talked about travellers,' one of the the women tells me later. We sit in her diminutive caravan kitchen, her hand resting on her swollen belly. The child is expected soon. It will be the fifth. We drink strong black tea, and she explains the history of travellers. 'They were Irish people driven out of their own homes during the time of the famine, who started living rough, and now they're used to it, like. Travellers won't live in houses— too closed up for them, you know.'

Outside, clothes are stretched across a row of hedges to dry, and nearby a girl in red is washing her hair. She is surrounded by copper and steel pots and pans that flash when they catch the skittish sunlight.

I am introduced to Ned Keenan. On our way to his caravan, we pass through piles and piles of rusted scrap metal. There is a cold north wind coming off the back of the mountains. 'Plenty of fresh air up here,' Ned says, standing at his door. 'About all there is.' Ned was born in the South and came to Belfast fifteen years ago. He is the father of sixteen children, and his oldest son, Patrick, is to be married today. All round the caravan site, the clan arrives: dark men combing down their shaggy forelocks, hosing off the grime from the tarmac or washing away the smell of horses with Fairy Liquid.

'Travellers is wild, wild folk,' warns a girl with eyes that are terribly mischievous, as she polishes her Sunday shoes on the steps of the caravan. 'It takes a wedding or christening to bring it out.'

Later, at the wedding, there are the Keenans, the McCanns, the Donahues, the Connors, the Gavins, the Mahons and the Dundons. 'There are our people,' a girl tells me, pointing to one side of the caravan site. 'But they aren't our kind,' pointing to the other side. Even though everyone here lives, in some measure, outside society, there is a social hierarchy.

The more well-to-do among them, explains Miss Ann Fitzmaurice, the head teacher at the school set up especially for the travellers' children on the Falls Road, might sell caravans or deal in antiques. Others sell scrap, horses or carpets. Some work on the roads, tarmacking or paving. Quite a few drive big cars. 'The wealthier ones can clear off any time,' Miss Fitzmaurice says. 'It's difficult, in any case, to keep the children in school. The parents always take them out as soon as they're fourteen, if not before: many people here can't read.'

Most of the travellers are Catholic, she explains, and are viewed by the North as the South's problem. Inevitably, though, the children of a typical family of travellers will have been born in the North and the South—some have lived in England as well. The South has made some efforts to build permanent camping sites—with running water, electricity and toilets—but not enough to keep up with demand. And prejudice is strong: it wasn't that long ago that the Mayor of Limerick cleared travellers off a field with a shotgun. They are curious, Lear-like pilgrims, trying to protect their right to shovel six tons of tarmac in a hour, to head South for several months each winter, to take to the hills when it suits them, to cough and shiver as the wind shakes their fragile mobile shelters. When a traveller dies in his bed, they burn the caravan afterwards, so that no bad memories linger. They are shy, and they are not permitted into most bars and social clubs. They do not vote. They do not takes sides in the war. When trouble starts on the road, the barricades go up around the caravans to keep the bullets and the bricks out.

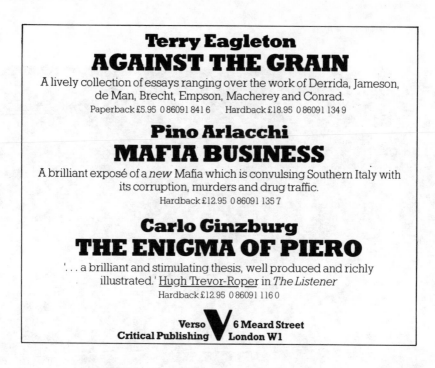

Primo Levi

The title of this piece is not intended to be tendentious. I don't mean to suggest that to be able to write imaginatively it is necessary, or even desirable, to start out in a trade which bears no relation to literature. I am telling you simply that this was what destiny had in store for me. That is: how I became a writer without having chosen to, and without having consciously prepared myself for it.

I studied to become a chemist, and worked as one for thirty years, before, during and after the war; but I turned, unexpectedly, into a writer because during the war I was sent to a German extermination camp. It would be cynical to say that this was a piece of luck. It is the kind of fortune one shouldn't wish on even one's worst enemy. But, with hindsight, it provided me with an extraordinary experience, a rare observatory on human behaviour, and an enormous reservoir of 'raw material'. In short: a paradoxically great store of riches.

During my year in Auschwitz I collected such a mass of things that pressed on me to be told that, after returning home, I felt almost obliged to write them down. My first book, *If This is a Man*, is a concentration camp story; its history is long and strange. I had been driven, almost forced, to write during the actual days of my imprisonment. I scribbled hurried notes with a stump of a pencil on shreds of cement sacks. I knew very well that all this was useless, for it was practically impossible to preserve these fragmentary records. Indeed, it was madly dangerous, because the Germans were extremely watchful for any signs that news was being smuggled out. They were only too aware of the deadly import of the massacre going on daily in Auschwitz and elsewhere. The mere act of writing was considered suspect; if the written matter referred in any way to what happened in the camp, the punishment was a public hanging.

Still, my urge to write was intense: not only in order to tell, to bear witness, but also to relieve myself of a burden. Of course, this urge was not mine alone: everyone felt it. Everyone felt a compulsion to tell his story, a need second only to hunger. Curiously, this need was reflected in a highly specific dream experienced by those in Auschwitz: the Camp dream. The details might vary, but the kernel was always the same. You had miraculously returned home; you were with your family; you were telling your story, hurriedly, furiously, with intense pleasure...and then you noticed that your wife, your father, your mother weren't paying any attention. In fact, they seemed not to hear: after some moments they vanished or, more cruelly, turned and went away.

I'd be grateful if dream psychology could give me an 'authoritative' explanation. My interpretation is simple. This dream enacted a deep, painful frustration: it said, 'I need to tell as I need to eat—and I cannot; I am forbidden to.' I yielded to this need as soon as I returned home. At the beginning, I did it just in talk, button-holing anyone who was to hand, but I soon realized that it was more appropriate, more 'economical', to write my memories down. Anyway, I did not perceive I was writing a book—much less did I intend to become a writer. I was a chemist, and I had resumed my trade, which gave me a reasonable income and a career. Writing was an accessory, a duty, a deliverance, a compulsion, a therapy, sometimes a pleasure: certainly not a job. Indeed, I wrote with no plan in mind. It suited me to begin at the end—that is, I wrote my first book almost exactly back to front, setting down the most recent episodes first, which were fresher in my memory.

The time was not ripe for this kind of story. The book was accepted by a small publisher, had a flurry of good reviews, was read by some thousand readers, and soon forgotten. I went on with my daily job, without resentment or frustration. I had not aimed for literary celebrity, and I felt at ease with myself for having done my civic duty as a witness, and felt relieved of the burden of slavery.

About ten years later the situation changed. All over Europe the wounds of the war were healing. The true horror of the Nazi occupation had emerged, and a new generation was growing up, eager to learn and understand. My dormant book was accepted by an important publisher, enjoyed success in Italy and was soon translated into four or five languages. I was encouraged enough to write a sequel—the story of the long journey home we made through a Soviet Russia and Eastern Europe devastated by the war. The book was called *The Truce* and was successful too, but still I refused to be treated as a fully-fledged writer. A writer is someone who sits full-time at his desk, earns his bread by writing, is concerned with problems of style and language, and aspires to recognition. At that time, my way of life couldn't have been more different. I spent all my working hours in a chemical laboratory or in a factory, of which I became technical director and later general manager. This was my real work, and I didn't feel alienated by it—on the contrary, its events, its problems, even its failures and worries were 'raw material' as the Camp had been, stuff to be put aside for some future use.

Around 1970, however, I realized that things could change. The time for my retirement was not far away. I suspected that the reservoir of my Camp memories was virtually emptied, but at the same time I was realizing that writing, even if only done in your spare time, was for me more than merely recording my most dreadful experiences. It was, or it could become, a new skill or a tool to convey to the reader other concepts.

Why not try to write about my daily work as a chemist? I felt indebted to my technical trade, and eager to transmit its features to the layman, but also hindered from making the attempt until I had broken my ties with chemistry conclusively in 1975. Why? I don't know exactly; perhaps in this, as in everything, you have to step back and gain some distance, to get a more balanced and comprehensive view.

What I had vaguely in mind was to cross-breed two trades: chemistry and writing. It seemed to me that in the immense panorama of modern literature something was missing. Where my profession should have been, at least in Italian literature, there was a void, a blank area. I speak here of my profession in the broad sense of the word and refer not just to chemistry, but the whole range of modern technological trades.

In novels or short stories, you could read about warriors, sailors, kings, thieves, prostitutes, countesses, ancient Romans; about love, vendettas, crime, bug-eyed monsters and more. But never any reference to industry—and this to me seemed strange, almost shocking: a void waiting to be filled, an empty ecological niche. You read of course about cars, planes, even spacecraft, real or fantastic, and computers, but almost nothing about the immense body of human thought and toil hidden behind, and representing an essential feature of, our present civilization.

What does the layman know about living in a modern factory, facing a technical or a financial problem, working in a chemical laboratory? Why not try to turn this experience into literature, as Conrad did navigation, and Jack London searching for gold in Alaska?

I did not feel encouraged. Italy is an old country with a complex history of small states quarrelling among themselves and with the Church. The Church has been enormously influential, and has always adhered to tradition and mistrusted science. Thus for centuries culture was identified with art, music and literature, while science and technology were belittled, frowned upon. Leonardo and Galileo were brilliant exceptions. Croce, our leading philosopher of the time, had flatly stated that scientific problems were false problems. Only humanistic knowledge could give you a cultural *formation*, whereas exact and natural sciences give you merely *information*. In the illustrious panorama of Italian literature there was no trace of our trade—of the transmuters of matter.

These were the considerations that led me to write my third book, *The Periodic Table*. The title is defiant: the 'periodic table' is the table of the chemical elements, in the square configuration developed by the famous Russian chemist Mendeleyev. I went a step further: each chapter of the book bears the name of, and centres on, a chemical element—iron, lead, titanium, sulphur...It was a challenge—daring to offer the reader a book, a novel, drawn from such 'unpoetic' matter. Matter is by definition unpoetic. Chemistry is arid, prosaic stuff, good only for manufacturing plastics, cosmetics, explosives and poisons.

But for us, the transformers, matter is something very different. It is the antagonist *par excellence*, never dead, always mysteriously alive. It can be your friend or your enemy, your slave or your master; sometimes obtuse, sometimes cunning, always obstinate. You are engaged in a lifelong struggle with it, and you can come out either the conqueror or the vanquished. Matter is also a judge, and the most impartial one of all. It never forgives your errors, and very often punishes them severely. When you transgress, it strikes back, like Conrad's sea.

Moreover, for the experienced chemist, elements and compounds tend to assume a character, a personality, like human beings. Many of them are tied to his own professional past by the firm bonds of anecdote, like the memories recalled by specific odours in

Proust's *Recherche*. Many are apt to give rise to metaphors, in the same way that animals are used metaphorically in literature throughout history. Many 'shop' terms, like *distilling, filtering, crystallizing, precipitating*, have for us a subtler sense than for the layman, and can convey to the reader, overtly or implicitly, an image or a state of mind.

In my experience the scientist-writer enjoys another particular advantage. His job has trained him in two virtues, precision and concision, that are appreciated by any reader. And what is chemistry, after all, but the art of weighing, recognizing, separating and putting together? Each of these operations has its exact counterpart in the art of writing.

Despite its heretical nature, or perhaps because of it, *The Periodic Table* has proved successful in Italy, in the United States and in Britain. I have received many letters, mostly from young readers, and each contains a tell-tale sentence: 'If I had been taught chemistry *this* way, I would have decided to be a chemist.' I think this best demonstrates my point. There is no wall between science and literature, just an old-established furrow that modern man, or a modern writer, ought to try to fill, or at least cross. When I am asked, 'Why do you write, being a chemist?', I feel qualified to reply: 'I write *because* I am a chemist.'

The successful experiment of *The Periodic Table* encouraged me to take a further step, to try another hybridization of technology and literature. I am convinced that such hybrids are fertile.

For centuries, all over the world, languages have drawn their pith from human work: from the mill, horsemanship, agriculture, mining, fencing and many other ancient crafts. We still speak of 'striking while the iron is hot', although blacksmiths have almost completely disappeared; we still say that something proceeds 'full sail', when sailing ships vanished a century ago, or have been reduced to an expensive sport.

But languages never stop developing. Today's trades are fantastically more numerous and more complicated than those of our forefathers. Everywhere, the jobs and crafts of ancient villages have been replaced by thousands of new specializations. Each tends to create its own jargon. New terms, similes, metaphors are born in the factories and laboratories, and enter common speech. I was in contact with the specialized jargon peculiar to factories for many years, and I was fascinated by the idea of writing a book centred on modern industrial work and its language.

Through my trade I eavesdropped on quite a bit of this speech, and found it rich and strong. I was also in touch with the unique breed of men who spoke it. They actually did not know any other language, although their way of life led them to travel round the world, and even though they spoke a good many foreign languages. I refer to the world-wide, nomadic tribe of machine-fitters.

My hero had to be a machine-fitter. Of course, when you set out to manufacture a character, you have to descend from the general to the particular. Your character must be an individual, localized in time and space, with individuated whims, tics and background. My man had to be a worker, but not one who sits on an assembly line. He had to be quick at his job, proud of his skill, good at trouble-shooting, even, when necessary, a good fighter. And, after so much literature about Naples and Venice, about the glory of ancient Rome and the beauties of Italy, he had to be a modest Turinese like me. In fact, he had to come from the rural sector of Turin, and his speech had to be a mixture of vulgar diction and the kind of technicalities you hear in every workshop. He was to speak to me about his travels abroad, his assembling of oil derricks, suspension bridges, cranes, and all the rest.

Once more, as you see, an experiment, a literary anomaly. And once more, an unexpected welcome from an unusual group of readers: those readers who do not read much, the workers themselves, wrote me enthusiastic letters: 'Look, for the first time in my life I'm finding in a book the stuff I'm grappling with every blessed day.' In addition, the austere Italian critics recognized that this book represented something new, an innovation in language, and another attempt to bridge the gap between the so-called 'two cultures'. Because of its linguistic character, *La Chiave a Stella* has been difficult for the valiant William Weaver to translate. The English title will probably be *The Monkey's Wrench*; publication is expected in the United States within the year.

Since its very beginning, literature has dealt with love, sex and violence, and it will certainly continue to do so. But new subjects keep emerging, and it would be a pity to overlook them. We live in a world that is populated more and more by machines—and one in the full swing of an electronic revolution whose effects will be much more radical than those of any political revolution. Is a writer permitted to ignore all this, to segregate himself from the present and look for shelter in the past?

The great writers and poets of the past, whom we all admire, are 'ancient' to us, but were 'modern' to their contemporaries. We ought to imitate them—but not mechanically: not by mimicking their style, which is the style of their times. Rather we ought to imitate their effort to keep pace with the events that surrounded them.

In past decades in Europe there used to be lively discussions about engagement. Has a writer the right to abstain from politics? Personally, I think that a writer, *in his everyday life*, has the same rights and duties as his fellow citizens, but that, *when writing*, he must be completely free to choose the subjects and the moral code that best fit him. He must not be subjected to any restraint. Leave compulsions and restraints to the countries where civil rights are ignored or disregarded.

But I also think that if a writer shuts his eyes to the reality of what is happening now, he risks missing the greatest change of direction mankind has made since the invention of the steam engine. He must be critical of every misuse and abuse, but if he is blind to what happens in the fields of astrophysics, new technologies or computer science, he will no longer be able to understand his more up-to-date neighbours. He will be an old man, a left-over, an outsider in this world. For the first time in history, his fifteen-year-old children will outwit him.

GRANTA

BACK ISSUES

Notes on Contributors

Richard Ford is the author of three novels, *A Piece of My Heart, The Ultimate Good Luck* and, most recently, *The Sportswriter*. Work by both Richard Ford and **Jayne Anne Phillips** has appeared in *Granta* 8: 'Dirty Realism' and *Granta* 12: 'The True Adventures of the Rolling Stones'. Jayne Anne Phillips is the author of *Machine Dreams* and *Black Tickets*. 'Fast Lanes' is available in a limited edition, with drawings by Yvonne Jacquette, from Vehicle Editions. **Richard Russo** teaches fiction-writing at Southern Illinois University. *Mohawk*, his first novel, will be published in September. **Ellen Gilchrist** is the author of a novel, *The Annunciation*, and three collections of short stories. 'Memphis' will be included in the latest collection, *Drunk with Love*, which Little, Brown publish in September. **Robert Olmstead** is writer-in-residence at Dickinson College, Pennsylvania. His first collection of fiction, *Riverdog*, will be published next spring. **Joy Williams** is the author of two novels, *State of Grace* and *The Changeling*, and is completing a third, *Willie and Liberty*. She lives in Florida. **Louise Erdrich** has written two novels, *Love Medicine* and *The Beet Queen*, from which 'Knives' is taken, and which Henry Holt publish this Fall. **Richard Rayner** is Assistant Editor of *Time Out*. He is a frequent visitor to Los Angeles. **John Updike**'s new novel, *Roger's Version*, will be published by Alfred Knopf in September. 'Getting The Words Out' is part of a longer work-in-progress. **Adam Mars-Jones** is the author of one book of fiction, *Lantern Lecture*, and is now at work on a novel. His writing has appeared in *Granta* 7: 'Best of Young British Novelists' and *Granta* 14: 'Autobiography'. A second feature on Northern Ireland by **Nan Richardson** and **Gilles Peress**, covering the events of this year, will be published in the next issue of *Granta*. A book of their combined work on the province will be published by Aperture, Inc, a non-profit foundation, which is seeking funds to support the publication. **Mary Benson** is the author of a biography of Nelson Mandela, published this year by Norton. **Primo Levi**'s new book, *The Monkey's Wrench*, is published by Summit Books in October.